# Dark Horizons

# Dark Horizons

By
Rae D. Magdon
&
Michelle Magly

Desert Palm Press

# Dark Horizon

## (Revised Edition)

By Rae D. Magdon & Michelle Magly

ISBN (book): 9781948327220
ISBN (epub): 9781948327237
ISBN (pdf): 9781948327244

Desert Palm Press
1961 Main Street, Suite 220
Watsonville, California 95076
www.desertpalmpress.com

Editor: R. Lee Fitzsimmons
Cover Design: Rachel George (http://www.rachelgeorgeillustration.com/)

Printed in the United States of America
Second Edition March 2019

# Acknowledgments

This book would never have been published without Lee and the folks at Desert Palm Press. They make the world better every time they put another story about women loving women into the world.

I would be remiss if I didn't thank my coauthor, Michelle. This story was a huge first for both of us, and I'm thrilled that our partnership and friendship has continued to grow and flourish since then.

# Chapter One

BULLETS WHIZZED PAST TAYLOR Morgan's head as she ducked for cover behind the nearest rock formation. Shots thudded into the planet's surface inches behind her, kicking up choking clouds of dust at her heels. She was safe for the moment, but she knew she had to keep moving before the ikthians got any closer. She popped a wasted ammo clip from her gun and jammed in a fresh one, frowning when she noticed that she only had a few rounds left. The ikthian gunners pursuing her didn't need to worry about ammo. They had plenty to spare after ripping through her squad.

"Damn bottom-feeders," she growled, scanning the barren wasteland ahead of her. The narrow canyon had no vegetation and almost no cover, but the winding path of the rocky cliff-face might offer limited protection if she used it correctly.

"Oof!" Taylor looked up, her eyes widening in surprise as one of her remaining soldiers crouched next to her. It was Jackson, miraculously in one piece aside from a bullet wound in his right shoulder. "Lieutenant Morgan, ma'am!" He raised the muzzle of the gun to his forehead in salute. "Good to see you in one piece."

"Likewise, Jackson," she panted. "How many ammo clips do you have left?" Jackson opened his mouth to answer, but before he could, the ground beneath them shook with the shockwaves of an explosion. It nearly split their boulder in half. "Shit, they have grenades, too?"

"And everything else we'd appreciate having right now." Jackson reloaded his own gun and fired a few rounds past the edge of their cover. "I don't know what happened to the others. One of the fish sent me flying as soon as the action started."

Taylor swallowed as she went over the body count in her head. Barkes had been the first to go. Plasma shot right through the stomach. The acrid smell of burnt flesh still stung her nose. Smith had died even more painfully, lifted up by a seeker as the alien flooded him with toxins. His screams had been the worst. Everyone else had been picked off in the firefight, and there were still at least four ikthian seekers tracking them. Not good odds.

"We're it," she told Jackson reluctantly. "There's a surface-side shuttle outside this canyon in the evac zone if we can make it. We've just gotta duck and weave."

Jackson glanced down the canyon. "You sure about that, Lieutenant?"

The sound of gunfire came closer, and a few of the bullets grazed the large rock they were crouched behind, scraping sparks from its surface. Taylor knew that the ikthians would waste no time killing them if they hesitated any longer. "What choice do we have?"

Taylor darted from her cover and let loose a barrage of fire. She aimed at the silvery silhouettes of the aliens standing at the canyon entrance. Jackson jumped up and joined her. The four assailants immediately ducked, and as soon as they dodged to the side, Taylor gave the signal to Jackson.

"Move!" They ran to the next bend in the pass and ducked out of sight just as the ikthians resumed firing. "See? No problem."

Jackson grinned at the understatement. What they both really needed were more grenades and a lot of ammunition, but without supplies, a quick retreat was their only option. Taylor checked her weapon, making sure it was ready to fire if the ikthians came any closer.

"I think we've got an opening!" Jackson said, popping out from the cover and firing again.

Taylor followed, and they sprinted for the next curve of the canyon wall. "We just need to keep them out of our line of sight. We're doing great."

Jackson nodded as they moved to retreat further back. Unfortunately, someone else was already crouched behind the narrow outcropping of rock.

"Shit," Jackson shouted as he tripped over the huddled body. It was an ikthian woman, with silvery skin blanched to a pale, pasty color. Her deep blue eyes widened with fear as she cried out and scrambled away from them. Taylor froze at the sight of her. The alien's civilian clothes had torn at her right rib, revealing a jagged cut and dark, clotted blood.

While Jackson scrambled away from the alien, he accidentally backed into the line of sight of the enemy seekers. One of them grabbed for him, aiming a gun at his head as its hand clutched his throat.

"Jackson!" Taylor screamed. She reached out for him, but stopped short. The seeker's hold on Jackson was even more deadly than the gun pointed at his head. If the ikthian sent its toxins through his skin, his entire body would shut down.

Desperately, Taylor grabbed the wounded ikthian woman and dragged her up from her hiding spot. She pressed the barrel of the gun into the alien's temple and held her against her chest as she walked back out into the canyon opening. "Let him go," she ordered. She didn't know if the ikthians had updated translators, but even bottom-feeders could understand what her threat meant.

"Lieutenant, run," Jackson shouted. "You can't negotiate with them."

"Shut up, Jackson. That's an order." Taylor pulled the ikthian closer and pressed harder with the gun. The four seekers at the opposite end of the canyon lowered their weapons, but the ikthian holding Jackson didn't let go. "Let him go, or I space your friend." Taylor's finger moved to the trigger. The ikthian in her arms didn't struggle, but her breathing came in labored gasps, and she whimpered whenever Taylor's hand brushed against her wound. The alien must have lost a lot of blood. She didn't even try to use her toxins to escape.

Taylor's grasp shook a little. Her new hostage had no weapons or armor. She could tell that she was holding a civilian, some innocent that she had just threatened to blast into oblivion, but it was to save Jackson. *This woman is just a bottom-feeder,* she told herself. *Just a stinking alien. Not worth my time.* Her heart pounded with the rush of adrenaline. She had to get off the planet. Had to get Jackson home safe.

One of the ikthians made a noise, a shriek, and Jackson cried out in agony. Taylor watched, horror-struck and unable to look away as he began to spasm. His skin bubbled, melting and blackening before her eyes as his entire body went rigid. His mouth opened in a final scream before he slumped to the ground, muscles still twitching.

Taylor squeezed the grip of her gun tighter. Time to make good on her promise. She just had to pull the trigger. Boom. It would be all over. One less ikthian in the galaxy. But as much as she wanted to, she couldn't shoot a civilian, even if it was an alien.

Taylor's military training took over. The seekers had her outnumbered and outgunned. She needed to run if she didn't want to end up like Jackson. She grabbed the ikthian by the arm, careful not to touch her skin, and dragged her away, out of the canyon and onto the open plain. They sprinted to the waiting shuttle, though Taylor felt the ikthian stumble more than once behind her.

The pilot sat lounging in his seat, but as soon as he saw Taylor running with an ikthian in tow, he fired up the engines. She could hear the battle cries of the enemy following them and dragged her hostage along faster. The door to the shuttle slid open just in time, and Taylor flung the prisoner aboard, only catching a glimpse of the seekers emerging from the canyon as she slammed the door shut. She banged a fist against the pilot's cockpit. "Get us in the air!"

She barely had time to grab onto a handrail before the inertia of take-off pitched her and the prisoner from side to side. Taylor braced herself against one of the benches until the shuddering stopped, keeping a close eye on the ikthian. She slumped onto the floor, too weak to stand.

Once they broke free of the planet's orbit, Taylor dug through the cabin's emergency supplies and found a suppressant collar. If the ikthian tried to use her toxins or pheromones, it would deliver a painful, debilitating shock. It was a barbaric tactic, but necessary if Taylor expected to survive the shuttle ride home.

She approached the prisoner slowly, just in case she tried to escape. The ikthian shrank away, but didn't attempt to harm her. Taylor knelt over her and grabbed her by the shoulder. "Hold still, and don't even think about poisoning me, or I'll find a worse way to chain you up," she growled. Even though this one hadn't tried to attack her, ikthians had just slaughtered her entire squad. She was all out of sympathy for them.

The alien said something in her own language, a series of melodious vowels, but she didn't allow Taylor to put the collar on her. She probably knew it would hurt her if she tried to use her abilities. This time, the ikthian gestured to her wound, and then the collar.

"You want medicine?" Taylor asked.

The ikthian nodded.

Taylor reached under the nearby passenger seat for a first aid kit and opened it up next to them. When her captive reached for the supplies, Taylor pulled them out of reach. "Collar first."

The ikthian dropped her head and allowed Taylor to put the collar on. As soon as it was locked in place, Taylor pulled a syringe full of narcotics out of the kit. It was rated for use on seven different bipedal species, according to the naledai who had supplied them with it. Before the ikthian could object, Taylor injected her with the drug and watched her go under. The pupils of her eyes widened for a moment, almost eclipsing the blue before her eyelids fluttered shut.

Taylor smoothed out the blot of blood on the ikthian's neck where the syringe had punctured her. Faint creases in the silver skin showed where gills used to be on the previously aquatic creatures. Evolution had reduced them to cartilage. Taylor frowned as she set the needle aside and dug out some gauze. Up close, she had to admit that the alien looked startlingly like a human. Sometimes, it amazed her that such deadly creatures could look so much like the people they slaughtered.

Rae D. Magdon & Michelle Magly

# Chapter Two

TAYLOR GLANCED BACK AT the prisoner for the fifth time during the shuttle ride back to Earth. Upon being searched, the ikthian had possessed no identification, and none of their admittedly limited databases had turned up ID scans of her fingerprints or retinas. For all Taylor knew, she could be a common civilian, or an invaluable asset to the Coalition.

"Final approach to Earth," the pilot said. "Brace for impact."

Taylor grabbed the railing as the shuttle entered the atmosphere and started shaking. The cabin bucked, and she used the opportunity to steal another glance at the prisoner. Her face didn't betray any of her emotions, if ikthians even expressed them like humans did. Instead, she stared at the opposite wall with her head held high. The sharp angle of her jaw and high cheekbones gave her a look of grace. No traces of pain or grogginess remained. The sedative had worn off long ago, and Taylor had already numbed and bandaged her wound. Perhaps she was in denial of her capture, or perhaps she didn't consider the humans a true threat. She didn't even attempt to tamper with the toxin suppressor around her neck.

With a sigh, Taylor forced herself to look away from the ikthian again. This one lacked the usual markings so many members of her species sported, although the spiked front of her crest faded from silver to purple at the edges. Taylor wondered for a brief moment if the color shift occurred naturally, or was tattooed on.

Humanity knew fairly little about the ikthians, aside from the fact that most other sentient races functioned as little more than slaves to their empire. Earth remained one of the last resistance groups, along with a handful of naledai colonies and a hidden group of rebels on Nakonum, the naledai home planet. It was lucky that Earth was far away from Korithia, the ikthian home planet, or their attempts at mustering a defense might not have been so effective.

"This is shuttle Grizzly Alpha-071, requesting permission to dock at San Diego Military Defense Grid." The pilot's chatter drew Taylor out of her thoughts. She looked down at her gun and scuffed armor, trying to decide if she looked presentable enough. After the clusterfuck her mission had become, she was lucky to be seeing Earth again. No one else on her squad would, and in exchange, one very unfortunate ikthian would become the Coalition's newest prisoner. Taylor almost felt sorry for the woman.

*Alien*, she corrected herself. Even though they looked similar to humans, ikthians were far from it. Taylor could only imagine what interrogation techniques the Coalition would employ. She didn't always approve of the more inhumane methods they used, but there was little to complain about if it saved human lives. They were currently fighting an extremely one-sided war. Any and every advantage was needed.

"Permission granted. Over."

Taylor sighed. In another minute, they would land, and she would be forced to give a full report to her superiors. Worse still, she would have to give her condolences to the family members of her dead squadmates. The Coalition had a form letter she could use if she wanted, but somehow, that felt too impersonal. After watching the men and women she had fought with being torn apart by the bottom-feeders, the least she could do was type a few paragraphs. Her superiors would argue that a captured ikthian would be valuable enough to make their deaths worthwhile, but Taylor wasn't so sure. Every time she closed her eyes, she just saw blood.

The prisoner jumped slightly as the shuttle came in for a rough landing. Taylor holstered her pistol and reached to unclip her safety harness. When they shuddered to a stop, she stood up and motioned for her prisoner to do the same. Although her hands were cuffed and she wore the collar, the ikthian wasn't restrained otherwise. So far, her body language had been the exact opposite of aggressive, and she had obeyed the few brief, wordless commands Taylor had given her without any sign of resistance.

The shuttle doors opened to reveal the familiar sight of the Coalition's San Diego military base, and Taylor inhaled deeply. The squat grey buildings weren't much to look at, and the scent of plasma exhaust from the engine was unpleasant, but she was too relieved to care. She hadn't been sure she would she would see or smell Earth again.

As she exited the shuttle, she noticed a small crowd waiting for her on the landing pad. Captain Michael Roberts, Taylor's superior officer and mentor, waited with an entourage of troops to act as escort. Taylor saluted, and the company of soldiers saluted back before Roberts nodded for at-ease.

"Lieutenant Morgan," he said as Taylor and the ikthian disembarked. "Welcome back." He eyed the prisoner with suspicion. "Congratulations on a successful mission, and I offer my condolences for your squad."

Taylor nodded. Perhaps it was just the shock of losing her squad, but the congratulations sounded hollow. "It was an honor to serve with them, Sir." She knew Roberts detested the high number of casualties they were taking in this war, but she knew he detested becoming a slave to the Dominion even more. He had been one of the first soldiers to work successfully with naledai operatives on counterattack initiatives.

Roberts signaled two guards to step forward. They each took one of the prisoner's arms and led her off the landing strip. Both Roberts and Taylor watched them take her away before turning back to one another. "Come with me, Lieutenant. We have some things to discuss."

Instead of following the two guards to the prison, Taylor and Roberts headed toward the main base, a much larger complex of interconnected buildings. "Is there a problem, Sir?"

The captain glanced at the soldiers accompanying them. "Let's save this chat for my office." Without any further comments, the two finished their walk to the main base, where the escort parted ways with them. They made the rest of the quick trip in silence, and Roberts didn't speak until the door was firmly shut behind them. He slumped into his office chair with a groan, allowing his fatigue to show on his face, but Taylor remained standing.

"To be honest, Lieutenant, we're amazed you came back alive at all."

"Do you mean this was a suicide mission, Sir?" Taylor asked.

Roberts offered Taylor the chair across from him, but she chose to remain standing. "I mean that this was ordinary reconnaissance until the ikthians showed up. We thought you all were dead. It's a miracle you managed to stumble into that noncombatant, and a miracle she was valuable enough for them to stop shooting."

Taylor shifted her weight from her left foot to her right. She felt awkward standing before her commanding officer without Jackson and the rest of her squad. The final moments of his life kept replaying in her head. His screams. The way the poison had torn him apart. She thought about the ikthian, too. She could still feel the alien clutched in her arms, could still feel the heart that beat too fast in fear, and could still see the wide, pleading blue eyes staring at her. "About that, Sir. What will the upper brass do with an ikthian prisoner?"

Roberts shrugged. "It's hard to say. The last ikthian prisoner anyone managed to retrieve was over six months ago. Our intel is a little old." He sighed and leaned back in his chair. "But if she turns out to be useful, it makes you a damn hero, Taylor. You deserve a rest. A vacation on some island, peace and quiet, no one to give you a hard time..." The captain's thoughts seemed to wander. He was no doubt picturing the downtime time he craved as well. "But we don't have time for that in the middle of a war."

"Understood, Sir." Although Earth itself was heavily guarded and hadn't seen any violence from the Dominion in almost a year, their outlying colonies were bogged down in a ground war that the humans were slowly losing. It was a constant struggle to defend the borders of the solar system, and the ikthians grew more and more irritated by their defiance with each passing year. They were patient creatures, but they considered the humans impudent.

"Take the rest of the day off, Lieutenant," Roberts said. "The brass will debrief you in the morning. Besides, I think they want a little time to interrogate the prisoner first."

Taylor frowned. Something about the ikthian she had captured still didn't sit right with her. She wished she knew why the seekers had stopped firing during her escape. Ikthian seekers were known for being relentless in the pursuit of their quarry, and they were nearly always successful.

"It's odd that they gave her up like that," she mentioned.

Roberts studied her for a moment before propping his feet up on the desk. "So what does that tell you about the prisoner?"

"Well, it says a lot, considering the ikthian was wounded when I found her." Roberts nodded, encouraging her to continue. "And she didn't make any attempts to kill me, which means she was either too weak or thought her chances were better here. Maybe the seekers were going to kill her. But if that's the case..."

Taylor's thoughts wandered. The whole situation felt wrong, but Roberts watched her with an expectant stare, as if the answer lay in plain sight. "Some things are worse than death, Lieutenant. Our prisoner was most likely running away from whatever that is."

"You think they needed her for interrogation?"

Roberts nodded. "I think she knows something." He glanced out the window of his office, observing the San Diego coastline in the distance. "And it's important enough that the seekers want her back alive."

"What will the others want to do with her?" Taylor asked.

Roberts frowned, a crease developing in his forehead. "Well, that's the problem. The generals will want to trade her back for resources, and the politicians will want to do a hostage exchange. Both are safer options in the long run." He ran a hand through his graying hair. "But you don't need to deal with this, Taylor. That's what I'm paid for. You should go enjoy the rest of your downtime."

"I'm not sure what I'll do with an entire day off," Taylor said, her tone slightly less formal now that Roberts had basically dismissed her.

Roberts smiled, standing up and putting a hand on her shoulder. He had always been close to Taylor on a personal level as well as a professional one. Over the years, he had become more of a mentor to her than a strict superior officer. "I'm sure you'll find some trouble to get into," he said, letting his hand drop as Taylor headed for the door.

On her way out, Taylor paused and turned back. She remembered the prisoner pinned to the shuttle floor, bleeding out. Jackson dying right before her eyes again. "Sir? What's going to happen to the prisoner after she's interrogated?"

"That depends on what she has to tell us. Hopefully, it will be something useful. I expect you here at 0800 tomorrow, Lieutenant."

Taylor saluted and left the office, not entirely sure why she had asked that question. The prisoner was only an ikthian, after all.

# Chapter Three

AS TAYLOR EXITED THE building and stepped outside, the sun warmed her face and caught her eyes with its bright gleam. The sky had cleared despite the tendency for early morning fog, and she tried to manage a smile. San Diego's weather was better than most places, but it still had a fair share of cloudy days. Still, she couldn't complain. At least she was alive to see them.

Before going across the field to the mess hall, Taylor decided to stop in her quarters and change out of her armor. It would be a good idea to leave her weapons behind before she did any more wandering. Clearing a checkpoint with an assault rifle or pistol was a pain.

It didn't take her long to arrive at her bunk. The room was small, but it was all hers. Taylor was grateful that her rank afforded her more privacy than the communal barracks. Once she had set her weapons aside, she stripped and hopped into the shower. Until the shuttle had picked her up, she had been groundside for several days with very little in the ways of comfort. The warm water soothed her aching back, but she tried not to linger. Wandering thoughts were the enemy at the moment.

As she finished drying her hair with a worn towel, her stomach growled. Food had also been a scarcity on the mission, though the meals in the mess hardly counted as food either. She threw the towel away in a hurry and began pulling on a fresh pair of fatigues. Even though her stomach was still tied into knots, she knew she had to put something in it. Her body felt weak after what she had endured.

Once she reached the dining hall, Taylor stepped in line with the rest of the soldiers waiting for their dinner. She stood in her spot patiently, feeling extremely out of place. After days of dodging bullets, the chatter of the mess hall was disquieting.

"Hey, when did you get back?"

It took Taylor a moment to realize someone was addressing her. She recognized the voice and turned to smile at Rachel Harris, one of the other soldiers stationed at San Diego base. They had become fast friends years ago, when Rachel had first transferred to Earth from one of the Coalition's border colonies. Her striking appearance, with smooth dark skin and a messy braid that always seemed to come undone, had even caused Taylor to develop a bit of a crush on her at first before Rachel had politely let her down.

"Maybe an hour ago," Taylor answered. She turned back to the line and accepted her tray of rations. "How are you?"

Rachel gave a dismissive shrug. "I've been on base. I don't have stories to tell. But you? You just got back from the front lines. Now that's something I want to hear about...if you want to talk about it, that is." Her hesitant tone suggested that rumors had already managed to circulate through the ranks. Taylor wasn't surprised. Of course, the whole base knew something had happened before she had even gotten her first meal.

"Let's find a table first," Taylor said, deliberately dodging the question. "You hungry?"

Rachel made a disgusted face. "You know, I could never do seconds for C rations."

"Good point." The two of them found a table in one of the far corners of the mess hall, somewhere that would discourage people from coming over and talking.

"So, you want to talk about what happened?" Rachel was blunt by nature, but since it was usually paired with empathy, Taylor didn't mind her direct way of speaking. In fact, she usually preferred it. It was one of the reasons they got along so well.

"There's not much to tell. Seekers took out my entire squad. The bottom-feeders cut them down like animals. I'd rather not think about it for a while."

"Can't blame you," Rachel said as she stared at Taylor's plate. Apparently, she had changed her mind about seconds. Taylor pushed the tray into the middle of the table so that Rachel could steal a piece of her nutrient dessert bar. She had never been particularly fond of them anyway. She remained silent for a few seconds, considering how much she should tell Rachel. No doubt news of the prisoner would spread like wildfire through the base, and Roberts hadn't ordered her to keep any of the information classified.

"I barely got out in time," she said eventually. "I ran into another ikthian—a civilian, I think...and when the seekers saw me with her, they stopped firing long enough for me to get onto the evac shuttle."

Rachel's eyes widened. "So it's true? There's an ikthian on base?"

"I guess they have her in interrogation now," Taylor said. "I'm not sure how much help she'll be. Like I said, I think she's a civilian."

"None of the ikthians are civilized," Rachel said, and Taylor nodded her agreement.

Thinking about the ikthian made Taylor's stomach twist in an unpleasant way, so she changed the subject. "So, how have things been back on base?" she asked as Rachel chewed her stolen bite.

"Same. Doom and gloom about the war effort. The brass keeps trying to cover it up. Andrew turned out to be a good lay." The confident smirk on Rachel's face indicated that Andrew had been more than a good lay. Taylor shifted uncomfortably in her seat. "What?" Rachel protested. "I didn't give any gross details."

Taylor shook her head. "I'm just not good company right now," she mumbled. She took one more bite of her rations, but the sandy texture did little to convince her of its edible status.

"So why don't you make way for some better company?" Andrew's rough, deep voice was the only warning Taylor got before the private slumped down onto the bench next to her, causing the whole table to rattle.

Taylor glanced over at him, trying to decide if his muscles had gotten even beefier in her absence. "Seriously, Andrew? Not in the mood."

"Hey, relax. I know I'm not your type." He winked at Rachel from across the table. "Besides, I've got other beautiful ladies to flirt with."

"Perhaps one beautiful lady?" Rachel asked, placing emphasis on the 'one'.

Andrew ignored her, eyeing Taylor's tray of half-finished rations. "Anyone eating that?"

Taylor wordlessly passed the tray over to him. He began making short work of the remaining food. "So, they say you captured an ikthian," Andrew said around a mouthful of ration bar.

Taylor tried to shrug it off. "I guess the entire base is already talking about it. Yeah. We stumbled on her in the middle of a firefight."

"I've never seen an ikthian in person," Andrew said.

Rachel's eyes narrowed, and her lips twitched into a brooding frown. Taylor recognized the expression on her face. Even though Rachel had been stuck on base for several months, she had seen action before, and she had faced the Dominion's forces. She knew what they were capable of. "Hope you never have to, Andrew. Their toxins can kill you in less than a minute, and they train their children as warriors from birth."

"It's hard to imagine. They don't look that intimidating."

"Spend a day on the front lines," Taylor said. "You'll see." The face of the ikthian she had captured pushed itself into her thoughts. She had looked very young, and if she had been human, Taylor would have guessed her age to be mid-twenties at most.

"Tell that to my superiors," Andrew said as he finished the nutrient bar Rachel had started. Neither of them objected. "Anyway, there are so many rumors about the ikthians that I can never be sure what's true and what's made up."

"I've heard that they'll fuck any alien species," Rachel added, making a disapproving face.

What little of Taylor's appetite remained vanished completely.

Andrew opened his eyes wider, a look of disbelief on his face. "Really?"

Rachel flipped her braid over her shoulder. "I seriously doubt you're going to be kidnapped by ikthians and forced to have sex with them any time soon. Besides, they drug your mind. They release pheromones to make you attracted to them."

"Still doesn't sound so bad to me," Andrew said. "They're gorgeous."

"They're deadly," Rachel insisted. "Do you really want to have sex with something that can kill you just by touching you?"

Suddenly, the echo of Jackson's screams filled Taylor's ears. She remembered the way he had died, his body jerking and twitching in the seeker's grip as the toxins flooded his nervous system. It took her several moments to find her words. "Let's hope the one I captured doesn't try that." For some reason, even though she could picture Jackson's death clearly, she couldn't imagine the timid ikthian prisoner harming anyone.

"Yeah, that's a bit of a libido killer," Andrew admitted, standing up as well. "But that's all right. I have...other opportunities." He gave Rachel a meaningful glance.

Taylor tried not to watch the two of them make eyes at each other. She stared at her empty tray instead and stood from the table. "Well, I'll let you guys explore those opportunities."

"Aw, come on. We can cool it a little longer." Andrew stood up and tried to block Taylor's path, but she stepped around him.

"I just got back from hell, Andrew. I'm tired."

"Oh." She could hear the disappointment in his voice, but knew he wouldn't press her to stay any longer. She took the food tray back to the front of the mess hall and left for her quarters. As she passed other soldiers, some of them cast sidelong glances at her. She knew they were only wondering what had happened on the latest mission, but their stares felt accusatory anyway.

Taylor left the mess hall and hurried across the field, heading back to her own quarters. This time, her room was a bleak mess of discarded clothes and dirty, dented armor. She managed to scrounge up enough energy to throw some of her fatigues into the laundry chute before collapsing on her bunk. The small bed was barely wide enough to hold her sprawling limbs. She closed her eyes, expecting to see Jackson again, but her mind kept wandering back to the ikthian she had taken prisoner. The memory of her numb stare haunted Taylor until she fell into a fitful sleep for the night.

Rae D. Magdon & Michelle Magly

# Chapter Four

HANDS GRIPPED MAIA'S ARMS, pushing her through a dark room and slamming her onto a cold table. She cried out as one of the humans forced her face to the side, pinning her to strap her arms and legs down. Light flooded the room, and she saw operating tools gleaming under the fluorescent bulbs. She swallowed. Her throat was too dry. She had tried to tell the humans she needed water, but none of them had listened. They didn't understand her language, or if they did, they were denying her on purpose.

A cold cloth came in contact with the back of her neck, and more fingers, pressing, prodding. The skin had gone numb, but she could still feel the pressure. "Hold still." The words echoed uselessly in her head. They could mean anything. She pulled against her restraints, but they remained securely in place.

One of the humans knelt in front of her. He held up a speck of an electronic chip and brought it to his neck, pantomiming the actions he would take on her. The humans were going to do something to her. "I don't understand," she said, but the words meant nothing to him.

The human lifted his shoulders and walked away. Maia thought about talking again, but before she could get any words out, she felt the pinch of a needle at her neck. Her vision began to blur. She groaned and tried to raise her head, but her muscles refused to cooperate.

Fuzzy colors swam in front of her eyes, but the fingers at the back of her head remained, prying at her neckfolds. It almost seemed like they were searching for something. A sharp edge began slicing through the top layer of skin. Somehow, Maia knew the sensation was painful, but her brain refused to transmit any feelings at all except for the same strange, uncomfortable pressure.

*My translator,* she suddenly realized. *They're replacing my translator.* Her arms pulled weakly beneath the restraints again, trying to stop what was happening to her. Although she couldn't understand the humans anyway, the thought of having her words taken from her was terrifying. Without her translator, only another ikthian who spoke her dialect would be able to understand her, and who knew when she would see her own people again? Part of her never wanted to, since most of them were trying to kill her.

A few moments later, the blade at the back of her neck pulled away. "The damn things even have gills," a voice beside her said. Although the cadence of the words still sounded awkward to her ears, Maia could understand them. "I've never worked on a fish before."

"Come on, let's get this over with," another voice said from nearby. Through the colorful streaks in her vision, Maia saw something white being passed over her head. "Stop the bleeding. I don't want to keep touching it."

More words came, but Maia's hearing started to fade. Icy liquid rushed down the back of her neck, chilling the length of her spine. Blissful numbness removed the last traces of discomfort along the side of her neck, and she let out a sigh of relief even though she knew that she was anything but safe. Her hands went limp in their restraints, and a comforting blackness began to swallow up all of the blurry colors before her eyes.

She blinked, trying to push back the approaching darkness. Her vision darted everywhere, searching for a hint of what the humans might be doing next, and her eyes caught at a window. More humans stood on the other side of the glass pane, watching her. Though her vision swam, Maia had to marvel at the genetic variance in the creatures. They stood there, each one a different shade from the other. Even the fur on top of their heads, strange enough on its own, was different. She spotted a human with spiky black fur and darker skin than some of the others. That one looked familiar, almost like the human who had run into her on Amaren.

Maia blinked again. It was the same human who had captured her. She gasped as she felt something prod the back of her neck, and the human's gaze met hers through the window. Maia remained focused on those dark eyes. The human looked hurt somehow. Perhaps saddened? Or maybe Maia was projecting her feelings onto the human. She had no idea how they behaved, or how they felt. In fact, she was having a hard time holding onto her own thoughts at the moment. The more she fought against the creeping chill and the darkness threatening to press in around her head, the more she seemed to slip away.

The world faded, and the cold sensation spread. Maia took a deep breath and blinked, but her eyes didn't open again after the lids shut. It seemed too much of a struggle.

\*\*\*

"Why are her eyes closed?" Taylor asked, pointing at the ikthian beyond the window.

"They put her under for the rest of the procedure," Roberts said. "They don't want her to move and mess up the flesh-knitter."

Taylor watched one of the surgeons run the head of what looked like a pen over the incision. The tip glowed brightly and left an infused seam of skin in its path. "Why didn't they drug her for the first part?" It had been unsettling to watch the ikthian stare helplessly up at her during the procedure. The surgeons could have at least tried to explain what they were doing better. The civilian was probably terrified.

Roberts shrugged. "It's hard to tell how much will put her under without damaging her in some way. We only have naledai advice on their anatomy. We're lucky enough that they adapted a translator upgrade."

Taylor tried to imagine what it would be like to have a conversation with the ikthian. "What do they have to say, usually?" She knew that there hadn't been an ikthian prisoner on base for several months, but surely there had been some communication with their previous captives.

"Water."

She glanced over at Roberts. "What?"

"They always ask for water." He folded his hands behind his back and stood a little straighter. "They were once aquatic, Morgan, remember?"

Taylor looked back at the silver-skinned woman. Her mouth hung open slightly, and she no longer twitched when the surgeons prodded her. They had to be finishing soon. "Will she ask for water?"

"Most likely. They can never drink enough of it." Roberts gestured with one hand, rubbing a forefinger and thumb together. "It's the lack of humidity." The concept made sense, but it also made Taylor a little uneasy. "It's an opportunity for the prisoner to show a willingness to cooperate," Roberts continued. "They have needs we will provide for, but they need to work with us in exchange."

Although her captain's explanation made sense, Taylor still felt some sympathy for the prisoner. She wasn't sure why, especially since her entire squad had been butchered by the rest of her kind. Her brow furrowed as she remembered what had happened on Amaren, and she turned away from the window. The ikthian seekers had demonstrated their understanding of mercy when they had killed Jackson. "She had better have something," Taylor said, a little more harshly than she had intended. "Please tell me she's useful, at least."

"Your squad didn't die for nothing, Lieutenant, even if capturing an ikthian wasn't part of the plan," Roberts said. "We're going to interrogate her tomorrow."

"I want to know what she was doing on Amaren, and why those seekers were after her," Taylor insisted. "I've never seen ikthians hunt and kill their own kind before." Unable to resist the temptation any longer, she glanced back through the window, staring at the limp, unconscious form of the ikthian lying on the operating table. The doctors appeared to be finished with her, but her limbs were still restrained.

Roberts clapped a hand on Taylor's shoulder, breaking out of his role as her commanding officer for a moment. "Don't worry. We'll find out what she knows, and why she was running away."

Taylor lowered her gaze to the floor, staring at the toes of her boots so that she wouldn't have to look through the window any longer. She doubted that any information the alien could give them was worth the cost.

# Chapter Five

"STATE YOUR NAME."

ALTHOUGH the words were in an alien language, they sounded clear in Maia's head. Gingerly, she touched the place along her crest where they had implanted her translator. It worked just like it had before, but with an addition. Apparently, the humans had modified it with their own language parameters. It was too soon to say whether that boded well for her or not.

"State your name," the amplified voice said again. They hadn't sent an interrogator in to question her, relying on a speaker system instead, so Maia had no one to look at as she answered.

"Maia."

"Your House Name," the voice prompted.

Maia swallowed. Her throat and skin felt sore from the room's dry air, and her stomach was clenched tight with fear. For one frantic second, she considered lying. It was far too dangerous for her to return to the Dominion, but if these humans didn't find her important enough to preserve, they might throw her away to rot in a cell, or worse, kill her. Telling the truth would be the best move. As long as she stayed alive, there was a slight possibility for escape.

"Kalanis."

There was a long pause as whoever watched her considered the answer. Obviously, it wasn't what they had been expecting. Maia's family name was well-known and well-respected, even among aliens, and she hoped that it would be enough to protect her this time.

Being captured by humans wasn't the worst thing that could have happened to her. Even though they were at war with her species, the humans hadn't harmed her so far. The soldier who had stolen her from the battlefield had inadvertently saved her life. The seekers pursuing her were under strict orders to bring her in alive, but her usefulness would end once the Dominion had access to her research.

As Maia recalled the events of her capture, she was surprised at how clearly she was able to picture her savior's face. The strong, rounded jaw, blunt nose, and severe eyes had seemed terrifying at first. Maia could still remember the first moment her rescuer had taken off her protective helmet and tucked it under one muscular arm, her pistol still clutched in her other hand. And the way the human had watched her during her procedure. Maia thought she had seen pity in those eyes.

"Your name is Maia Kalanis? Irana Kalanis's daughter?" the voice asked, interrupting her thoughts.

"Yes," Maia said. A few weeks ago, her biggest worries had been achieving tenure and soliciting funds for her genetic research. Now, she was the most wanted ikthian in the entire Dominion. Even the fact that she was Irana's daughter wouldn't be enough to spare her life now that word of her latest research had gotten out. She hadn't expected her reports to the University to blow up in her face so spectacularly.

Maia stared down at her cuffed hands. The humans had kept the collar around her throat as well. She wasn't cut off from her natural defenses, but any attempt to poison someone would result in pain, a lot of it. She was no warrior, but her mother had forced her to participate in all the necessary defense training. Unfortunately, everything she had learned required the use of her toxins. She had no chance of escaping without them, and even if she did, where would she go? Not back to the Dominion. They would just send the seekers after her again.

"Have you sent any transmissions since your capture?" the voice asked.

Even though there was no physical interrogator, Maia looked around. There were cameras in the room somewhere. She wanted the humans to believe her. "No."

"Have you received any transmissions since your capture?"

"No."

"Is the Dominion aware of your current location?"

"No."

Maia wondered if the room was monitored somehow aside from audio and video feed. Perhaps they were checking her heart rate or stress hormone levels to try and determine if she was lying. Her heart was beating so fast that it wouldn't matter, and her mind was still cloudy with fear and the last of the sedatives. She had no idea what she was going to do next.

"What was your purpose on Amaren?"

"Research." She was pleased when her voice only shook a little. "I am a scientist." Amaren was a small, backwater world sitting right in the middle of contested space, and aside from its mineral deposits, the only useful resources there now were the genetic samples she had been trying to collect from fossilized remains.

"State your area of specialization."

"Genetics," she answered quickly. "I study the genetic variations and matches inherent in several sentient species." Maia scolded herself for rattling off so much information. The humans didn't care. What did she think this was, a review board?

"Are you a member of the Dominion's military?"

"No."

"Did your research contribute in any way to the Dominion's military intelligence?"

"No," Maia answered, hesitating only briefly. "I am a civilian." Hopefully, that would be enough to earn her at least a little mercy from her captors. Her mother had pressed her to change her specialization to something more 'useful' several times. With her name and connections, Maia had been offered several jobs, but she had always refused. It was the only form of rebellion she had ever taken.

The voice didn't reply right away, and Maia began to calm down. So far, her answers hadn't seemed to upset the humans, although it was impossible to read any emotion in the mechanical voice coming through the speakers.

Perhaps because her mind was swirling with so many emotions, her thoughts returned to the human that had taken her captive. She had heard the woman's name only once when her superior greeted her as they departed the ship. Taylor. It was a silly thing to remember. So much else had been going on at the time, but for some reason, the human—Taylor—had stuck in her mind. Maia wondered if she would ever see her savior again. Taylor had remained silent but observant during the installation of her translator, and Maia could still remember the intensity of her gaze.

"You will stand up and proceed to the door now," the voice said when it returned, startling Maia even though she had been waiting for it. She glanced nervously around the dark, barren room as she climbed out of the chair and walked toward the door, not wanting to disobey any orders yet. She tried to let her hands fall down to her sides before remembering that they were still cuffed together. Eventually, she just held them in front of her as she waited.

The door opened a few moments later, and four armored guards carrying assault rifles stepped into the interrogation room. None of them were Taylor. None of them had her same inquisitive stare. Two lowered their weapons and took her by the arms, escorting her out as the others kept their rifles trained on her. Maia had no idea what she had done to earn such caution.

The guards led her down a narrow, dimly lit hallway, completely silent except for the sound of their boots tracking on the concrete floor. Maia didn't try and examine her surroundings, afraid that the guards would notice and object, but she did memorize the turns they were taking. Right, left, then left again. Finally, they arrived at another solid metal door much like the first. One of the guards removed his glove and pressed his hand against the scanner. The door slid open with a whoosh.

This new room was slightly better, but not by much. It was still uncomfortably dry, and very small, although the darkness didn't bother her. It had a chair, a cot, and what looked like a toilet and a sink, but no other fixtures. The guards unlocked her cuffs, but kept her collar in place before locking her in the new cell. Maia was relieved when they left. She preferred being alone anyway, and if her guess was right, the humans would try to interrogate her again soon. So far, aside from informing them of her name and giving them a brief overview of her job, she hadn't given them any useful information.

Unsure what else to do, Maia walked over to the sink against the far wall. She tested the taps, pleased when she discovered that they worked. Grateful to have a clean source of water, Maia cupped her hands under the tap, taking several long sips before splashing the rest over her face. Some of her discomfort receded. There was no mirror above the sink, but Maia knew that if there had been, she would have appeared exhausted.

Once she finished her attempt at washing and soothing her dry skin, Maia wandered back to the small, sheetless cot that had been shoved in the opposite corner. She lowered herself down, sitting on the edge and crossing her legs. It was far from comfortable, and bolted to the floor, but better than nothing. She stretched out along its length until her feet touched the wall and stared up at the blank, empty ceiling. The only thing she could do now was wait.

# Chapter Six

TAYLOR JERKED FORWARD, HER heart battering frantically against her ribs as she tried to outrun the seekers. Something darted out from a dip in the canyon wall, blocking her way. They collided, and Taylor drew in a sharp breath as she realized it was the ikthian civilian. She stared at Taylor, blue eyes wide with fright, but wasn't looking at her. Instead, the alien seemed to be looking through her. Through her at Jackson, who was trapped against a seeker's chest.

In less than a second, Taylor had her gun pressed against her captive's skull. "Let him go," she yelled. She pressed the gun harder against the civilian's temple. The seekers stared back at her, guns leveled. "Let him go, or I'll kill her."

The ikthians laughed. One caught her gaze and stared intently at her. Taylor panicked and tried to look away, but an invisible force gripped her head, holding her eyes in place. The seeker sneered. "You won't shoot her. You can't. You're too soft. You won't even trade a life for a life."

"Don't listen to them, Lieutenant," Jackson called out to her. "You can't listen to them." As he spoke, his body started to twitch, and his skin melted from his face, leaving only blackened bone behind.

She still couldn't pull the trigger.

"You're weak, human," the ikthian spat. They laughed as Taylor continued to stand with the civilian trapped against her chest, frozen in place.

Taylor shot up in bed, panting raggedly. Her heart hammered, and she brushed a sweaty lock of hair away from her damp forehead. She glanced at the clock, trying to catch her breath as her pulse returned to normal. Only one minute remained until her alarm went off. With a sigh, Taylor reached out and silenced it. She staggered out of bed, slouching over to the washroom and running herself a cold shower. Even though her bathroom was small, it was also private. She was relieved to have a shower all to herself, especially now. She needed a few minutes to herself after witnessing Jackson's death a second time, even if it had only been a dream.

"That damn prisoner had better be worth it," Taylor muttered as she began scrubbing her skin with a cloth, wiping it free of sweat. But even as she said it, she knew that Jackson's death had been her fault. She was the officer in charge. It had been her drop. Those soldiers had been her responsibility. She had failed them.

After vigorously washing her hair and scrubbing her skin, Taylor turned off the water and began to towel herself dry. She returned to the bedroom, kicking aside piles of used clothes in search of something to wear. Roberts was expecting her in his office at 0800, and from the tone he had taken with her yesterday, it was important. There would probably be at least a few of the upper brass in attendance. Taylor's stomach lurched at the thought of explaining herself to them. She hoped they would be too interested in the prisoner she had brought home to interrogate her about the failed mission and her dead squadmates.

Once she had pulled a fresh pair of fatigues over her still-wet skin and cleaned most of her dirty laundry off the floor, Taylor made her bunk and headed out the door. Her meeting with Roberts started in fifteen minutes, and she wanted to get there early.

Fortunately, the walk over to the main building only took her ten. She ran into Roberts on her way to his office and gave him a crisp salute, straightening her spine. "Captain Roberts, Sir!"

"At ease, soldier," Roberts said, giving her a smile. "This debriefing is going to be fairly informal. The brass mostly want to congratulate you. What you did out there impressed them."

"What I did?" Taylor had considered her survival and capture of an ikthian dumb luck. Apparently, the story sounded better than that to the higher-ups, even if the rest of her squad had been butchered along the way. A darker part of her thought she should have died with Jackson and the others. Their deaths were certainly not worth a commendation.

"You're the sole survivor of an ikthian instigated act of aggression. Your quick thinking not only got you out alive with valuable intel, but with a wealth of untapped knowledge from your ikthian prisoner."

"Oh, did the interrogation turn up something?" Taylor asked as she and Roberts resumed the short walk to his office.

"Not much, but it has potential to be something big." They stopped right outside of the office door. "Things are changing for you, Taylor. Not all of it will be easy, but I think you've handed us a piece that might actually help us win the war."

Taylor swallowed. "Really, Sir?" She didn't dare to hope.

"I'll let the brass tell you."

The door to the office slid open and they both walked inside. Taylor instinctively saluted when she noticed who was waiting for them. She had been expecting someone from the upper brass to show up, but not three out of the Coalition's five generals. General Joseph Hunt stood in the center of the group. He was an older man with several creases in his forehead. It gave his stare a certain severity. He nodded to them in acknowledgement, and they lowered their hands.

Once at ease, Taylor's eyes immediately darted to a familiar pale figure. They had brought the ikthian with them. She stood in the far corner, looking out a window that only provided a view of the building across from them. She still wore the torn, stained clothes that she had been found in, and Taylor scanned the pale skin for any markings or irregularities. It didn't look like they had given her any rough treatment.

"Lieutenant Morgan," General Hunt said.

Taylor glanced back at the general and fought down a blush. Had they noticed her staring? "Yes, Sir?"

"We would like to extend our congratulations on your successful capture of Maia Kalanis."

Taylor's eyes widened, and she couldn't help looking back at the ikthian again. *I captured a Kalanis?*

The ikthian looked over at her with the same blank expression from yesterday, and Taylor swallowed. What little intel the military had gathered showed that the Kalanis family was made up of powerful ikthians, equivalent to something like a dynasty or a corporation by human standards.

"Thank you, Sir," Taylor said crisply. It was somewhat disconcerting to put a name to the alien, but she ignored her discomfort.

"We've already read your report," General Hunt said, recapturing Taylor's attention. "But we wanted to hear what happened from you in person." Her detachment, led by Captain Roberts, was under General Hunt's command, so technically, he was her boss's boss. His presence alone let Taylor know just how serious the situation was.

"Yes, Sir. The mission parameters were simple: reconnaissance on a world called Amaren. Mostly unpopulated, some active volcanoes, but we had reports that the ikthians were using the mineral deposits there to fuel their fleets. We hoped to cut off their supply line. When we arrived, we ran into a group of seekers almost immediately. I managed to contact the evac crew, but they had already butchered most of my squad."

Taylor paused, trying not to replay Jackson's death in her mind. She took a deep breath. "There was no possible way to salvage the mission. I retreated, and on my way to the rendezvous point, I captured the ikthian. When the seekers saw her, they stopped pursuit, and I was able to return to the ship." She glanced over at the ikthian, Maia, who was looking everywhere but at her. "I guess I know why they didn't fire on me now."

"The Kalanis family is very influential in Dominion controlled space," General Ines Moore said. She was one of only two female generals in the Coalition, and Taylor knew that she had taken the hard route to get there, serving plenty of combat time before taking a leadership position. "We think that we can use this one as a bargaining chip, perhaps even open negotiations. Taking her alive has given us an invaluable asset."

"And that asset needs to be guarded," another voice interrupted. Taylor hadn't noticed a fourth figure slithering around behind the generals, but she recognized him immediately once he stepped in front of them. She had seen Chairman Bouchard's smarmy face on more than enough news broadcasts concerning his lead position on the Council of Defense. His self-important attitude was even more off-putting in real life. If her capture of the ikthian had politicians crawling out of the woodwork in addition to the generals, things were even more serious than she thought.

The third general in attendance, Lee, cleared his throat. "What the Chairman means to say is that the prisoner will need to be monitored. Unfortunately, this base doesn't have proper holding facilities."

It took a moment for Taylor to realize what the general was implying. "You want me to guard her, Sir?" she asked, a little skeptically.

"During the negotiations, yes," said General Lee. "We can't afford to lose such a valuable bargaining chip. It makes sense for you to guard her, since you were the one to bring her here, and your squad was killed in action. You will set up a guard rotation outside her quarters, provide for her basic needs, and go with her whenever she is outside of the room. Upon completion of this assignment, you will receive a promotion."

That caught Taylor's attention. She wondered for a moment if she had only imagined it. "I'm sorry. But did you say...?"

General Hunt nodded. "Assuming that Kalanis makes it through to the end of negotiations, you'll be promoted to Captain."

Bouchard interrupted once more. "We've decided to move the prisoner out of interrogation, since it isn't suitable for long-term imprisonment. She needs a humidified environment, or her health will be negatively impacted." He spoke with a diplomatic tone that only made him sound more insincere. It was obvious that he didn't care what happened to Maia as long as she was still around to bargain with. "She will be confined to a recently vacated captain's quarters, since it has the necessary controls and the highest security clearance. It's a little...opulent for a prisoner of war, but it is the best we can do. At the very least, it will allow you to stay there in comfort as well." Bouchard paused and looked from Maia to Taylor.

"I cannot stress how important this task is," General Lee said. "I don't care what methods you use to restrain her or keep her in line. They are completely at your discretion. But if she dies or escapes and we are unable to make use of her in our negotiations, there will be serious personal consequences for you."

Taylor didn't know what else to say. She looked once again at Maia, but the ikthian still showed no sign of a reaction to her fate. Taylor would have wondered if ikthians showed emotion at all, but she had seen several looks of pure anger directed at her on the battlefield, as well as the sick joy some ikthians got out of poisoning humans with their toxins or mowing them down with assault rifles. Taylor felt her nails biting into her palms and unclenched her fists. She hadn't even realized she had tightened them.

"Do you have any questions, Lieutenant?" General Hunt asked.

Taylor looked over at the general and tried to think of what she could possibly ask that was appropriate. Hundreds of questions ran through her head, all of them centered on her confusion over the situation. She didn't understand why she had been selected to look after an ikthian prisoner, but if she really could help them end the war, Taylor owed it to her squad to do her best and follow the generals' orders.

"I have no questions, Sir."

General Hunt nodded. "Very well. Report to the top floor of the officer's barracks at 0900. Bring your gear and personal items. You'll be bunking there. The prisoner will be waiting for you when you arrive. At that time, she will be transferred to your custody."

"Yes, Sir."

"You're dismissed," Bouchard drawled, but Taylor remained in place until General Hunt gave her a nod of approval. With his permission and another salute, she turned and left the office, resisting the nearly overpowering temptation to look back over her shoulder at the ikthian on the way out.

# Chapter Seven

IT ONLY TOOK TAYLOR a few minutes to throw her things into a camouflaged duffel bag. She was minimalist by nature, and she didn't have many personal items. Aside from her clothes, medals, and toiletries, nothing much was left.

Once the room was almost bare, she opened the top drawer beside her bed. There, within easy reach, was one of the few luxuries she allowed herself—a realistic looking, sensation transmitting strap-on. She had no intention of using it with someone else any time soon, since there weren't a lot of available women on base, but the military was strained these days. There was no guarantee that her bunk would remain empty. If they decided to give someone else her quarters, the last thing she wanted was an expensive sex toy left out for someone else to find. Taylor tossed it in the bag with the rest of her things, throwing several pairs of underwear from the same drawer on top of it.

After everything was packed, Taylor slung the bag over her shoulder. It was heavier than she had expected. She headed through the door, walking in the direction of the elevator. She couldn't really say that she would miss her old room, she thought as she waited for the lift's doors to open. She liked living on her own, and had appreciated the private shower, but her old quarters were not anything special.

Her stomach churned with guilt at the thought of receiving such an easy assignment in response to the slaughter her squad had faced. Based on their few interactions, Maia seemed to be the quiet, careful type. If she tried to escape, it would be a long and drawn-out process. Taylor could tell there was intelligence in those shimmering blue eyes. Maia wouldn't waste time trying to overpower or threaten her. *Perhaps seduction, but...*

The thought jarred her. It was true that the ikthians had a promiscuous reputation, and often chose to mate outside of their own species if rumors were to be believed, but Taylor still wasn't sure where the strange thought had come from. Maybe Rachel had been right, and the stories about ikthian pheromones were true. Taylor shook her head in an attempt to clear her mind and took the elevator up to the captain's quarters.

Finally, the lift stopped and she stepped out, glancing down at her boots as they scuffed over plush carpeting. "Damn. Even the floor's nicer up here." The few buildings on base that weren't molded concrete had been something else before the war. These officer's quarters happened to be part of an old hotel previously used for visiting families staying with injured soldiers in the medical ward.

There were five visible doors spaced throughout the hallway, but Taylor knew which one she wanted immediately. Two guards in black body armor were posted on either side, assault rifles clutched to their chests. Adjusting the strap of her duffel on her shoulder, Taylor approached them, and the pair saluted.

After nodding at them, the guards lowered their arms. "I've got it from here, boys," Taylor said. They stepped aside and allowed her to enter the quarters. Once inside, she initiated the lock sequence for good measure. The door had already been coded to her fingerprints, retinal scans, and wrist communicator. No one could get in or out aside from her and whomever else General Hunt had given clearance. He had also given her the necessary codes to operate the prisoner's restraints and collar, though Taylor doubted she would need them.

The quarters were quiet as she examined her surroundings, and Taylor noticed that they were much more spacious than her previous bunk. Furniture had even been provided to fill the space. The living room contained couches and a low table, and a short hallway most likely led to the bedroom. The only thing missing was her charge, but as Taylor stood there scanning her surroundings, she picked up the sound of running water.

*** 

The shower was the first luxury that Maia had made use of in her new gilded cage. Although part of her desperately wanted to remain under the spray forever, breathing in the blissful steam and letting it soothe her itchy, uncomfortable skin, she worked fast, knowing she would only have a few precious moments of privacy. She had no idea when the humans would interrupt her again, but she decided it was safe to close her eyes and take a few deep breaths. Even though her species hadn't lived beneath the water for millions of years, she still needed more moisture than this planet afforded. Her home planet of Korithia was covered in water and scattered islands, dense with humidity and tropical weather.

With a sigh, she returned to washing her skin, wincing whenever she touched a bruise or scrape that hadn't fully healed. Once she had scrubbed the dirt of the last several days away, she turned off the faucet and stepped out into the steamy room. She grabbed a towel and ran it over her body quickly, not bothering to brush aside all the droplets that clung to her arms and legs. She wanted to dry off and change back into her clothes before the human—Taylor—arrived. This would probably be her last opportunity for a moment alone. She wanted to cherish it.

Maia set the towel aside and opened the bathroom door. The cool air on her wet skin made her shiver, so she hurried into the bedroom. She stopped in her tracks, however, as soon as she spotted the human sitting on the bed. She gasped and immediately covered herself with both arms. Her captor's gaze lingered, and Maia's cheeks burned with embarrassment. She moved to go back to the bathroom and fetch her old, ruined clothes, but the human spoke.

"Wait." Taylor rose off the bed. "Come here."

Maia hesitated before moving back into the bedroom, still keeping her arms wrapped around herself.

"So...you're not that different underneath the armor," Taylor said. The words sounded stilted. Whatever she had been doing in the bedroom, she had obviously not expected a naked ikthian to come running in.

Maia's heartbeat throbbed in the dip of her collarbone. There was something in the human's stare that she couldn't read. For a moment, Maia almost expected Taylor to reach out and try to touch her.

Instead, Taylor looked away. "You don't have any clothes aside from the ones you came in, do you?"

Maia shook her head. She had never been so concerned about her state of undress, but she had never been in such an embarrassing or compromising position before, especially in front of an alien. She wondered what her new guard intended to do.

"Here," Taylor said, reaching for her duffel bag. "I have some spare fatigues. They might not fit you well, though," she warned, studying Maia's figure. This time, her examination seemed more clinical.

Maia frowned. Although she was much shorter overall, her breasts were larger than Taylor's, and her hips were far more generous. The human's clothes were sure to hang off her in some places and pull uncomfortably snug in others.

"Thank you," Maia whispered as Taylor withdrew a shirt and a pair of pants and passed them into her arms. They would have to do.

She dressed quickly, all too aware of Taylor's watchful eyes as she pulled the shirt over her head. This human had been kinder to her than the others, relatively speaking. Still, her broad shoulders and muscular arms clearly marked her as a soldier. Maia would have been able to tell that about Taylor even if she hadn't run into the human on a battlefield. She knew that as long as she had the toxin suppressor on, Taylor would easily be able to overpower her.

"I'll try and see about getting you something that fits better," Taylor said as Maia pulled up the pants, struggling to get them around her hips. There were several inches of material at the bottom that covered her feet.

"I...thank you," Maia repeated, not knowing what else to say. She glanced around the room, avoiding Taylor's eyes. When she chanced another look, she caught the human staring at the bed.

"Guess we'll both be sharing these quarters," Taylor said. "Do you want the bed?"

Maia's heart thumped harder. She was expected to share living space with the human? "I..." Still, words failed her. She had delivered talks at academic panels and scientific conferences before, but how was she supposed to communicate with this human? Her captor? The alien that had refused to kill her even when the seekers showed no mercy?

Maia had never thought much about humans before, too absorbed in her work to form an opinion on them one way or another. Although they had been a distant part of her research, she had focused mainly on naledai, rakesh, and other better-known bipedal species closer to Korithia. But Taylor made her pause.

The shape of her body was similar to an ikthian's, which wasn't surprising considering the genetic similarities her own research had uncovered in all Milky Way species, but the differences that did exist were striking. Taylor had no webbing between her fingers, no fringe and no gill marks, and the dark fuzz on top of her head was particularly fascinating. Unlike naledai fur, it only covered a small portion of her body. Maia bit her lower lip, suppressing the sudden urge to reach out and touch.

Unfortunately, Taylor noticed where she was staring. "You like my hair, huh?" she asked, running one of her own hands through the dark, spiky strands. "Hair?" Maia repeated, studying the human's head more intently.

"Yep. We all have it." Taylor brought her hand back down. She paused for a moment as if she were considering something. Finally, she seemed to come to a decision. "Do you want to touch?"

Maia thought about Taylor's offer. Even though she knew it was irrational, she desperately wanted to touch the human. Her scientific curiosity got the better of her, and she nodded once.

Taylor bent her head. Slowly, Maia reached out with one hand, gingerly touching the soft strands. Her eyes widened as she ran her fingers through them, and she gasped. She hadn't expected it to be so soft, or so ticklish. It was a strangely tactile experience. Soon, she found herself lightly scratching over Taylor's scalp. The human allowed her to explore for a few moments before straightening back up, forcing Maia to pull her hand away. She found herself slightly disappointed that they had broken contact so soon.

"I...I wasn't going to poison you," Maia blurted out before she could stop herself.

Taylor took a step away, clearing her throat. "I know. The collar, remember? Mutually assured destruction."

Maia did remember. It hung around her neck, a heavy, constant reminder of her present situation. In spite of that, she was surprised Taylor had allowed any physical contact between them. The other humans she had encountered had gone out of their way to avoid touching her whenever possible for fear of being poisoned.

Taylor broke the awkward silence between them. "Have you eaten anything since you arrived on base?"

Maia's stomach began cramping uncomfortably when Taylor mentioned food. She was starving.

"I'll go get us both something," Taylor said. "Wait, can you even eat human food?"

"Yes," Maia said. "Your food should be compatible with my digestive system."

Taylor shrugged. "All right. I'm going then," she said, taking another step away. "I'll be back. The guards are outside." She walked out of the room, leaving Maia alone again.

Maia heard the door to the apartment hiss open, and then slide shut as it locked back into place, sealing her into her new prison. She sat on the bed and crossed her arms, unsure why she felt more alone now than when she had first been brought to Earth.

# Chapter Eight

THE APARTMENT WAS QUIET when Taylor finally returned, carrying several boxes. She looked around the living space but saw no sign of Maia. Shifting the food to one arm, she shut the door and locked it. She set the boxes she had retrieved down on a coffee table, figuring she could at least show Maia that humans were civil regarding their meals.

The next place to check was back in the bedroom. Taylor kicked off her boots and walked slowly down the hall. As she had expected, she found Maia sprawled across the bed with her eyes closed. Taylor paused for a moment to study her again. Everything about Maia and their interactions so far only confirmed Taylor's first suspicions. She was a scientist, a civilian with little to no combat experience, if human scientists were an acceptable comparison.

Maia's silvery skin, almost pale white, hadn't looked so jarringly alien when she had emerged from her shower earlier. Taylor had been shocked at the sudden appearance, and then angry at herself later when she fetched the food. Her prisoner wasn't something to be gawked at. She was to be considered dangerous and treated with the respect owed a prisoner of war. Allowing Maia to touch her had been especially stupid, collar or no collar.

It was probably her rattled nerves. She still could see the canyon walls when she blinked. The images were burned in behind her eyelids, and Maia only made the memories more potent. The ikthian's presence got Taylor's blood pumping, as if she should expect a squad of seekers to break in at any moment and finish her off. But now, with Maia lying on the bed, Taylor couldn't feel the same overwhelming sense of panic from before. Something about the sleeping ikthian looked so peaceful, and the furrowed crease in her forehead made her look almost human.

As if she knew Taylor was watching, Maia groaned and rolled over, limbs splaying across the covers. The light streaming through the window highlighted her softened features. Often, Taylor had wondered what ikthians felt, if they ever did. The look on Maia's face was one of pure exhaustion. It was as readable as any human's expression. Taylor's throat tightened. The similarities were unsettling.

Maia groaned and stretched an arm out, her hand clutching a fistful of bedsheets before relaxing once more. Her body shifted so the light fell across an extended arm, drawing attention to the unusual color of her skin once more. Taylor had the sudden urge to touch, much like she had wanted to when Maia first appeared in the bedroom.

*Morbid curiosity,* whispered a voice in her head. *It's hard to believe her skin could kill me if she wasn't wearing the collar.*

Despite all the warning signals going off in her head, Taylor reached out with one hand, trailing her fingertips along Maia's bare arm. Her flesh was incredibly soft despite its slightly scaled texture, and also temptingly warm. It was difficult to believe that such beautiful skin could be so deadly. At least she was safe as long as Maia kept her collar on.

Even as her mind warned her to stop, Taylor continued her exploration, sliding her fingers down and brushing the crease of Maia's elbow. Maia stirred, but didn't wake up. Gently, Taylor took Maia's hand in hers, running her thumb over the center of the ikthian's palm. Maia had five fingers, just like her, and though there was webbing between them, she had nails similar to a human's.

Taylor lowered Maia's arm again when she began to stir further. The ikthian's blue eyes fluttered open, and Taylor was embarrassed that she remembered the color so easily. For a moment, Maia's peaceful expression remained, but her face fell as she realized where she was. She blinked rapidly when she noticed Taylor standing near her but didn't pull away or start.

"I brought some food for you," Taylor said.

Maia sat up, looking around for the promised nourishment. Her stomach growled. "Where?" she asked.

Taylor suddenly realized that Maia's voice was lovely. Even if she was mostly hearing the translation that the chip in her ear sent to her brain, the sound had a certain lyrical quality to it.

"Living room." Taylor walked out of the bedroom and let Maia follow her to the low table where the stack of boxes waited for them. She sat down on the couch and gestured for Maia to do the same. When Taylor offered one of the boxes, Maia took it. "Eat as much as you want," Taylor said, watching as the ikthian opened the package. "I know you must be hungry. You haven't eaten since I took charge of you."

Maia peered into the box, and her eyes widened with surprise. The first thing she picked up was a sandwich. "What is this?" she asked, holding it up and inspecting it with a doubtful look on her face.

"It's a sandwich," said Taylor. "Meat, cheese, lettuce…not ringing any bells?"

Maia shook her head. "There is no sound of bells, but this should be fine for me to eat. We have similar fare on Korithia, although with different ingredients."

Taylor opened her own box. Apparently, even a translator couldn't help Maia identify human idioms. She took out her own sandwich and wasted no time devouring it. When Maia finally took a bite from her food, Taylor paused in chewing and asked, "Any good?"

Maia swallowed before answering. "Why do you care what I think?" she asked, her tone harsher than Taylor had expected.

It threw her off for a moment, but she recovered and explained, "Well, I want to make sure you can eat it. I wouldn't want you to starve to death on my watch. My superiors would kill me." For some reason, the mistrust in Maia's voice had upset her.

Maia didn't respond. Instead, she peeled apart the bread in her sandwich to take a closer look at what she had just taken a bite from. After picking at the lettuce and tomatoes to make sure they were edible, she took a second bite. Once she was satisfied that the sandwich was safe to eat, she began chewing rapidly.

Finally, after she had eaten half the sandwich, she paused long enough to give Taylor her opinion. "It is good," she said quietly, staring down at the sandwich. After a pause, she added, "I was hungry."

"The fridge is stocked with basic provisions any time you need something," Taylor said. She pointed to a storage unit in the corner of the room. "I won't always be around to feed you, so you should get used to taking meals from there as you need." She passed another object to Maia, a bottle filled with water. "Here. You'll probably need something to wash your food down."

Maia took the bottle and undid the top. Hesitantly, she drank, and then let out a heavy sigh. She downed half of the bottle without pausing for breath, and Taylor remembered what Roberts had said about ikthians and water. She would have to make sure that Maia had access to plenty of it.

Once Maia had finished her sandwich and water, she handed back the empty bottle and wrapper. Taylor set them on the table before settling back against the couch. The silence that followed made her shift uncomfortably in her seat. She tried to think of a conversation starter, but there was really nothing she could discuss with Maia. Being around the ikthian caused a clash of emotions that she didn't know how to deal with, and she spoke without thinking. "You know, I never thought I would be spending time like this with an ikthian. Before, they always just tried to kill me. Every single one of them."

A strange look crossed Maia's face, and Taylor began to regret her statement. Maia had never acted violently toward anyone since her capture. Perhaps it wasn't fair to lump her in with the seekers.

"And have you killed many ikthians?" Maia asked.

"The Dominion invaded our solar system and demanded that we submit. What else would you expect us to do?"

A crease formed in Maia's brow. "I suppose if another alien species tried to take control of my home planet, I would fight," she finally said. "But I am only a scientist. Not a soldier."

"If you're a scientist, what were you doing in a war zone?" That was probably what intrigued Taylor the most about Maia. The comment Roberts had made in his office had stuck with her, and if anything had come up during Maia's interrogation, none of the generals had seen fit to mention it.

"Research," Maia answered vaguely, and Taylor instantly knew there was more that the ikthian wasn't telling her. Perhaps she would mention it to Roberts the next time Maia was taken for interrogation. Despite her curiosity, it wasn't her job to question the prisoner. She only had to guard her.

* * *

After a few minutes, Taylor stood up and set the rest of the boxes beside Maia. "I'm going to take a shower." Without waiting for a response, she headed toward the bathroom. Maia's eyes lingered on Taylor's departing figure, watching the muscles shift with every movement.

Once Taylor was gone, Maia stood up and stretched. She was still extremely tired, even after the short nap she had stolen while Taylor was gone. She wandered back into the bedroom and looked around. Taylor had never finished their conversation about the bed. That probably meant she wanted to sleep on it.

Maia picked up one of the many pillows and clutched it to her chest, wandering back into the living room. The couch they had sat on to eat didn't look like it would make a particularly comfortable sleeping place, but she wasn't in a position to be choosy. She left her newly claimed pillow behind and returned to the bedroom to grab the top sheet from the bed as well.

After a few moments, she had fashioned herself a passable bed on the couch. As she expected, it wasn't very comfortable, definitely meant for sitting rather than lying down, but it was a vast improvement on the cot she had slept on before.

Maia tucked herself into the sheet, wrapping it around her body like a protective cocoon. The sound of running water drifted in from the washroom, reminding her of rain. She sighed and buried her face in the pillow, blocking out some of the light. The room wasn't damp enough either, though it was certainly better than the prison cell.

She wished this was all a dream. That she had never submitted that final report to the Dominion. That she had never been forced to run for her life. That she hadn't been captured and interrogated by humans. And then there was Taylor. She was endlessly confusing, and Maia had no idea what to make of her strange behavior. Perhaps all humans were equally strange.

For now, all she could do was try and appease her captors, particularly Taylor. Escape seemed impossible. Her only hope was to stay alive and pray that the negotiations were unsuccessful. Maybe she would be held indefinitely as a war asset. So far, her House name had earned her food, water, a shower, bedding, and a personal guard who hadn't yet harmed her. Sadly, it was one of the kindest things her mother had done for her in recent years.

The water shut off, and Maia waited with the sheet clutched around her. A few moments later, Taylor peeked into the living room, obviously looking for her. "If you're going to sleep out here, I'll turn off the light for you," she said, tapping a pressure pad beside the door.

Maia had hoped the dark would make it easier for her to sleep, but the couch still remained too uncomfortable. Her neck already hurt, despite the leverage the pillow gave her. She tried rolling over, sleeping on the opposite end, curled up on one cushion, but nothing worked.

Two hours later, she gave up and stood from the couch with a sigh. Reluctantly, she crept into the bedroom. Taylor didn't seem to notice. The human slept peacefully, unmoving beneath the covers. Carefully, Maia pushed the sheets aside and sat down at the edge of the bed. She lay down with her own sheet and pillow, keeping as far away from Taylor as possible as she tried to get comfortable. Once her fear of waking the human faded, she was able to fall into a fitful sleep that eventually turned into a deep, dreamless slumber.

# Chapter Nine

TAYLOR WOKE THE NEXT morning with someone soft and warm lying in her arms. She groaned and pulled the unfamiliar body closer, placing a gentle kiss on the woman's shoulder. Her hand stroked lazy circles over her bed-partner's back as she tried to remember whom she could have possibly fallen asleep with. Whoever it was had the softest breasts...

Her eyes fluttered open, and as Maia's pale form came into focus, her memories of the previous day came flooding back. She stiffened, and Maia released a low moan. Heat crawled into Taylor's cheeks as the ikthian blinked up at her. For a second, they just stared at one another in confusion. Then, they scrambled awkwardly apart.

Maia curled into a ball, tugging the sheets up to her chin. "I...I am sorry," she stammered. "The couch was uncomfortable, and you did say I could use the bed if I wanted..."

"You're welcome to it," Taylor said, standing up and looking away. She wanted to give Maia some privacy even though the ikthian had fallen asleep in the over-sized clothes Taylor had given her the day before. "Just let me know. I'll take the couch."

Taylor went in search of new clothes without saying another word. She had left some of them scattered across the floor, but they were mostly used, so she tossed them in the laundry chute and went rummaging around for a fresh change of pants and a shirt in her duffel bag. Sometime today, she needed to unpack properly. That could be accomplished after she established some space between herself and Maia. Waking up with the ikthian draped over her had been the last thing Taylor had expected, but what upset her the most was her own reaction. Instead of feeling concerned for her own safety or angry at Maia, she felt embarrassed for getting into the situation in the first place. She should have insisted on taking the couch.

*What am I thinking? She's a prisoner. An ikthian. Her people killed your squad, remember? Why are you letting down your guard like this?*

But try as she might, Taylor found it difficult to lump Maia in with the seekers. She wasn't sure what about the ikthian put her at ease, but although being in Maia's presence could be incredibly awkward, Taylor felt with a certainty deep in her bones that Maia was harmless. She was even glad that her superiors had ordered her to give Maia the gold-star prisoner treatment. The thought that Maia might have been confined to one of the barren cells under the base instead was strangely upsetting to consider.

As she peeled off her shirt and pulled a new one over her head, Taylor wondered what her fellow soldiers would say if they had witnessed her display this morning. It was often the standby joke to tease soldiers about charming exotic women into their beds. Captain Roberts got the worst of it by far, considering how many missions he worked in cooperation with the naledai military. It was even worse with ikthians. Their reputation as sirens was already firmly established.

Thinking about Roberts made Taylor remember that she hadn't bothered to check her datapad since the night before. She had been too busy to read her messages. She hurried over to her dresser, where the tablet still sat, and activated it, frowning when she noticed several missed calls and even more messages. She read the first one, and her stomach sank when she saw that it was from Captain Roberts.

*'Report with the prisoner to interrogation at 0700. Building D-05, floor 2.'*

Taylor checked the time and breathed a sigh of relief when she saw that they still had an hour to prepare. If she hurried, they wouldn't be late. "Get up," she said, her attention returning to Maia. "We have to be somewhere this morni..." Her voice cut off as Maia stood up, letting the sheet fall from her body. It was a distracting sight, even though she still wore the clothes that Taylor had given her the day before. Taylor shook her head and turned away. "I'll leave you to prepare." She walked out of the bedroom and waited for Maia to join her in the living room.

Once both of them were up, they still had time to spare, so Taylor dug out some of the food from yesterday and prepared a quick breakfast. Finally, thirty minutes before they had to be in the interrogation block, they left the officers' quarters. Taylor had to cuff Maia's hands with magnetic wrist restraints, though she knew it was a somewhat excessive precaution. Without the use of her toxins, Maia would be dead before she escaped San Diego base, and even if by some miracle she managed it, she had no chance of successfully leaving the planet. Maia was currently the only ikthian on Earth, as far as Taylor knew.

The base wasn't necessarily quiet early in the morning, but the soldiers and personnel who were up and about had destinations in mind. Still, they all spared a moment to stop and stare at Maia. Groups of men and women leaned in close to one another, muttering too quietly for Taylor to hear, but they always glanced away when she responded with a challenging stare.

Taylor was so focused on shepherding Maia past a particularly large cluster of onlookers that she hardly noticed two soldiers walking straight toward her from the opposite direction until she nearly ran into them. The only reason she stopped was because Maia came to a halt first, and Taylor swiftly realized she was standing face to face with a familiar wall of muscle.

"Hey, Andrew."

"Lieutenant," Andrew said with a grin. "Sergeant Bower here was interested in seeing the ikthian."

Bower was another rather muscular soldier, but unlike Andrew, he tended to leer at women in a way that made Taylor's skin crawl. He looked over Maia's body with little reservation. "Just like a human," he muttered. "That's what the rumor is, anyway." He reached out to touch Maia, but she flinched away.

"Are you an idiot, Sergeant?" Taylor barked, catching his arm with her own and knocking it aside. "She could kill you with one touch if she wanted." If she hadn't been so angry, she might have been embarrassed, considering her own hypocrisy when it came to physical contact with the prisoner.

"She's got the collar on," Bower drawled, apparently unconcerned. "She won't use any of her juice unless she wants her brains scrambled."

"*Your* brains are scrambled, Bower. Anyway, I need to take the prisoner to Building D. Just leave before I have to file an incident report about this."

"Building D is close enough," Bower said. "Besides, I haven't gotten to satisfy my curiosity yet."

"Uh, maybe we should get going," Andrew said, clearly uncomfortable with how the situation was escalating.

"Not yet." Bower stopped staring at Maia long enough to cast a brief look at Andrew. "Come on, it's not every day you get to see an alien up close and personal, especially an ikthian. I hear they'll breed with any species at all, even animals."

Taylor had heard similar things before, but hearing Bower say them to Maia caused her fists to clench. She glanced at Maia briefly to make sure she was all right and noticed that her eyes had narrowed. Still,

Taylor doubted she would try anything. Obnoxious as Bower was, he was right about the collar.

"Not this one, Sergeant," she said firmly, taking a step forward to position herself between Maia and Bower. "And from the way she's behaving, she obviously doesn't consider you an option."

"Have you gotten a chance to test her out yet?" Bower stepped to the side so Taylor no longer obstructed his view. "Those pheromones must be good if you're this possessive already."

"Drop it, Bower," Taylor snapped. "She's a prisoner, not some piece of meat for you to gawk at with a hard-on."

Bower kept grinning. "You had me going for a minute there. Come on, Lieutenant. It's just an ikthian. Didn't they wipe out your squad? It doesn't deserve your charity." He pushed Taylor aside, grabbing for the collar of Maia's shirt. "I think it needs to be knocked down a few pegs, actually."

Taylor reacted instinctively. She drew her weapon, aiming the nose straight at Bower's head. "Just try and touch her, and I'll do a lot worse than pull rank on you," she growled, her finger twitching on the trigger.

A gurgling noise escaped Bower's mouth, but he wasn't the first to speak.

"Hey, hey, Taylor!" Andrew lunged forward, urging her to lower her arm.

Taylor aimed her pistol away from Bower, but that didn't stop him from glaring angrily at her. "You fucking bitch," he growled, his voice hoarse.

"Sorry, I didn't hear a 'ma'am' attached to that," Taylor said. She was done with him, and he would be reported for insubordination if she had any say. Quickly, she turned to Maia. "Are you all right?"

Maia started, seeming to snap out of a daze. It was as if she had retreated within herself for protection. "I think so."

"Come on." Taylor led her away before Bower could recover, slipping inside the first available building and hurrying for the elevator. Once they were safely inside, Taylor felt like she could breathe again. She stared at the elevator doors as the two of them waited through the slow ride to the bottom.

Maia broke the silence first. "Thank you."

"Just doing my job," Taylor said flatly. When the ikthian's expression fell, she tried a different approach. "Look, if you're going to escape and kill anyone while you're here, make sure you poison him first. He deserves it."

Maia's eyes widened at the comment, and Taylor wondered if she understood that it was a joke. "I have no intention of hurting anyone here."

Taylor snorted. "Well, that's a first coming from an ikthian, but I believe you. Anyway, you don't need to thank me. Bower obviously had it coming."

"This is not the first time you have come to my rescue," Maia said. "Back on Amaren, when you intercepted those seekers...you saved me."

Something about the way Maia looked at her left Taylor speechless. There was admiration in her voice, but her blue eyes held something like hope. Either way, Taylor knew it was unwarranted. "I don't think I saved you from anything," she said truthfully.

The elevator opened, and they stepped into the hall. Maia sighed. "Perhaps you will understand one day."

Rae D. Magdon & Michelle Magly

# Chapter Ten

THEY ARRIVED AT BUILDING D-05 after a few minutes, and Maia noticed several guards in black armor waiting at the door to escort them the rest of the way. Taylor kept one hand around her elbow, guiding her firmly, but the grip was loose enough to allow her some comfort. Maia glanced nervously at the other humans that had fallen into step beside them before returning her gaze to Taylor, hoping for some reassurance. Taylor squeezed her arm, and Maia let the tight, tense line of her shoulders relax slightly.

It wasn't long before they reached their destination, a nondescript room on the second floor. Three men in uniform were waiting inside, and Maia recognized them, although she wasn't sure of their names. The muscular, dark-haired human on the right had been there to meet them at the landing pad during their arrival on Earth. The silver-haired human in the middle was a high-ranking official of some sort, judging from the medals on his chest. Maia remembered the pale man with a naked head on the left as well. All three had been present when Taylor had been assigned as her guard.

"Lieutenant, just on time. We're about to open negotiations with the Dominion," the dark-haired man on the right said. He smiled at Taylor, and Maia noticed that she smiled back. Obviously, they were friendly. "Chairman Bouchard is particularly eager to get the ball rolling."

"Of course, Captain Roberts." The man with the naked head, Bouchard, cleared his throat. "I see the prisoner is in...presentable condition, Lieutenant Morgan."

"Yes, Chairman," Taylor said. She turned to the silver-haired man. "She's been fed and introduced to her new quarters, General Hunt, Sir. So far, she hasn't acted aggressively or attempted to escape."

General Hunt nodded. "A wise move. If her mother and her people come through for her, she won't have to. I just hope we can stop at least some of this bloodshed."

Maia listened intently. She hadn't spoken to her mother in some time before her capture. Irana did have some affection for her, although she didn't entirely approve of Maia's career choice, or her current status with the Dominion. The thought of going back into such a dangerous situation made Maia's stomach clench. She hoped that the negotiations would fall through. Anything the humans did to her was bound to be less gruesome than the Dominion's punishments for traitors.

"We all want that, Sir," Taylor said. "Just tell me what I need to do, and I'll take care of it."

"For now, take the prisoner inside," General Hunt ordered. "We're going to record proof of her capture and send it to the ikthians."

Maia allowed Taylor to lead her further into the room, and she began to take in her surroundings. Like the first interrogation chamber, this one was cold and dry, harshly lit with blank concrete walls. A chair was bolted to the floor in the middle of the room, and a vid recorder floated nearby. Taylor led Maia over to the chair, and she sat down without instruction.

"Taylor, over here," said Roberts.

Taylor returned to the captain's side as they prepared the vid equipment, and Bouchard moved to stand beside Maia. "Someone fix this damnable microphone," he said. One member of the camera crew took a step forward, and Maia noticed the nervous glance he shot in her direction. "We haven't got all day," Bouchard snapped, the wrinkles in his forehead becoming even more pronounced.

"Yes, Sir." Cautiously, the man stepped forward and fixed the small microphone attached to Bouchard's suit. His hands trembled, and he deliberately looked away from Maia's chair. Unlike that other horrible man, Bower, this one seemed terrified of her in spite of her restraints.

"Stop behaving like a child," Bouchard said as the man tried and failed to correct the mic. "She's harmless, and she cannot release toxins as long as she is wearing the collar. It will shock her if she tries."

The technician swallowed nervously, but pushed on with his task. Finally, he finished and scurried away to rejoin the camera crew, leaving Maia alone next to Bouchard.

"Lieutenant Morgan," General Hunt said, gesturing to the empty space opposite Bouchard. "Please join the Chairman behind the prisoner."

Maia's gaze met Taylor's as she left the rest of the group and walked around the chair. She resisted the temptation to turn and watch Taylor's movements as the human stepped into place behind her. A hand rested on her shoulder, and Maia tensed before she realized it was

Taylor. For some reason, it comforted her.

"All right," Bouchard said. "Get ready to record. We'll edit later."

"Recording," the man behind the floating camera said.

"I am Chairman Bouchard of the Human Council for Defense." Maia had no idea what to do with her facial expression. She knew she should stare directly into the camera, but she was hyperaware of Taylor's presence behind her. She also didn't want to think about who would be viewing this footage back on Korithia.

"We have captured Maia Kalanis, the daughter of Irana Kalanis. So far, she has not been harmed."

Maia's shoulders tensed, and she felt Taylor squeeze slightly, as if to comfort her.

"She will remain unharmed if you agree to open negotiations with us, and cease attacks on all human and naledai forces while the negotiations are in progress." For some reason, Bouchard's voice set Maia on edge. She would have to ask Taylor about him later.

Before he could continue, General Hunt held up his hand, motioning for the camera to stop recording. "That's really all we need, Chairman. We stated our demands, and we proved that the prisoner is in our custody."

Bouchard looked disappointed, but Maia breathed a sigh of relief as Captain Roberts nodded his agreement. "Short and sweet. I like it. Now, we just have to wait for their answer." He looked past Maia and addressed Taylor directly. "Good work, Lieutenant Morgan. You can take the prisoner back now. We'll contact you if we need anything else."

The walk back to her prison was slower than the journey to the interrogation had been, Maia observed as Taylor led her from the room. Unfortunately, more humans were out and about this time. Maia's skin crawled as she felt countless pairs of eyes watching her. It was even worse than before. She hated being stared at, and she instinctively pulled closer to Taylor. Although her captor was a human, she was also Maia's only protector. What if Taylor hadn't been sympathetic when Sergeant Bower had grabbed for her? The outcome might have been very different.

When Taylor had first captured her, Maia assumed she had traded one hell for another, though the humans seemed content to wait and see how useful she could be before throwing her away. The time she had spent with Taylor had convinced her that remaining with the humans on Earth would be safer than returning to the Dominion, but the hate in Bower's eyes was more than enough to remind her that she was still among enemies.

A thought occurred to her, rising unbidden in her mind. What if someone else had found her in the canyon? Any other human would have shot her without a second thought, but Taylor had hesitated. Without her, Maia knew she wouldn't have left Amaren alive. Perhaps that was why she found Taylor so intriguing, even beyond her usual scientific curiosity about other species. The human had saved her, even though she had no reason to do so.

# Chapter Eleven

MAIA FELT A WAVE of relief as soon as the door to the captain's quarters closed behind them. Even though it was technically her prison, she felt safer inside the barracks than out among the soldiers.

"Here, give me your wrists," Taylor said once they were alone. Maia offered them, staring down at Taylor's hands as she undid the cuffs. The human's hands were less elegant than she had expected, calloused and scarred in a few places with uneven white marks, and of course there was no webbing. A question rose in her mind before she could stifle it. How would those hands feel on her skin?

"Are you okay?" Taylor asked, and Maia forced herself to look up into the human's face. She was a little surprised that Taylor seemed able to read her emotions. Based on her experience with the humans so far, most of them thought that ikthians were little more than animals. Even a few of Taylor's comments had been hurtful.

"I am all right," Maia murmured dismissively. She didn't like the involuntary reaction her body had to Taylor's presence. The more time she spent around Taylor, the more confused she felt. She should have been worrying about being a prisoner of war, about the Dominion's attempts to find and kill her, but instead, she found herself wondering what Taylor thought of her. It was disconcerting to say the least.

Apparently taking Maia at her word, Taylor shrugged and headed for the washroom, leaving her alone with her thoughts. Not sure what else to do, Maia sat on the couch, trying to process the uncomfortable realization that Taylor's departure had lowered her mood, even though she had only gone into the next room.

*She's your only company. Of course you have grown attached.* The lone thought flickered through her mind, though Maia knew she was just trying to rationalize away her feelings. That was something her colleagues had always criticized her for. There had to be a rationalization for everything.

"And why shouldn't there be?" she had always replied. "This galaxy has yet to prove that things simply 'happen'. There is always an order to be distilled from the chaos." The basis of Maia's research had been on this slightly paranoid belief, and in the end, she had been right. Even now in Taylor's company, she could only find more evidence mounting to support her argument. It didn't take a geneticist to observe the similarities between their species, but it had taken Maia's research to prove it meant something.

However, her interest in Taylor extended beyond scientific curiosity. The way her blood rushed every time the human touched her was a clear indication. Maia wondered for a moment if this was her own doing. Perhaps if she had taken the time to gain more romantic and sexual experience instead of burying herself in her work, she would have been able to handle this situation better.

Ikthians almost never had sex with aliens, despite what the rumors on Earth apparently claimed. Some of the protectorate nations were more accepting of the practice than others, but it was considered foolish and demeaning to pursue romantic endeavors with other species. Her people firmly believed that they were the pinnacle of evolved life, predestined to surpass all other races, and the theory dissolved quickly if ikthians started mating and raising families with other species, even if they were of equal intelligence and capability, as Maia's research had indicated.

The humans were quickly proving themselves to her. Taylor, at least, was perfectly capable of the same wide range of emotions that her species felt, and showed a level of intelligence equal to most ikthians. She also had a certain surety and bluntness to her that Maia found somewhat annoying, and, she had to admit, attractive in an irritating sort of way.

The sound of the door opening gave Maia a few moments of warning before Taylor's return, but it wasn't enough time to try and will away the hot blush staining her cheeks. It didn't help that Taylor had decided to emerge wearing less clothes than she had left with. Her uniform was gone, stripped away to reveal a plain white compression shirt and a loose pair of undergarments that cut off at mid-thigh. There was a strip of olive skin between them, positioned at exactly the right height to highlight Taylor's navel and the line that bisected her abdominal muscles.

"I'm going to work on some things," Taylor said, walking right past Maia. She watched the human move, aware of how the water droplets rolled over the curve of her muscular arms. Taylor slumped into a desk chair and pulled herself up to the wooden tabletop. Maia was surprised to find that she enjoyed watching Taylor's hands activate the graphic interface. For some reason, the deft movements of her fingers were a point of interest. Maia shook her head and stood up, deciding to follow Taylor's example and head for the shower. Her skin was feeling dry anyway.

"I will be in the washroom," she said. Taylor barely nodded as she kept working. As far as guarding her went, the human was fairly lax in her duties, but she had probably assessed Maia to be low risk. Maia had already considered searching for a weapon in the apartment, but aside from Taylor's gun, which she always kept close, there was nothing for her to use. The apartment had been combed over quite thoroughly before she had arrived.

Maia stepped into the steam-filled room and breathed deeply, the moisture immediately soothing the aches in her body. Earth was far too dry for her liking, she had decided, but this room provided some relief when she needed it. She shut the door and stripped down, turning on the flow of water before stepping into the shower. At least humans had these devices, but more than anything, she wanted a proper body of water to go swimming in. She knew Earth had oceans, rivers, and lakes, but she doubted the humans would let her near one just because she felt a little homesick. For now, the water cascading over her body was more than enough to sate her.

Maia ran her hands over her parched skin, enjoying the steam as it caressed her arms and legs. She found herself remembering the way Taylor's hands had looked. The sure, steady movements. The small scars. The large palms. Maia reached up to touch her own shoulder, remembering the way Taylor had gripped it with a reserved sort of strength while the camera recorded them.

It took Maia a moment to realize that her other hand had started to wander, tracing patterns over her stomach and drifting undeniably lower. She leaned back, bracing herself against the side of the shower and enjoying the cool, firm wall against her flesh. It was a strangely pleasant contrast to the warm droplets trailing down her limbs.

She debated with herself for a little while, letting her fingertips hover just below her navel. Why was she suddenly thrumming with energy? Why was her skin so exquisitely sensitive? They were not new feelings. Despite her inexperience, Maia was somewhat familiar with physical desire and how her body worked. But why was this happening now? She was a prisoner, and although she had escaped from the seekers and the Dominion, her life was still in danger.

*Perhaps,* Maia thought, *I am mistaken.* The hand that had hesitated on her lower abdomen began moving again, sliding downwards to cup between her legs. Her breath hitched when her fingers met wetness and welcoming heat. *No, not mistaken.* Before she could talk herself out of it, she closed her eyes and tilted her head back, tracing her outer lips until they began blossoming apart. The steady, insistent throb that had started low in her stomach began spreading downward to meet her fingertips.

"What am I doing?" she murmured, so softly that she could barely hear herself over the hiss of the shower. But then Maia found the tight ridge just above her entrance and began circling, flicking over the sensitive tip. Suddenly, she didn't care. Not about what was causing her strange spike in desire, or her current situation. At least for the moment, none of it mattered.

As her hand moved faster, she tried to conjure up a face from her memory, someone suitable to think about. One of her old schoolmates, although they had long since drifted apart. The particularly attractive professor she had studied with for two semesters, back before she had started working for the University. And, finally, someone completely imaginary, a face with dark eyes, a strong chin, and a shock of dark hair. *Wait, hair?* Maia was so startled by where her mind had wandered that she almost stopped the motion of her hand.

Her heart thumped crazily against the cage of her ribs, and her fingers slipped. *No.* This was wrong. Taylor was an alien, not to mention her guard. The human might have inadvertently saved her life, but she had still taken Maia captive.

It was just the stress of her situation, Maia decided. She closed her eyes again and allowed her fingers to press firmly against the swollen bundle of nerves. A shudder ran through her body, and she bit her lip. Yes, she needed this to take the edge off her stress. That was all. The human's figure just happened to be a sexually pleasing one. Lust and proper emotional desire were two very different realities, and Maia trusted that her attraction to Taylor would remain safely within the realm of lust.

She groaned, giving in to temptation and slipping two fingers inside herself. Perhaps if the humans and ikthians had found peace instead, she would have come to Earth on a scientific study. They would have made Taylor her escort in between lectures, and sometime during her busy schedule...

Maia could picture it vividly. Taylor would pin her against the shower wall, hands gliding down from her shoulders to cup her breasts. She swallowed a moan as she rocked forward on her own fingers. Taylor would part her legs and slip two fingers inside her just like this, taking her with frenzied passion.

The thought alone, so utterly forbidden and impossible, was enough to bring her release crashing down on her sooner than she expected. Maia gasped as her inner walls fluttered around her fingers, and she rocked into the heel of her palm, desperately trying to relieve the pressure.

As her contractions faded, so did the pleasure. Her clouded mind returned to Earth, in this steamy shower, where she stood alone. She shook her head. "What is wrong with me?" she whispered. Maia had never fantasized so intensely about someone before, especially not an alien she knew next to nothing about. If she took the time to learn about Taylor, surely her stress-induced infatuation would vanish.

Maia removed her fingers and resumed washing. A friend of hers had once said that relationships ended when both parties realized neither would live up to the other's expectations. The same would hold true for her infatuation with Taylor. She was Maia's guard, and the largest obstacle between her and freedom. Taylor would never sympathize with her, and she would certainly never help her escape the base. That alone would put enough distance between them.

Maia shut off the water. She still felt tightness deep within her chest every time she breathed. She wanted to know more about Taylor, as disappointing as the outcome would inevitably be.

Rae D. Magdon & Michelle Magly

.

.

# Chapter Twelve

TAYLOR GROANED AND HIT the 'delete' button again. The screen in front of her wiped, and she flexed her fingers on top of the old-fashioned touchpad. She had no idea what else to type. Most of her colleagues simply dictated through the microphone, but she couldn't seem to find her voice, let alone her words. She had gone through perhaps five attempted drafts for this letter with little success, and it was only the first one on the list. It was addressed to the significant other of Private Barkes, whom Taylor had never met before her mission to Amaren. Barkes had never brought up personal details with the squad, a fact Taylor only realized after sitting down to write the damn letter.

With a sigh, she started typing again, this time trying to describe the battle scene. *Private Barkes fought bravely to ensure the safety of the squad.* Taylor considered deleting the line. The seekers had taken them completely by surprise, and most of the squad were butchered before they could put up a proper fight. Only she and Jackson had escaped the initial ambush.

Taylor rubbed her temple and leaned back in the uncomfortable chair. Although losing Jackson, Barkes, and the others weighed heavily on her, she had no words of condolence for their grieving family members, and she hated herself for it. She could feel pressure building behind her eyes. *Damn it.* The last thing she needed was to be on the verge of tears.

As she wiped a hand across her eyes, she heard the door to the bathroom open. Taylor hunched over the interface and tried to concentrate on the letter. If she kept her face low, perhaps Maia wouldn't see the tear streaks forming on her cheeks. Taylor felt like she was going insane. She had to be. Nothing had ever made her cry so easily. She hadn't even cried right after her squadmates died, but there had hardly been time to think about it. Now, sitting at this desk, she had to write a letter that somehow conveyed a sick message of hope, respect, and remorse for her fallen comrades. She drew in a shaky breath and forced herself to type another meaningless sentence.

"Taylor?" The voice behind her sounded inquisitive, concerned.

Taylor wiped at her eyes again, but she didn't turn to face Maia. "What do you want?"

There was a moment of silence, as if Maia was unsure whether or not to continue. Even while staring resolutely at the datapad, Taylor could sense her hesitation. "I was wondering why you were crying," she said at last.

For a moment, Taylor fooled herself into believing that there was sympathy in Maia's voice. She sighed, blinking away the sting in her eyes and hoping no fresh tears would fall. "It's nothing," she said, more gruffly than she had intended. She wasn't in the mood to talk about the loss of her squad, or the seemingly impossible task of writing letters to their family members.

Maia crept further around Taylor's chair. She didn't force eye contact, but she pressed slightly into Taylor's personal space. "I do not know much about humans, but I doubt that they cry over nothing. I did not even know your species was capable of crying before now."

Taylor sighed. Part of her wanted to unburden herself, but it seemed almost disrespectful to talk about the loss of her squad with an ikthian. Maia certainly didn't act like the seekers, who slaughtered without mercy, but she was still the enemy.

After a moment of conflict, Taylor finally turned her chair to face Maia, not bothering to hide her face anymore. She had to talk to someone, and even though Maia was an ikthian, she had witnessed Jackson's death. Perhaps she would be able to relate in some small way.

"You know I lost my entire squad on Amaren." Taylor set her datapad back on the desk and switched off the terminal's interface. "The seekers killed them all. Since I was their commanding officer, I have to inform their families." She swallowed, trying to fight the sudden thickness in her throat and praying that her voice wouldn't break. "They all got a brief memo to let them know what happened as soon as I reported in, but...I have to write letters. Something more personal."

Taylor looked into Maia's blue eyes, and was surprised to see them swimming with sympathy. It was more emotion than she had ever seen on an ikthian's face before. She didn't know how to react. Finally, she decided to continue. "The worst part is, I don't know what to say. I worked with them. I respected them. I would have given my life to get them off that rock safe. But I didn't really know them. Not the way their families did. Now, I wish I had. At least then I would have something to say besides: 'I'm sorry I got them killed.'"

Maia placed her hand on Taylor's shoulder, much like Taylor had done for her earlier. The contact made Taylor jump, but she made no move to pull away or push the hand aside. For some reason, it comforted her. "It is not your fault. The seekers were not even pursuing your soldiers in the first place."

Taylor ran the back of her hand across her face again, wiping away the last stubborn streaks of her tears. "Don't say that. It was my fault. It was my job to get them out of there alive, and I failed."

"No," Maia whispered. "The seekers were after me." Although she didn't step away, she pulled back a few inches, almost as if she were retreating. Taylor felt the comforting weight of Maia's hand leave her shoulder, and for some reason, she wanted to reach out and take it back. Instead, she remained seated and resisted the impulse.

"That doesn't change the fact that a bunch of bottom feeders mowed them down for nothing." Taylor swiveled her chair back around and picked up her abandoned datapad. She had to finish these letters before tomorrow, no matter how difficult it was. After all they had lost, it was the least her squad's family members deserved.

Maia started to say something, but Taylor didn't meet her gaze, her face fixed with concentration. She typed a few more useless words, sighed, and erased them again almost as soon as they appeared on the screen.

"I know you are upset," Maia began, but stopped when Taylor let out a snort.

"Damn, I wonder how you figured that one out?"

Maia frowned. "I came over to help you, but that seems pointless if you are going to behave this way."

"Well, I didn't ask for your help anyway," Taylor snapped. She knew she was being petty toward Maia, but she had little sympathy left at the moment. She tossed her datapad aside. She was sick of writing these letters. "You're right. It is your fault my squad is dead. Whatever stupid quarrel is going on between you and the rest of your stinking race, it killed my people."

She knew the words were a mistake the moment she said them. Maia looked livid, and Taylor felt a spike of fear. Even with the collar on, Maia was still dangerous.

"You involved yourself with that quarrel when you made me your prisoner to save your comrade," Maia said, and Taylor could hear the tightness of anger in her voice. She leaned back in her seat, shocked at the obvious display of emotion from her usually demure prisoner. "And even that poor attempt failed. The seekers would have slaughtered you if they did not need to torture me first."

"Maia," Taylor said, unsure how else to calm her.

"This quarrel is beyond any feud between races. At least you know your soldiers are dead and not being tormented for information. At least you know you are safe on your own home-world."

Taylor saw tears welling in Maia's eyes. She reached forward to grab Maia's hand, but the ikthian stepped back. She took a breath and closed her eyes for a moment. When she opened them again, the tears were gone. "I apologize," she said, the pitch of her voice softening. Taylor sat still, mouth open in slight shock. "I scolded you for an ill temper and lost mine instead."

"No, it's okay. I started it." Taylor got up from her chair and grabbed her datapad. "Would you like to sit down? You look like you have some things on your mind."

"What?" Maia asked.

"You seem to be upset," Taylor clarified.

"Oh." Maia crossed her arms and took another calming breath. "I suppose I am."

Taylor led her over to the couch, and they sat down together. She was relieved to see that Maia had calmed down. She didn't know how she would have handled a sobbing ikthian. "I'm sorry I snapped. I forgot that you're a civilian probably on the verge of a breakdown. God knows I would be if I had been captured by ikthians."

"You would be dead, if you were lucky," Maia said in her usual serious tone.

Taylor laughed. The tension had broken, and she felt much better than she had before starting the letters. "Well, there's a vote of confidence for me."

Maia shook her head. "I was merely stating a fact. If they thought you could provide them any useful information, the Dominion would..."

"Hey," Taylor said, resting her hand on the ikthian's forearm. "Let's not think about what the Dominion would do to either of us if we were on Korithia instead of Earth."

"That is probably for the best," Maia sighed. "It is far from ideal, but being held captive by humans is preferable to being dragged home by the seekers."

Taylor wanted to ask Maia to expand on the cryptic comment, but she suspected her prisoner didn't care to talk further. Instead, she waited to see if Maia would volunteer an explanation on her own. When Maia didn't speak up, Taylor changed the subject. "Hey, thank you for trying to make me feel better. It's not something I would have expected from an ikthian, especially one that's my prisoner."

Maia offered a small smile. "You are not what I expected from a human, either," she confessed.

"I'm not sure whether that's a compliment or an insult." Taylor returned the smile. She stretched, trying to ease some of the stiffness in her shoulders and spine before she pushed herself up off the couch. "I'm going to try and finish those letters." She headed back toward the desk and her discarded datapad. "I think I know what to say now."

Maia rose from the couch as well. "I think I might try and sleep," she said, gazing at the open door leading to the bedroom.

"I won't be far behind you." Taylor activated the datapad's screen. Her fingers hesitated for a moment, and she glanced back over her shoulder. "Maia? It wasn't your fault my squad died."

"Yes, it was," Maia whispered. "But...thank you for saying that anyway." She turned and made her way to the bedroom before Taylor could respond.

# Chapter Thirteen

TAYLOR SLAMMED ANOTHER AMMO clip into place and hoisted her assault rifle back up to her shoulder. She aimed at the distant target, let out a breath, and fired a short burst of shots directly into the dummy's chest. The cluster of bullets hit in a controlled scatter with a satisfying *rat-tat-tat*.

"Not bad, Taylor," Rachel said, holding her own gun at the ready. She grinned, narrowing her eyes as a smirk tweaked the corners of her lips. "That is, if you were still in training." She turned back to the target, took aim, and fired off a series of clean shots. All of the bullets landed squarely in the dummy's forehead rather than the scattered chest shot Taylor had gone for.

"I get it, Harris. You rock. I suck." Taylor shot again, this time clipping the target's shoulder. "Damn it," she growled. Usually, she was a much more consistent shot, but she was on edge this afternoon, and her concentration was blown.

Maia had been taken in for another interrogation, and Taylor found herself increasingly worried by the ikthian's absence. It wasn't like the brass wanted to hear about Maia's research anyway. After talking with her that morning, Taylor learned that the interrogators had already asked about her findings, but were much more interested in her lineage.

Instead of dwelling on it further, Taylor waited to fire another round. Rachel took another shot that landed right between the dummy's eyes, so Taylor gave up, locking the safety in place and putting her rifle down. "You win."

Rachel pouted. "Aw, come on, you usually last a little longer than this. What's bugging you today?"

Taylor kicked the dirt with her boot and picked up her gun again. If shooting targets would stop Rachel from asking questions, maybe it was too early to call it quits. "Nothing is bothering me," she said, although it was a lie. She wanted to spend more time with Maia. *No, that can't be it. Maybe I'm just upset that they might be torturing her.* Maia wasn't like other ikthians; she was a person, and if the interrogators treated her like anything less...

"Something is obviously bothering you," Rachel said. "Is it the twenty four hour watch they dumped you with? I mean, I know we're short-handed, but it's unfair to expect you to watch a bottom-feeder all day, every day."

Taylor cringed at the word 'bottom-feeder', even though she had used it plenty of times herself. Maia was anything but that. The empathy she had shown yesterday proved it. "I appreciate the downtime, don't get me wrong," Taylor said, gesturing at the shooting range. This had been her first moment alone with a friend for a while. "But I just think they're wasting time in the interrogation today."

"Who?" Rachel asked.

"The people interrogating Maia." Taylor sighed and pulled the spent ammo clip from her gun.

Rachel blinked, as if she was surprised to hear that the alien had a name, and even more surprised to hear Taylor use it so casually. "So, you're on a first name basis with it now?" she asked, her tone edged with disapproval. She fired a few more shots into the dummy's head, and Taylor watched it snap back in response. "Damn it," Rachel muttered, "this thing won't last long before someone breaks it. Wish they would spring for a proper holo-arena."

"No money," Taylor said, secretly relieved that Rachel hadn't expected an answer to her first question. She didn't want to think about the curious way her relationship with Maia was developing. "This war is bleeding us dry."

"True," Rachel agreed, popping out her own spent ammo clip and replacing it with a sharp motion of her hand. "I haven't been off-planet for a while, but I've heard stories. They're barely equipping squads with what they need to complete their missions anymore."

Taylor lowered her weapon, turning away from the targets. "A lot of bullets and guns won't save you if the ikthians get the jump."

"At least we're not as bad off as the colonists," Rachel pointed out, following Taylor's lead and lowering her own gun. "My family's out there. They wanted to come back home, but the Chair of Defense issued an executive order saying Earth couldn't take any more refugees."

Taylor scowled at the mention of Bouchard, but decided not to say exactly what she thought of him. It would only feed Rachel's worries. "They're still alive?"

Rachel nodded. "For now. But if something doesn't break soon...who knows?"

"We just have to hope..." Taylor caught herself just before she used Maia's name again. It was a dangerous habit to get into. "We just have to hope that the ikthian can help us. The brass seems to have high hopes."

"She'd better," Rachel said, narrowing her eyes. "She cost you your entire squad. It would be nice to see something good out of it."

Taylor swallowed thickly, glancing at her gun to disguise the conflicted expression on her face. She remembered back to the night before, when Maia had talked about her own people with such obvious fear. For just a moment, Taylor wondered if there was a way to use Maia and negotiate for a ceasefire without turning her over to the Dominion afterwards. She had made it clear that the ikthians were not going to be kind to her if she was returned to Korithia.

After a moment, Taylor noticed that Rachel was staring at her, and she quickly looked back up, trying to disguise the awkward pause. "Yeah. It would. At least then I'd have something to tell the families...I wrote all the letters of condolence yesterday."

Rachel winced. "Damn. I don't think any of them would have blamed you for taking another few days to get your head together, especially since you're babysitting our ticket out of this mess."

"It isn't terrible," Taylor said. "She's not bad company."

Rachel set her gun down. "Did you just say that? Really?"

Taylor avoided meeting Rachel's gaze. "What? She's just a harmless civilian."

"It's the reason your crew is dead," said Rachel. She put a hand on Taylor's arm. Though it was supposed to be a comforting gesture, Taylor had to resist shrugging the touch off. "And even if one ikthian might have some civility, this one is going to end up dead or traded away, so don't you dare tell me you're growing attached to it."

The callous words made Taylor back away. She hated to admit it, but Rachel was right. Maia was probably not going to get out of this situation alive. "I'm not," she said, trying to reassure her friend. "And she's not an it. Just because she's a political prisoner doesn't mean we should treat her like dirt. We'd be no better than the bottom-feeders if we did."

Rachel's eyes narrowed as she considered what Taylor had said. "But there's more than civility here, Taylor. I'm your friend. Don't play me off like some fool."

Taylor picked up her assault rifle and brought it over to the weapons bench, beginning to disassemble it. "I'm not. And there's nothing more to me and the prisoner than what you're putting into it."

Rachel placed a hand on her shoulder again. "Are you sure? Taylor, look at me."

Taylor looked up from her half-assembled rifle and met Rachel's concerned stare. "What?"

"I don't want you getting in trouble, okay? Sometimes I worry about you."

"Don't worry, then. I have it under control." This time, Taylor did shrug off the friendly touch. She grabbed a rag from the weapons bench and began wiping down the dusty parts of her rifle. She hadn't given it a proper cleaning in a while, anyway.

"There shouldn't even be anything to have under control," said Rachel. "That's my point."

"Don't worry," Taylor said again, more insistently. "I have a job to do, and I'm going to do it."

"Okay, okay." Rachel raised her hands in mock surrender, shifting back and turning to begin disassembling her own weapon for cleaning. "Just...be careful. Even though it—"

"She," Taylor interrupted.

"She," Rachel corrected grudgingly, "might not seem like the ikthians that killed your squad, she's still one of them. You don't really know her. And if there's some way we can use her to protect Earth, it doesn't matter how nice she is. We need to look out for our own people first."

Taylor sighed. Deep down, she knew Rachel was right, but her friend's logic didn't ease any of the conflict she felt. "Yeah. I know." Still, she couldn't help picturing Maia's face as she resumed cleaning her weapon. Even though Maia was an alien, her expressions were so familiar. So human. Taylor's hands shook over her gun. Thoughts like that would only make it more difficult when Maia was sent away from Earth.

# Chapter Fourteen

MAIA'S FIRST INSTINCT WAS to rush out to the living room when she heard the door open. She could tell it was Taylor by the way the human grumbled. A clattering noise filled the small apartment as Taylor began tossing aside pieces of what Maia could only assume was her armor.

"You don't have to stare. This stuff just feels like crap," Taylor grumbled at the armed guards outside. Unable to resist, Maia peeked past the bedroom door and watched. She almost laughed when she saw the identical expressions of confusion on the guards' faces. Apparently, they hadn't been expecting Taylor to strip practically in the middle of the hallway. A piece of Taylor's armor nearly hit one of them as she continued to pull off the heavy layers, and both of them edged away, wisely deciding that Taylor could handle herself.

As soon as they were gone, Taylor turned and shut the door, activating the lock code. "You'd think the whole base has no more confidence in me," she muttered, kicking aside her chest plate without bothering to pick it up.

Maia didn't know how to respond to Taylor's irritable mood, so she chose to remain standing with her hands cuffed in front of her. She hadn't said a word to the guards when they had insisted on binding her wrists for the interrogation. They hadn't harmed her otherwise, but she was still relieved when Taylor stomped over and punched in the code to release her.

"Why the hell do we even bother restraining you with these anymore?" Taylor asked, pulling the open cuffs away and tossing them onto the table. "What do they think you're going to do while the collar's on? Scratch someone's eyes out?"

Maia rubbed her wrists, massaging the place where the cuffs had chafed her skin. "I think they were simply following instructions, Taylor." She walked to the couch and sat down. Perhaps if she could get Taylor to stop moving, the human would begin to unwind.

Taylor continued pacing. With no more armor to fling, she made sweeping gestures with her arms. "It's the principle of the thing." Her hands balled into tight fists. "They act like... like..." Taylor's pacing slowed as she searched for the words she needed. "Like you're someone they can't trust."

Maia frowned. "Why should the guards trust me?" The couch sagged as Taylor sat down next to her, and Maia swallowed. She felt the heat of Taylor's thigh press against hers, and the muscles in her core tightened.

"I don't know." Taylor seemed frustrated with her own response. "How did the interrogation go?"

"More of the same. I am afraid I could not tell them anything useful." Maia had decided it was in her best interest to remain cooperative with the humans, but none of them seemed interested in asking questions about her research or what her standing with her people was. Even when she tried to interject, they simply silenced her and moved on. Apparently, the generals had decided they wanted her as a bargaining chip, not a war asset.

Taylor's forehead creased with concern. "They didn't hurt you, right?"

"No." Maia paused, considering her next words before asking, "But why did the guards take me instead of you?"

"I had a few hours of leave."

"How did you spend your free time?" Maia asked, curious what could have put Taylor into such a foul mood.

"Shot some practice targets with a friend of mine. It was supposed to be relaxing."

"But it was not," Maia finished.

Taylor slumped back against the couch. Her hands flopped down at her side, her fingertips inadvertently brushing Maia's thigh. "We argued, mostly about you."

Maia's heart rate picked up. "Oh? Why is that?" She hoped she didn't sound like she was prying, but she couldn't help being curious. Knowing that Taylor had been thinking and talking about her made Maia feel a little better about her own fascination with the human.

"My friend thinks I'm crazy for trusting you, but I can't help it. You're..." Taylor's words broke off as her gaze lingered on Maia's eyes, then traveled south, staring.

*Is Taylor looking at my lips?* Maia wished she knew. Instead, she felt a blush bloom over her face and neck.

Taylor's hand settled more firmly on her thigh. "You're not a monster."

Maia leaned closer to Taylor. For what purpose, she didn't know, but she trusted her body's instincts. For a moment, both of them held perfectly still. Maia's hand moved slowly to Taylor's thigh, and the human drew in a sharp breath before blinking and standing up. She cleared her throat and took a few steps back.

"You know..." Taylor's voice wavered as she spoke, though she rested a hand on her hip in a gesture of confidence. "The bedroom is probably more comfortable. There isn't anything to do in here anyway."

Maia opened her mouth, but closed it again. She wasn't sure if Taylor meant to dispel the tension pooling between them, or heighten it with the suggestion, but the statement was telling. Maia stood up from the couch. She thought about objecting, but eventually decided that there was no denying the powerful draw she felt. She had to face it, one way or another. Hesitantly, she followed Taylor back into the bedroom.

Taylor flopped down onto the bed instantly, lying back and resting her hands behind her head while Maia took a hesitant seat on the edge of the mattress. It took all of her willpower to keep her eyes averted. For a moment, she wondered if she should just confess her insane attraction. Surely Taylor would realize the immediate danger of their situation and hurry to put distance between them.

Her sprawled position was already giving Maia unacceptable ideas. She longed to lean forward, to pin Taylor's arms together and remove her fatigues. She would have the freedom to study Taylor's naked form, to explore every inch of her with hands and mouth.

*What is wrong with me?* Maia wondered yet again, but there was no making sense of the fantasy. It simply was, and she found that she couldn't dismiss it. *It has to be the stress of being held prisoner here. There is no other explanation.*

"Maia?" Taylor said.

Maia looked up, startled as she snapped out of her daydream. "What?" Her heart hammered with nervous energy.

Taylor rose by crunching her abdominal muscles, adjusting herself into a seated position in the middle of the bed. "You keep staring at me like you have something on your mind."

Maia tried to speak, but her voice stuck in her throat. This was an unwise decision to say the least. Logically, she knew that confessing was a horrible idea, but her illogical side, the part of herself she usually kept smothered with statistics, was urging her to say something. Although most of the humans had treated her with basic dignity, for which Maia considered herself fortunate, Taylor was the only one who had shown her any sort of kindness. She deserved to know.

"I must be going crazy," Maia murmured under her breath.

Unfortunately, Taylor heard. "Look, I know you're technically a prisoner, but if something is bothering you, you can tell me. I'll try and make it better." She gave Maia a soft smile. "You've already done the same for me twice, and you didn't have to. I don't think most prisoners are nice enough to listen to their guards' problems."

Maia had no ready reply for that statement, and her face heated with a deep blush. Taylor seemed to take her silence for hesitation, or perhaps even worry. She leaned forward, making Maia's heart beat even faster.

"Is it because of the interrogation, or me? I can leave you alone, if you'd rather—"

"No. No, it is not that. I just..." She tried to explain, but her words refused to come when she needed them most.

"Just what? Has anyone been treating you badly?"

"No," Maia said, even more emphatically than the first time. With growing dread, she realized that Taylor was going to keep guessing at what the problem might be until she either stumbled upon it, or frustrated her into confessing. Maia sighed, staring down into her lap. Earlier, when Taylor had put a hand on her thigh, she had fought the urge to reach out and stroke the contours of the human's strong fingers.

"Then what is it?"

Since Taylor wouldn't be dissuaded, Maia decided to say the one thing that was guaranteed to stop the questions—the truth. "I find myself having strange reactions to your presence," she blurted out, wincing as she realized how awful her wording sounded.

Taylor blinked in confusion. "Strange reactions?"

Maia forced herself to continue. "When...well, it is probably the same for both species. It would not surprise me, considering our genetic similarities. Physical attraction plays a key role when selecting a person to mate with...er, that is...I mean..." Maia resisted the temptation to hide her face in her hands. She had always been awful at this sort of thing.

She finally found the courage to look at Taylor and was surprised to see that the human's olive skin had darkened. This time, the reddish-brown tinge reached all the way to the tips of her silly and adorable looking external ears. Maia had hoped Taylor would be able to interpret her ramblings, but unfortunately, the human looked just as embarrassed as she felt.

"For reasons I cannot explain, I find myself drawn to you. I am sorry, and I understand if you wish for me to sleep in the other room tonight."

Taylor cupped Maia's face, seemingly asking for something. Permission, maybe? Her warm brown eyes filled Maia with confusion and longing. She remained frozen, uncertain, but Taylor moved closer. She dipped her head and caught Maia's lips, cutting off her soft gasp of surprise.

Maia stiffened at the unfamiliar sensation, but quickly relaxed as she grew used to the pressure of Taylor's mouth. It brushed hers with a few gentle pecks at first before Taylor pressed forward with her tongue. Without conscious thought, Maia kissed back. She started hesitantly at first, but after a few moments, she grew bolder. She grabbed Taylor's shoulders, pulling her close. They needed this. They just needed to get it over with so they could go back to being prisoner and guard.

"This is insane," she said when they finally broke apart, their faces still hovering less than a breath away from each other. Taylor laughed and nipped the fullest part of Maia's lower lip, tugging to coax her mouth open again. The tease was too much. Maia practically pulled Taylor on top of her as they sank onto the mattress together. Her hands were everywhere at once, running up and down the broad expanse of Taylor's back, trailing over the dip in her spine, caressing her hips.

Taylor broke away from Maia's lips, kissing along her neck. "Let's not think about that right now," she whispered. Before Maia could respond, Taylor's hand slipped under her shirt, trailing curiously over her stomach. Maia shivered and arched into the touch, her muscles flexing against Taylor's palm.

"We'll only do this once," Taylor breathed. Maia shivered at warmth of Taylor's mouth against her skin. She wanted to feel that mouth all over her body, even in places she hadn't imagined. "Once, and then we won't have to anymore."

Maia nodded, though part of her knew that they were making a terrible mistake. For once, the rational part of her brain had completely shut off. "Just once," she agreed before Taylor's lips descended on hers again. Maia had very little experience with kissing, and she certainly hadn't expected it to be like this—all heat and smoothness and bruising force that made her long for things she didn't understand. She whimpered into Taylor's mouth, and her hips pushed upwards against the firm thigh that had somehow wedged itself between her legs.

"This needs to come off," Taylor panted. She tugged at the hem of

Maia's shirt, trying to pull it over her head. Maia raised her arms and sat up, attempting to help. She had absolutely no idea what she was doing, but Taylor didn't seem to care. Taylor was moving so quickly that Maia didn't have time to do anything but make encouraging noises in response. She shivered as she realized that unless she said 'stop' or pushed her away, Taylor would continue until she had taken what she wanted.

As soon as Maia's shirt came off, Taylor tossed it aside. Neither of them cared where it landed. For a split second, both paused to catch their breath. Maia blushed as Taylor stared at her exposed flesh. She couldn't remember the last time she had been naked in front of someone else, aside from the embarrassing incident outside the shower.

Taylor hurried to tug off her own shirt and compression top, and heat throbbed between Maia's legs. Taylor's skin was wonderfully soft, a different texture than her own, but undeniably pleasing to touch. She knew it would feel even better when they were both completely naked and tangled up in each other. Her eyes widened as she watched Taylor strip to the waist. Taylor was perfectly formed, all toned muscle and broad shoulders. The smooth expanse of her torso, her small, firm breasts, and the obvious line that bisected her abdominal muscles were all incredibly tempting.

Before Maia could make further study, Taylor climbed on top of her again, pinning her to the mattress and nipping at the column of her throat. In the middle of the string of kisses trailing down towards her chest, Taylor paused to bite her shoulder. Maia let out a cry of pleasure as she rocked down against Taylor's thigh. When Taylor's warm lips folded around the tip of her breast, Maia rolled her head back onto the pillows. Taylor's tongue scrape against the stiff point, teasing it with the edges of her teeth, and Maia had the sudden urge to run her hands through Taylor's hair and pull her closer. She gave in, sinking her fingers into the thick tangle of black and pulling a little too tightly.

Fortunately, Taylor was too distracted to notice. She only grunted in response before kissing her way across to Maia's other breast. "Fuck," she sighed, pulling up just far enough to stare at Maia's flushed face. "I need you. I don't care who you are."

Even though she knew she shouldn't, Maia cupped the back of Taylor's neck. She squeezed slightly, urging Taylor to keep going. "Please," she begged, shocked by the need in her own voice. Both of them fumbled to pull their pants and undergarments off, parting for a brief moment to kick their clothes away before coming back together.

Maia wrapped her legs around Taylor's waist and rocked forward. This time, bare flesh met her own. She gasped when Taylor pushed back against her with just as much need. Her body ached for more, for something that she knew Taylor wasn't yet doing. None of her research could have prepared her for this, an emptiness that made her throb with desperation. "Please," she whimpered again. "I need...something, anything."

Taylor's hand ran up along the sensitive skin of Maia's inner thigh before pressing between her legs. "Oh God," she whispered. Maia shuddered as warmth spilled from deep within her, spreading over Taylor's exploring fingers. At first, she was embarrassed, but when she looked up into Taylor's face, she saw only desire reflected back at her. She shivered as Taylor spread her folds with two fingers, obviously examining her. Maia wondered just how different her own anatomy was from a human's, but she knew it wouldn't be a problem when a confident smile spread across Taylor's face.

"I was right," Taylor drawled, looking down between their bodies. "Not too different at all."

Maia gasped as Taylor's fingers found the curved ridge of her clit, rubbing it in slow circles, coaxing it out of its delicate hood. She dug her nails into Taylor's back, trying to draw her closer. She had no idea how Taylor knew just how to touch her, but it made her feel like her heart was about to batter its way out of her chest. Sounds she barely recognized tore from her throat, and she pushed against Taylor's hand, quivering every time those magical fingers rolled over her. She spread her legs wider, well past caring that they should not be doing this.

Taylor's fingertips glided down, and Maia stiffened as they tested the tight ring of her entrance. Soon, she forgot her hesitation and began rocking against Taylor's hand, pleading for more with each push of her hips. Taking that as permission, Taylor slid forward, and Maia clamped down tight around her fingers, adjusting to the new fullness. The stretch burned a little, but it was also blissfully wonderful, and she wanted more. When she let out a low groan of encouragement, Taylor added a second finger and curled forward, catching against a sensitive spot along her inner walls.

Maia bucked in response to the pressure as Taylor's mouth found her shoulder, and lights swam in front of her eyes. She clamped her thighs tight around Taylor's wrist, desperate to keep Taylor's fingers deep inside of her. Taylor tried to adjust, but Maia could only cling to her broad shoulders and beg her to keep going. Nothing had ever felt more blissful than those fingers rubbing against her. Her body burned, and pressure pounded inside of her until she was close to spilling over, but something held her back. She needed more.

"Please," she gasped, unable to form the words she needed.

"I know. I'm working on it." Taylor redoubled her efforts, causing Maia to cry out again and lose all concentration. She tried to speak, but she couldn't warn Taylor as the last of her control slipped away. Maia rocked against Taylor's hand, taking her fingers as deep as possible. When the pleasure grew almost unbearable, Taylor's thumb pressed hard into her clit, curling against her inner wall at the same time.

The sensation started out as a faint throb, but soon, Maia was overwhelmed with powerful contractions. Her core fluttered around Taylor's fingers, and she tilted her head back. Her mouth fell open in a silent scream as pleasure ripped through her, and slick heat spilled from deep inside of her, slipping into Taylor's hand. *If I had known it would feel like this,* Maia thought, before she was swept away by a fresh round of pulses, *I would have agreed to do it more than just once.*

Maia's tremors soon faded, growing weaker each time they coursed through her body. Taylor kissed along her shoulder and up her neck, whispering soft words of comfort as she came down from her spike of pleasure. "I'm here. I'm right here." For some reason, that comforted Maia more than anything else Taylor had given her.

Afterwards, they lay together for a few heartbeats, limbs entwined and bodies covered in sweat. Both of them panted, but Maia could still feel how tense Taylor was beside her. Taylor's lips caught Maia's cheek as she withdrew her wet, glistening fingers, bringing them between her own legs instead.

Maia's eyes widened with surprise and renewed arousal. She had been so wrapped up in her own pleasure and release that she had completely forgotten about Taylor's. Quickly, she shifted onto her side, cupping her palm over the back of Taylor's hand. "No." She moved Taylor's fingers aside and replaced them with her own. "Let me."

"You don't have to..." But Taylor didn't finish the sentence as Maia began exploring, hoping she could find the right spots. The alien thicket of black hair between Taylor's legs was coarser than the hair on her head, and much shorter, and it tickled Maia's fingers as she sought out the wetness underneath. Taylor groaned and shifted forward, spreading her thighs to give Maia more room to maneuver. "Oh God, more," she muttered, grinding against the heel of Maia's palm.

Maia's eyes grew even larger, and she smiled when she felt Taylor's wetness coat her hand. She pressed hard against the hot flesh, encouraged by Taylor's moans. The way Taylor's face contorted with pleasure was an intoxicating sight, and knowing she was the cause made Maia feel strangely wonderful. Taylor's body spasmed under her touch, and Maia raised her free hand, raking her nails along the human's flat stomach. She still wanted to taste that flesh with her mouth, but she put that desire aside for later.

Instead, she brought her hand to Taylor's hip and gripped hard as she slid two fingers inside, pressing deep into the velvety smooth flesh. They moaned together as Taylor's muscles contracted around her fingers. "So wet," she murmured, entranced by what she was doing.

Taylor rocked forward, causing Maia's fingers to slide in and out as she worked herself closer and closer to release. But it wasn't enough, and soon, Maia noticed the hard, pink bud standing out above Taylor's entrance. Hoping Taylor's body would respond the same way hers did, she swiped her thumb over it. The tight bundle twitched at her touch.

Taylor went rigid after the first pass, pushing even more urgently into Maia's hand. "Fuck. I...I'm coming." A second later, Maia felt contractions ripple through Taylor's body. Silken heat clutched around her knuckles, and wetness trailed down her wrist, but she kept her hand in place while Taylor pulsed against her.

Finally, Taylor's muscles went slack. She collapsed onto the mattress, breathing deeply as she recovered from the intensity of her release. Maia felt a surge of pride, and a slow smile spread across her face. Taylor smiled back, but her eyes drooped as she suppressed a yawn. "Are you tired already?" Maia asked, cupping the square shape of Taylor's jaw. Her stomach fluttered as Taylor nuzzled into her palm.

"Just a bit," Taylor said, her words thick with sleep. Maia settled against the human's side, sighing happily as one of Taylor's arms wrapped around her. "We shouldn't have done that, but it was...so much better than..."

As Taylor fell asleep in her arms, Maia's smile faded and reality began to set back in. She had just had sex with a human. Not just any human, but the one assigned to guard her. She had probably just made the worst mistake of her life. Still, as she studied Taylor's closed eyes and peaceful expression, Maia couldn't bring herself to regret what they had done. As impossible as it seemed, being with Taylor had meant something to her.

Maia rested her head on Taylor's shoulder, lying against her chest and listening to the steady thud of her heartbeat. Just for tonight, she would try to forget that Taylor was holding her captive. They would fall asleep together, not as guard and prisoner, but as two people who had just experienced an intense connection. There would be plenty of time to return to their usual roles tomorrow.

# Chapter Fifteen

THE NEXT MORNING, TAYLOR woke with a start. Her eyes snapped open, and she had to swallow down a surprised gasp. She was pressed against Maia's back again, and this time, both of them were completely naked. Everything that had happened the night before came back to her in a rush. Had it been pheromones? Had Maia discovered some way to use her powers even while wearing the collar? No, Taylor decided after a long moment of thought. Her attraction to Maia was genuine, no matter how ill-advised or unethical it was. The ikthian hadn't forced her, and she hoped Maia felt the same.

Taylor untangled herself from Maia's sleeping form as quickly and quietly as she could. She gave the ikthian a hesitant glance, debating whether to wake her or not. Maia looked so innocent and peaceful with her cheek resting against the pillow that Taylor couldn't bear to disturb her. Instead, she hurried to retrieve the clothes she had abandoned the night before.

Her undershirt was beneath the bed, and her pants were in a crumpled heap next to the side table. Once she had thrown them on, Taylor squeezed her feet into her boots, not bothering to bend down and unlace them properly. She needed time to think, and maybe even some advice. Unfortunately, there were very few people on base that she trusted. Captain Roberts was her direct superior, not to mention something of a father figure to her. There was no way Rachel would understand. Finally, Taylor settled on Andrew. At least he would be able to understand her attraction to Maia without immediately assuming it was some kind of trick.

Maia's scent still lingered around Taylor even when she retreated to the hallway and slunk past the guards on duty. She felt stifled in the enclosed space, especially during the elevator ride down to the main floor. As soon as the doors opened, she wasted no time escaping the building. Once she stepped outside, she took a deep breath, trying to expel the memory of the ikthian from her mind. Being with Maia had been good. Way too good, and not just because of physical release.

Taylor could have handled it better if it were a matter of mere attraction, but something else lingered under the surface.

She had to find Andrew and talk this through like a rational person. Unfortunately, she had no idea where her friend was assigned to work. She didn't know his schedule, since it changed from day to day, but she guessed he might be near the bunks or the mess hall. She decided to try the mess first, glancing nervously at every soldier she passed on the way.

Luckily, Taylor spotted Andrew talking to another soldier outside the building, waving a sheaf of papers with little regard for their condition. "Andrew," she called out, trying to get his attention.

Andrew looked over at her. His eyes widened. "Lieutenant!" He turned away from the man he was speaking with and jogged over to her. "Hey, I'm really sorry about the way Sergeant Bower acted the other day. I taught him a lesson after you left, I swear."

It took Taylor a moment to recall what had happened several days ago. She had too many other things on her mind. "Oh, yeah. Actually, I wanted to talk to you about something else…but not here."

Andrew nodded. "Okay. So, where to?"

Taylor thought about it. The mess hall definitely wasn't private enough, and Andrew didn't have a bunk to himself. Going back to the captain's quarters was out, since Maia was still asleep there. She finally came up with a solution. "My old bunk," she said, turning to head back the way she had come. "Hopefully it hasn't been reassigned yet."

"Works for me," Andrew said. "It's kind of on my way, and another minute won't hurt. I'm not in any hurry to get back to the clerk's office. Not exactly my kind of mission. I don't know why the brass even bothers keeping hard copies of their paperwork anymore. No one ever uses them."

The two of them walked in silence after that, returning to the officers' barracks. Although she looked outwardly calm, inwardly, Taylor was still panicking. She had no idea how she was going to explain to her friend that she had just had sex with an ikthian—even worse, one she was supposed to be guarding.

They arrived at Taylor's old bunk more quickly than she would have liked. Thankfully, a new officer hadn't been relocated to the space. It looked exactly the same as when she had left it.

"So, what's up, Taylor?" Andrew asked, making himself right at home despite the room's barren appearance. He plopped down on the bed and his bulk made the frame groan beneath him. "You looked pretty upset when you found me. Don't worry, I only noticed because I'm your friend. No one else would have."

He patted the space next to him, and Taylor took it. She sighed and hung her head between her slumped shoulders, resting her elbows on her knees. "Come on, it can't be that bad," Andrew said cheerfully. "It's not like you got into trouble with your prisoner, right?" Taylor didn't look at him, and he did a double take. "Tell me what happened. Now."

Taylor heaved a long, low sigh. "We...had sex." She still couldn't quite believe what she and Maia had done, even as the memories replayed vividly in her mind.

Silence stretched between them until Andrew adjusted his position on the bed, forcing several squeaks from the spring mattress. "Wait, you mean she seduced you? Used her pheromones on you?"

Taylor shook her head no and buried her face in her hands. The room suddenly felt too hot. "Oh God, Andrew," she groaned. "Those stupid vids are all propaganda. The ikthians might as well be humans...or, this one is, anyways."

"Whoa, really? You mean, like, they have all the same parts down there?" Taylor shot Andrew a glare. "Right, sorry. Not the point...you sure she wasn't trying to brainwash you or anything?"

"I...no. It was...I mean, over the last few days...she's just a person, and Rachel was getting mad at me for wanting to treat her with a little respect, and then Maia and I talked, and we decided to have sex just once to get rid of the tension." The rambling words that spilled from her mouth made little sense, but once she started telling the story, Taylor couldn't seem to stop the rest of it from bubbling out.

"And so you came to me because..."

"It didn't work. I want to be with her again. Badly. It was the best sex I've ever had, and it only lasted a few minutes."

Andrew laughed. "You sure she didn't drug you up? Sure, sounds like that from the way you're gushing about her."

"I'm sure," Taylor insisted, more certain of the fact than ever. "I wanted to be with her, she didn't force me. But I have no idea what I'm going to do now. I'm supposed to be guarding her, not fucking her. What if we, you know, get attached?"

"That good, huh?"

Taylor paused, considering how much she wanted to reveal about her encounter with Maia. Andrew was her friend, but he was also something of a pervert. Of course, she wasn't much better, since she was having sex with her alien prisoner. "Better than good. I wish I hadn't rushed through it so much, but something about her just drove me crazy. I told myself it would only be the one time, but..."

"Stop and think about it for a minute," Andrew said. He didn't seem nearly as concerned about the situation as Taylor was. "If you wanted to be with her, what's wrong with doing it again? She's hot and wants you. Not exactly a bad situation to be in, Taylor."

"She's my prisoner. Assuming she can even consent to sex with her guard, I shouldn't be spending time getting to know her."

"So? From what you've said, it sounds like your parts match up."

Taylor blushed as she remembered how good Maia had felt against her fingers. She felt like Andrew was missing something important that she was trying to tell him, and she was terrified of her feelings. They had the potential to do more harm than any amount of physical contact with Maia.

"So, what's the problem? Aside from the generals finding out you're fucking her and possibly demoting you, I mean."

Taylor groaned. "You want a list?"

"No, but if you want to tell me about how you fucked her, I wouldn't say no to a play-by-play...Ow! Hey, watch the guns," he complained as Taylor's fist collided with his arm. He rubbed the area even though the blow couldn't have hurt that much. "All right, all right, I get it. Damn, I thought finally getting laid might mellow you out."

Taylor glared at Andrew to let him know the crude humor wasn't appreciated. She wished Maia was human, or that Rachel wasn't so anti-ikthian. That way, she could go to her friend for some proper comfort. "I just wish I knew what to do," Taylor sighed. She ignored Andrew's exaggerated pouting. Although the apartment where Maia was imprisoned had felt stifling before, she wanted to return there as fast as possible. She felt drawn to Maia in ways that frightened her.

"That's up to you. But if it were me? I'd go for it. You only get so many chances to do crazy, stupid, awesome things in your life, especially in the military."

Taylor pushed herself off the bed, standing in front of Andrew as he continued to sit. "Well, this definitely qualifies as crazy and stupid." She studied Andrew for a minute as she considered her earlier thought. "Speaking of crazy and stupid, thank you for actually hearing me out. There aren't many people around...wait, there is no one else around I would have talked to about this."

"Aw, thanks, Lieutenant," Andrew said, tapping the forgotten sheaf of papers on his thigh. "I should probably get this pile on its way, actually, though I appreciated our discussion. We should talk about this kind of thing all the time." Taylor whacked him on the arm again. "I mean it. I'm just trying to be a good friend."

Taylor rolled her eyes and opened the door. "Sure you are," she said, though she knew Andrew was just teasing. He acted like a lecherous ass, but she knew it was mostly for show. "I'll see you later, okay?"

"Sure, Taylor," Andrew said. "Maybe you can invite me into your swanky new pad sometime." He gave her a wink as he stepped out into the hall.

"Yeah, you keep thinking that."

Andrew waved before walking off to finally deliver his papers. He would make a good officer one day, Taylor thought, though his talents were wasted on base. He belonged out in the field where he could do some serious damage, but his division had yet to be rotated out.

Taylor sighed and shook her head. She glanced down the hall, noticing that there were only a few soldiers walking around. It was past midday, but not quite evening yet. Most people were busy with their daily assignments. Taylor had nothing better to do than return to her quarters. "But I'm not going to expect anything when I get there," she muttered as she entered the elevator and hit the button for the top floor. "I'm just going to do my job. That's all."

# Chapter Sixteen

TAYLOR RE-ENTERED THE SUITE expecting Maia to be up and about, or at least in the shower. She wished she had taken one herself before escaping from the room. Hopefully, Andrew hadn't noticed her disheveled appearance and wouldn't forget his promise of discretion.

Concerned that there was no sign of her prisoner, Taylor made her way to the bedroom. Her eyes widened when she peeked through the door. Maia was still in bed, sprawled on top of the rumpled sheets. A slight smile spread across Taylor's face as she took in the ikthian's deep, even breathing. She was still fast asleep, just as Taylor had left her. And even while she was sleeping, Taylor felt the same tug of attraction as the night before. There was no way Maia could be exerting any sort of mind control over her at the moment.

Since Maia wasn't awake to notice, Taylor took the opportunity to study her more closely. During their wild, regrettable encounter, she had been in such a rush that she hadn't paused to admire the view. Now, Taylor wished she'd taken a little more time. If Maia had been human, her skin would have probably been a paler shade. Taylor could almost picture it. She would have been a very beautiful human by anyone's standards.

Something about the way Maia was positioned invited a closer look, so Taylor walked around the bed and surveyed her, taking note of the way her body curved, of where her hipbones caused two slight swells on either side of her pelvis. Everything from her beautiful fringe down to her webbed toes drew Taylor's gaze. And then there was the tempting flesh between Maia's legs. The similarity of their anatomy really was astonishing, now that Taylor took time to think about it.

She crawled onto the bottom of the bed, balancing on her elbows. There, she could see the details much more clearly. The lips between Maia's legs were completely hairless, like the rest of her body. They were a darker shade than most of her silvery-white skin, but her clit was no longer swollen. Taylor reached out to part her folds, but stopped. She had already tiptoed the edge of a moral line by sleeping with her own prisoner, and Maia couldn't agree to anything while she was unconscious.

Before Taylor could retreat, Maia whimpered. Her hips rocked forward slightly, and Taylor gasped as some of Maia's wetness rubbed onto her fingers. Without meaning to, Taylor ran them over Maia's clit, and she watched in wonder as it started to swell with need. Maia arched up from the mattress, bringing both hands to the back of Taylor's head. It seemed to take her a moment to realize what was going on, but when she did, she spread her legs wider. "Don't stop," she muttered, her voice still thick with sleep.

Taylor pulled her mouth away and lowered her fingertips to Maia's entrance. Now that Maia was awake, her reservations had vanished along with her resolve. She slid inside with two fingers, curling them forward and trying to find the same magical spot as before. Maia's sharp hitch of breath let Taylor know when she hit the right place. She dipped her head and took Maia's clit back into her mouth, lashing her tongue over the tip.

Maia's hips twitched, and more wetness flooded around Taylor's knuckles. Pleased with that reaction, she sucked more insistently at the firm ridge in her mouth, relishing the way it seemed to grow harder between her lips. It had been so long since she had gone down on someone, and she was determined to enjoy herself.

Slowly, she released her prize, placing a few more kisses on its tip. Maia's clit stood out from beneath its hood, and Taylor moaned softly as she ran the fingers of her other hand over it, making the ridge pulse. She took it in again and sucked greedily, enjoying the soft whimpers that came from above her and the slick heat pouring into her hand. With every pull of her mouth, Maia's inner muscles seemed to squeeze tighter around her.

Taylor pulled out, smirking as Maia groaned at the loss. "You're already close, aren't you?" she whispered, looking down at Maia's glistening folds.

Maia's only response was a quiet cry of need. "Please, Taylor. Do not tease me," she begged.

The sound of Maia's pleas tugged at Taylor's heart. She dipped her head again and took Maia's clit back into her mouth, causing the ikthian to let out a strangled sob of relief. Taylor slid her fingers back inside as well and began a gentle thrusting motion. The more she curled them forward, the more Maia's hips bucked. She released little gasps of pleasure with each thrust, writhing in an attempt to get closer. Taylor sped up the motion of her hand. She had meant to hold out longer, but she found herself getting carried away again with Maia's need.

"Come for me," Taylor said, breaking her seal around Maia's clit just long enough to whisper the words. Her free hand wandered up along Maia's stomach, nails raking over the twitching muscles there.

Maia's thighs trembled, and her hands tightened in Taylor's hair. "Oh, Taylor," she sobbed as she pulsed over and over. With each contraction, the tightness in her body loosened until she was a shivering mess.

Once the ripples faded to aftershocks, Taylor withdrew her fingers and placed a few kisses on Maia's inner thigh. "You liked that, huh?"

Panting and blushing, Maia draped an arm over her face. "Yes," she admitted, her voice slightly muffled in the crook of her elbow.

Taylor crawled up by her side and collapsed next to her. She ran a hand over Maia's stomach. "Hey, are you all right? Did I do something wrong?"

Maia shook her head. "No. I am just getting accustomed to...this. I told you to keep going." She removed her arm and met Taylor's eyes. "You were...you made me feel wonderful."

"So did you," Taylor murmured, with a small smile of satisfaction on her lips.

They stared at one another for a while, drawn into a reflective silence. Maia turned and reached out to stroke Taylor's arm. "We made a mistake," she whispered, her smile receding.

Taylor withdrew her hand, breaking the contact between them. She took a deep breath. "Yeah, I suppose we did."

"Taylor, we both know nothing can come of this."

"Yeah, I know."

Taylor sat up and deliberately shifted toward the other side of the mattress, but Maia followed, reaching out to clasp one of her shoulders and gently drawing her back. "That does not mean that I do not feel..." Taylor swallowed to loosen the knot in her throat as one of Maia's thumbs traced the line of her jaw. "Even though we cannot do this again, I want you to know that it meant something to me."

"If it meant something, why do we have to stop?" Taylor asked, even though she could come up with several answers to that question on her own. She knew it was wrong, but she was desperate for an excuse, any excuse. When Maia didn't answer right away, she sighed. "You're right. I'm sorry. I mean, I'm your guard..."

"This reaches beyond us, Taylor. You are hardly my guard anymore.

This planet is my prison, and you happen to be the person they elected to keep me company. But none of that matters. I will be traded away to the Dominion within a few weeks, and once I am taken back to Korithia, they will kill me."

The words seemed so final as Maia spoke them. Taylor felt her stomach twist into a hard knot. "Don't talk like that." The thought of Maia dying made her chest ache. "Maybe...maybe we'll just keep you on Earth. Maybe you have some information, something useful..."

"I doubt the rest of your species would care for my research," Maia said, her voice gentle, yet firm. "And humans certainly do not care for ikthians. It is obvious every time I leave this cell." Maia massaged Taylor's shoulder in an attempt to comfort her, but Taylor's muscles only bunched up further. "The negotiations will take several weeks yet. Perhaps something will change between now and then. We have no way of knowing."

Taylor nodded, letting her shoulders relax slightly. "Yeah, sure." Captain Roberts had been so sure Maia would provide them with something useful when they had first arrived on Earth. Now, Taylor was devastated that her mentor had been wrong.

"You will survive this, Taylor, but for now, we should refrain from being physically intimate anymore."

Even though she knew it was the right decision, protests rang in Taylor's head. Her eyes began to sting. Suddenly, she wanted Maia close to her. "Can...can I hold you at least?" she asked before she could think better of it. "Just for now?"

"Of course," Maia said, curling up against Taylor's chest as they settled back down onto the pillows. "Just this once, and then..."

"Then we stop," Taylor whispered, unable to hide the sadness in her voice. She breathed in Maia's scent and bent down to kiss the top of her head. If this was going to be their last moment of intimacy, she wanted to memorize every part of Maia that she could. It seemed like everything had happened far too quickly. Maia had only just come into her life, as odd and twisted as their relationship had started.

"Sleep well," Maia sighed against Taylor's throat, brushing the soft skin with her lips before she closed her eyes and surrendered to a fitful sleep.

Taylor remained awake for a long time afterward, listening to Maia breathe and trying not to think about how that kiss would probably be their last.

# Chapter Seventeen

DURING THE NEXT SEVERAL days, Taylor stayed as far away from Maia as possible. Maia had been right to remind her that any further involvement between them could only lead to pain. The first time, they had both been too desperate to pause and reason with one another, and Taylor wished she could dismiss the second time as harmless curiosity. She had wanted to know what Maia looked like, felt like, tasted like. But her hunger hadn't abated, and neither had the empty feeling in her chest.

The fact that an alien, an ikthian, had evoked such a strong reaction within her filled Taylor with confusion, longing, and regret. She questioned herself again and again, wondering if Maia was manipulating her, if she was manipulating Maia, or if she was going insane, but even when they were apart, her attraction, and her inner conflict, refused to fade.

For her part, Maia seemed listless and depressed. Taylor couldn't blame her. Her situation looked bleak, but Taylor was in no position to help her. Even when she did try to initiate conversation, Maia answered any comments and questions half-heartedly. She no longer seemed interested in talking, despite the longing looks she cast when they were in the same room together. Taylor began leaving food for Maia so she could take her own meals in the mess, although she kept an especially close eye on the guard rotation she had organized to make up for avoiding her job.

One evening, about four days after she and Maia had sworn not to touch one another, Taylor found herself sitting at a table with Rachel during the evening meal. The two of them spent most of their time talking about the latest military operations, but they exhausted that topic quickly. The news wasn't good, and Rachel looked like she had something else on her mind. She kept glancing at Taylor, mindlessly stabbing at bits of food left over on her tray.

"So, is it true?" she finally blurted out, breaking the silence in her usual blunt way.

"Is what true?"

Rachel looked around, making sure no one else was close enough to overhear them. "That you're having sex with the ikthian."

Taylor's eyes widened in surprise, then narrowed. "Andrew," she muttered, completely ignoring the rest of her food. She set her fork down on the tray with a loud clatter. "I'm gonna kill him."

"So, it is true," Rachel said, pushing away her own tray. "Taylor, I can't believe you. She's a prisoner and a danger to the human race."

Taylor held up her hands defensively. "First of all, I know what I did was wrong. Maia and I already agreed never to do it again. Second, she's a prisoner of war, not some all-powerful force of evil. She can't do anything to hurt us or destroy Earth all on her own."

Rachel looked at her with a furrowed brow. "It's trying to seduce you, Taylor. It would be safer if you just requested someone else take over the watch."

"Oh, you mean like I've already been doing for the past several days?"

"You're not taking this seriously," Rachel insisted. "She isn't human. Last time I checked, sex required skin contact, and you know what usually happens when an ikthian touches a human."

"Maia's not like that, Rachel." Taylor placed her hands on the table to keep them from shaking. "She didn't seduce me, and she isn't going to poison me. She's very much aware of the fact that she's probably going to die on this rock."

"You seriously just called Earth a rock? It sounds like it's gotten its claws into you already. Next thing you know, you'll be telling me it's wrong to keep one imprisoned."

"I'm not suggesting anything," Taylor snapped. "I'm a human first, and I remember that. It's because I'm human that I want to treat our prisoner of war with some respect...We don't talk much anymore, anyways."

"Whatever, Taylor," Rachel said. "You know I trust you, just...not the ikthian."

"And that's understandable. Hell, I should be able to sympathize more. I watched them kill Jackson even after I threatened to shoot Maia. The seekers didn't value either of their lives at all."

Rachel stared at her for several quiet seconds. "I know it's been rough, Taylor," she said after a long pause. "Just promise me you'll be careful, all right? Ikthians are dangerous. I'm worried about you."

Taylor sighed, but decided to indulge her friend's worry. "Aren't you always?" Rachel frowned at her, obviously still not satisfied. "If anything comes up, I'll go to you first, okay?"

Rachel took both of their trays and stood up. "Okay. I'll hold you to that."

Taylor didn't wait for Rachel to unload the food trays. Instead, she waved goodbye and left the mess, drawn back to work by a sense of restless guilt she couldn't seem to shake. The cool air had a slight bite to it, but Taylor hardly noticed the chill seeping through her clothes as she returned to the barracks. The evening sky above was a dark grey, too cloudy and rainy to show a proper sunset.

Before she reached her destination, the comm on her wrist buzzed. Taylor glanced down at the screen, noticed Captain Roberts' picture, and answered the call. "Captain. What can I do for you, Sir?"

"The ikthian leaders just responded to our message. They didn't agree to a ceasefire, but they definitely want to open negotiations. General Hunt is already in my office. How fast can you get here?"

"Give me five, Sir," Taylor said, ending the call and setting off at a jog. Her heart pounded, but not from the light physical exertion. Negotiations meant Maia might not be on Earth for much longer, and *that* meant...she didn't want to think about it.

Roberts was waiting for her outside his office when she arrived. "Look sharp, Lieutenant. The brass is present."

Taylor saluted. "Thanks for the warning, Sir." She checked her fatigues quickly to make sure she looked presentable. No stains from dinner, fortunately, but there wasn't much she could do about her mussed hair or the bags she knew were visible under her eyes.

"I want this to run as smoothly as possible," Roberts said. "If we're lucky, Bouchard will keep his mouth shut long enough for us to make progress."

Taylor's mood dipped even further. "He's here again?"

"I'm not happy about it either, but the politicians want eyes on this, and the generals think he's useful, so we'll keep our opinions to ourselves." Roberts reached out, straightening the collar of Taylor's shirt almost affectionately. "Ready, soldier?"

"Ready, sir."

They both entered the office, although Taylor allowed the captain to walk ahead of her. She closed the door behind them, coming to a smart stop and saluting. General Hunt was indeed present, and Taylor caught sight of Bouchard sidled up beside him, just like Roberts had warned her.

"At ease," General Hunt said, stepping out from behind Roberts' desk. "Lieutenant Morgan, I'm glad you're here. The ikthians have sent us an offer, and we want you to weigh in on the matter based on your time spent with the prisoner."

The request caught Taylor off guard. She didn't consider herself very knowledgeable about ikthians, unless someone was asking her how to kill them. Judging by the deep creases in Bouchard's brow, he was equally skeptical of the idea that she might have a useful perspective to offer. "I'm happy to lend what help I can," she said, speaking confidently only because she knew it would annoy him.

Bouchard looked as though he wanted to complain, but Roberts chimed in with his support first. "We appreciate it, Lieutenant. You've had more experience with ikthians than most of us. Like it or not, you're something of an expert, at least on the behavior of the prisoner you've been assigned to guard."

"Yes. The prisoner." Bouchard's frown made it clear that he didn't consider Taylor an 'expert' in anything. "As much as we appreciate your service, Lieutenant Morgan, I'm afraid one ikthian is a rather small sample size."

"If Doctor Kalanis is as important as we think she is, one is all we need," said General Hunt. "We received a recorded transmission from the Dominion a little under an hour ago." He approached the terminal at Roberts' desk, bringing up a holographic image of three ikthians. The miniature figures wore brightly colored robes, thin ones with overlapping folds that reminded Taylor a little bit of togas. Two sported large collars that extended up behind their heads, and the third wore a rippling hood that cast a faint shadow over her face.

"Are you ready to watch?" Roberts asked.

Taylor nodded. "Yes, Sir."

"Go ahead, Bouchard," General Hunt ordered.

Bouchard un-paused the terminal, and the holographic ikthians began to move. The one in the middle was tallest, draped in flowing sea-green, and her collar matched the color of her bright blue fringe. The ikthian on the right wore a purple robe with artfully cut, circular gaps along the shoulders and sleeves, and the beautiful pink pattern of scales upon her forehead was made even bolder by several thin black lines. The face of the hooded ikthian on the left, however, was bare except for a little mottling. Taylor picked up on a family resemblance immediately. She knew beyond a shadow of a doubt that this had to be Maia's infamous mother.

The first ikthian spoke in melodious tones, and a translation appeared at the bottom of the screen. Taylor's translator made it unnecessary, but she found herself reading along anyway. "We have received your message, and believe the evidence you have shown us regarding your capture of Maia Kalanis is legitimate. We wish for her safe return, and are willing to negotiate in order to ensure it. In the meantime, in a gesture of goodwill, we will cease all operations within Earth's solar system. That is all."

"Well, that was short and to the point," Roberts said as the holograms froze again. "What do you think of their offer, Taylor?"

Taylor maintained a thoughtful silence before voicing her opinion. "It's hardly an offer at all. The ikthians aren't focused on Earth right now, or the Luna and Mars colonies. None of them have had a drone strike in almost a year. The ikthians would rather keep pushing at the edges of our borders. They like applying pressure where we're weakest."

"Did you not hear the part of the message where they agreed to leave our solar system alone?" Bouchard interrupted.

"Then why do you think they make the offer, Lieutenant?" General Hunt asked, ignoring Bouchard's outburst.

"They don't want to risk killing Maia," Taylor said. "Doctor Kalanis, I mean. They know she's on Earth, and as far as they're concerned, this planet's her jail cell. It'd be pretty stupid for them to launch any heavy attacks while she's a prisoner here. Not if they want her alive."

Hunt sighed. "That's what I was afraid of."

"The ikthians have us grossly outnumbered," Bouchard said, "and just because they have not attacked Earth recently doesn't mean they will continue to leave our home world unscathed. Let the more distant colonies fend for themselves. We should take this opportunity to preserve our safety here before the Dominion forces us to accept protectorate status."

"That's not how we're going to handle this," Captain Roberts said with a rumble in his voice. "We can't just let our colonists take the brunt of the Dominion's retaliation. Putting aside how immoral that suggestion is, how do you think they'll react when they hear the news that they're being abandoned?"

"It doesn't matter. The colonies will only be useful if we continue to exist as a people here!"

"What about the naledai?" Roberts asked. "They're our allies. The information they gave us on the ikthians at the start of this war is one of the main reasons you're still here to complain about all this. Are we just going to withdraw all of humanity's support from other solar systems?"

"We have already given the naledai plenty of assistance—"

"Weapons and resources, barely any troops. And you expect us to take what little we've offered away? Their soldiers are still fighting and dying out there, even though their home world was invaded decades ago. The largest rebel cell on Nakonum is sending a special detachment to San Diego Base in a few days. What do you expect me to tell them when they get here, Chairman? That we're withdrawing our support?"

"Stand down," General Hunt ordered. Bouchard and Roberts glared at each other, but ceased their argument to let him speak. "We're here to discuss our response to the Dominion's message, not to decide the fate of our colonies. The Coalition Council can deal with that. If neither of you have anything else valuable to add, I suggest you stop talking."

Neither Roberts nor Bouchard challenged General Hunt's statement, but Taylor sensed they were both deeply unhappy. "We shouldn't respond right away," she suggested, when no one else seemed willing to speak. "The ikthians took their time answering us, so why should we seem eager to get back to them?"

"Because it will show we are serious about the negotiations," Bouchard protested. Taylor could see his jaw tighten as he glared at her. "Don't try to play politician, Lieutenant. That's my job."

"Your opinion is noted, Lieutenant Morgan," General Hunt said, before Roberts could challenge Bouchard again on Taylor's behalf. "Thank you for your insight, and you're free to return to your other duties. The generals and I will confer, and approach the Coalition with an official recommendation shortly."

"Yes, Sir." Taylor's gut told her that another long, loud argument would break out soon, and she didn't want to be here for it.

"Dismissed," Roberts said. "Good work, Lieutenant."

Taylor saluted both him and General Hunt. "Thank you, Sirs." Once the formalities had been taken care of, she slipped out through the door and hurried away from the office before the next shouting match started.

# Chapter Eighteen

MAIA EXAMINED THE HUMAN book she had borrowed from the sparsely filled living room shelf, rubbing one of its dotted leaflets between two fingers. The material was made from some type of fibers or pulp, of that she was certain. None of the symbols made sense to her, but the print and layout were interesting enough on their own. It amazed her that humans actually printed information on such fragile material. Before transitioning to digital mediums, ikthians had recorded important text on specially treated Baledon skins. Not only were they durable, but also waterproof, which was useful in a variety of circumstances.

*Baledon. I would give just about anything for a taste of that again.* Suppressing a wave of homesickness, Maia returned her attention to the book, bringing it closer to her nose. She had to admit, although the book itself seemed flimsy, its pages did have a pleasing smell.

The sound of main door opening and closing caused her to sit up in bed. Footsteps followed—Taylor's, judging by the familiar cadence—and Maia set the book aside just as the human entered the bedroom. A sheen of sweat covered Taylor's brow, and Maia tried to ignore the way she wiped her forehead and tugged off the outer layer of her fatigues, revealing her muscled form underneath.

"It's hot in here," Taylor muttered, apparently unconcerned with the amount of flesh she was revealing.

"I increased the humidity," Maia said. "I hope that is not a problem."

"You messing with the temperature in here is the least of my problems," Taylor sighed. Her eyes fell upon the book Maia had abandoned. "Are you reading that?" she asked, with a little more brightness in her voice.

"I cannot." Maia closed the book and set it carefully on the nightstand. "How are you?"

Taylor's faint smile receded even further, and Maia wished she hadn't asked. After a brief hesitation, Taylor joined her on the bed.

"Things aren't much worse than usual," she said, but her words weren't convincing. "Just got back from a meeting with the brass, and that's never fun. They...heard back."

Maia's eyes widened. "Really?"

"The ikthians sent us a short response, basically saying they want you back and agreeing to give us precisely nothing with a side of nothing in exchange."

"Oh." Maia stared down at the comforter, mostly in order to avoid Taylor's eyes. Part of her wanted to know what the Dominion's leaders had said, and to ask if her mother had been among them, but she decided that hearing more information would only worsen her mood. There would be plenty of time to worry about her fate later. Pondering the topic tended to drain her these days rather than frightening her.

"I'm not even sure why General Hunt wanted my opinion," Taylor said. "I don't know anything about ikthians other than how to kill them." She backpedaled instantly, seeming to realize how poorly her statement was worded. "I mean, I know you, obviously, but you don't spend your time telling me about your people, and, well..."

Maia looked up, forcing a smile. "I understand what you meant."

"Sorry. Anyway, nothing got resolved. It was just a bunch of arguing." Taylor let out a frustrated sigh and flopped back on the mattress, cupping her hands behind her head and staring up at the ceiling. The position put her arms on enticing display, but Maia forced herself not to look. "At least the Dominion's called a ceasefire on Earth until we come to some kind of agreement," Taylor continued. "I think it's only because they don't want to risk blowing you up, but still."

Maia's lustful train of thought veered off course, and she failed to stifle a gasp. The Dominion had never declared a ceasefire on another species' home planet before conquering it. There could only be one reason for that decision. They were still hoping to bring her in alive. She didn't know how much of her research was currently in the Dominion's hands, but if they needed her, it probably meant they didn't fully understand it.

*I suppose they wish to torture me until I agree to publish more favorable articles about the superiority of the ikthian species and our great genetic destiny.* Her research had proven the polar opposite conclusion, but Korithia's propaganda machine wouldn't allow itself to be restrained by silly things like facts and scientific evidence. The Dominion fed on the belief that ikthians had been biologically designed to rule the galaxy and its other inhabitants, and it was always ravenously hungry.

Maia suddenly realized Taylor had been talking to her. "I apologize," she murmured. "I was lost in thought. Could you repeat yourself?"

"I asked what you thought of the Dominion's offer to leave Earth alone."

"It is unexpected." Maia left off any more telling comments. She didn't want to contemplate how much longer her relatively safe imprisonment on Earth might last if negotiations were moving forward. "I assume your leaders did not accept the terms?"

Taylor rolled her eyes, a gesture Maia couldn't help but interpret as ikthian. Aside from their species' anatomical similarities, it really was remarkable how even things like body language had developed similarly between their two different cultures. "No," Taylor said. "Maybe the generals will get their shit together, but the Coalition can barely agree on which direction is up. So...you have some time."

Maia could tell Taylor was trying to comfort her, but the words sounded hollow and unconvincing. When she didn't respond, Taylor cleared her throat and changed the subject. "So, Rachel's still angry at me."

"Rachel is your friend, correct? The one who believed I would attempt to seduce you as part of my secret plot to kill you."

"Yeah." Taylor sat up, lifting the bottom of her shirt a couple of inches to wipe her forehead again. The glimpse Maia stole of her muscular stomach was a brief bright spot in their otherwise gloomy conversation. "She found out about us, since I told Andrew the first time it happened." Taylor looked embarrassed, and almost worried, but Maia couldn't bring herself to be upset over something as trivial as Taylor's lack of discretion. Not while her life was in danger, at least.

"I assume she objected."

"She thinks you're using your pheromones to seduce me."

Maia made a disparaging noise in her throat. "Then your friend does not understand my species as well as she thinks she does. Our 'pheromones', such as they are, have no effect on aliens, and their effects on other ikthians are so subtle that we are almost always unaware of them ourselves. They were used millions of years ago by our ancestors to communicate underwater. It is hypothesized that we found them useful for hunting in groups."

"Hunting in groups?" Taylor repeated, with obvious interest. "So, you were like the wolves of the sea?"

"I do not know what a wolf is, but the ancestors of modern ikthians were aquatic apex predators who hunted in matriarchal family pods. Anthropologists theorize that our highly social background is the reason we place such importance on the genealogy of our Houses."

Maia checked Taylor's face, half-expecting to see that the human's eyes had glazed over. Taylor, however, was listening intently. "No magic pheromones? Just a bunch of pretentious 'my family is better than yours' posturing?"

"That is accurate, yes," Maia said with a soft chuckle. "Honestly, I have no idea why humans believe us to be so sexually promiscuous. On Korithia and the other central ikthian worlds, mating with or even befriending an alien would be considered a severe social taboo. Such individuals are frequently ostracized."

"Obviously not a taboo that you buy into," Taylor said.

"I grew up on Korithia, so I believed in the inherent inferiority of other species for a time. When I became a scientist, however, my views shifted rapidly. I was intrigued by the genetic similarities between ikthians and naledai, specifically. They struck me as something beyond mere coincidence, and so I began my research. More recently, it has expanded to include humans, although that portion of my work was…interrupted."

Taylor fidgeted, running a hand through her hair. "Can I ask a question?"

"You may," Maia said, unsure whether to feel pleased or uncertain.

"Is that why you were, uh, physically attracted to me? The genetic similarities? Or even your interest in alien species?"

The softness in Taylor's voice bordered on vulnerability, and it touched something in Maia. Perhaps if she and Taylor had met under normal circumstances, in a galaxy where the Dominion wasn't at war with Earth, the two of them could have had a proper date. She reached up to adjust the collar around her neck. So much could have been different.

"I am not sure," she said when she realized Taylor was still waiting for an answer. "As I told you before, I was drawn to you. I did not spend much time thinking about why." She hesitated, then asked, "So…since it is not due to my nonexistent, alien-brainwashing pheromones, why are…were…you attracted to me?"

Taylor rubbed the back of her neck. "That's an interesting question," she said, obviously stalling. It made Maia smile. Perhaps she wasn't the only one who felt insecure. "It would be kind of shallow to admit that I like your body, but your physical appearance is…appealing."

Maia's face flushed. "Go on. And?"

"And I guess you've shown me a lot of unexpected empathy since I became your guard. You felt bad for me when I talked about losing my squad." Taylor's expression looked vacant, as though her thoughts were far away.

"This surprises you," Maia whispered. "Why?"

"I guess empathy wasn't something I thought I'd see in an ikthian," Taylor said after a thoughtful pause. "I spent so much time killing them that I never bothered to talk to them."

Before she could consider the consequences, Maia found herself reaching out to put a hand on Taylor's knee. The heat of her skin radiated through her fatigues, warming Maia's palm. "I doubt the ikthian soldiers you fought ever bothered talking to you, either. Do not blame yourself for killing them, Taylor. The seekers are trained for violence."

"You know, if someone told me a few weeks ago that I'd be feeling bad for ikthians, I would've called them crazy," Taylor muttered.

"You feel bad for my species?"

Taylor's hand found hers, grasping her fingers. "Well, I feel bad for at least one ikthian."

Maia looked up, staring into Taylor's wide, dark eyes. It took her a few moments to realize that their faces were drifting closer and closer together, but when she did, she froze with indecision. Their lips were only a breath apart. It would be so easy to lean in and let their mouths brush…

She jerked back, trying not to be too obvious. The moment was broken. She and Taylor let each other's hands go, leaving more space between their legs on the mattress. "So, which of the leaders contacted you to make demands for my return?" Maia asked in a bid to change the subject.

"There were three of them. They never said their names, so I don't know who they were…but one of them looked like you."

A jolt raced through Maia's heart, and suddenly its echo sounded unnaturally loud in her ear canals. "Oh?"

"Her face looked like yours," Taylor said, staring just a little too long at Maia's lips. Maia could feel Taylor's gaze travel up to meet hers, and a rush of heat came along with it. "And she had your eyes. She seemed sad. Worried."

"That would be my mother. She is…House Kalanis is important. I did not expect her to appear in the transmission personally. She is usually busy with speeches, or treatises, or some other task the Dominion has set for her." Maia had spent much of her childhood with private tutors while her mother traveled from world to world, making speeches and writing legislation as one of the Dominion's most formidable politicians, but there had been moments of happiness between the two of them. Those moments seemed so distant now as she paused and reflected on them.

"She's a politician?" Taylor asked.

Maia gazed down at her hands, twisting them in her lap and trying to ignore the stinging sensation behind her eyes. "Yes. She encouraged me to adopt her career, and she disapproved of my decision to study genetics instead, especially with an anthropological and evolutionary focus. Perhaps she sensed my unwillingness to let politics dictate scientific advancement before I became aware of it myself."

"So she tried to stop you?" Taylor's voice nearly startled her when it came from close beside her. They had scooted nearer to each other once again.

"Not exactly. She attempted to persuade me to shift my focus. When she realized that I was far too awkward to be a politician like her, she tried to convince me to work for the Dominion as one of their researchers. My decision to seek a permanent position at the university instead was yet another disappointment to her."

There were so many things Maia wanted to say, memories she wanted to share, but she knew that now wasn't the time, and Taylor was probably not the right person to hear them. Instead, she turned away, hoping Taylor wouldn't notice the tears welling in her eyes. "I...I..." It was all too much to handle. The memories of her mother, her feelings for Taylor, the torture she would endure and the death sentence she would receive once she was delivered to the Dominion.

*I will never see Taylor again.*

It was a bizarre thought, and one that Maia was far too confused to put into any kind of useful context. "Please, excuse me," she mumbled, rising from the bed and hurrying toward the bathroom.

Maia thought she heard Taylor call after her, but she ignored the sound of her name, shutting the door behind her and bracing herself against the wall. Her tears fell in a river, streaming down her cheeks as she cupped her face in her hands.

She would give herself a few minutes to cry, she thought as she tried to stifle her sobs. A few minutes. Then, she would try to forget.

Forget that she was probably going to be executed, and forget about what a disappointment she was to her mother. It didn't matter now, not when she was facing death in a matter of weeks.

The only things she didn't want to forget were the feelings she was developing for Taylor. Even though they already had a clear expiration date, they were the only bright spot amidst the darkness.

# Chapter Nineteen

"MAIA..."

MAIA HEARD TAYLOR call after her, but she didn't answer. Even when Taylor rapped on the door, she couldn't form a reply. She sank to the floor and wrapped her arms around her knees, drawing into a protective position and gasping for breath between sobs. The dryness of the air only made things worse. She needed water, but she didn't want to move.

Taylor eased the door open with a gentle push. "Are you okay?"

Maia felt a soft touch on her shoulder. When she didn't respond, Taylor stepped into the bathroom and knelt beside her. Maia looked up, tears flowing down her face. She didn't know what Taylor would think of her for showing such weakness. "Why would you ask me that?"

Taylor smiled, though worry still lingered in her eyes and at the corners of her mouth. "I'm concerned about you. Here." She turned on the shower, and just the sound of the water made Maia relax and breathe a little easier. Taylor turned back and held out a hand, offering it to her. "We should get you cleaned up."

Maia hesitated. She knew she shouldn't be seeking comfort from Taylor, but she took the human's hand anyway and stood up. Once she found her footing, Taylor let go and glanced toward the door. "I can leave you alone to shower if you want. I just thought..."

As Taylor made to leave, Maia reached out, clasping her wrist and pulling her back. "Stay," she whispered. "Please." Before she could think better of it, she leaned forward and brushed Taylor's lips with hers, needing the intimacy and comfort. Their mouths remained pressed together for a hot second before they pulled apart, uncertain what to do next.

"Okay, I'll stay."

Carefully, Taylor helped Maia out of her shirt, lifting it over her head. Maia removed her undershirt without assistance, but she allowed Taylor to help with her pants. It was slightly awkward, since Taylor had to crouch to pull the legs down, but eventually, Maia stood naked in the middle of the washroom, feeling incredibly vulnerable. Taylor had undressed her much like a child.

As Maia watched, Taylor peeled out of her own clothes. Soon, her pants, shirt, and underwear were kicked into a small pile behind the door. "Come on," Taylor whispered. She put a hand on Maia's shoulder, steering her toward the shower. Steam had already begun to fill the room.

Maia went in first, but she held open the door, waiting for Taylor to come inside. After a moment, Taylor joined her. At first, they both stood under the hot water in an awkward silence. Maia stared at the shower floor, her arms crossed over her chest. Eventually, Taylor grabbed a soap bar and washcloth and began lathering it up.

"What are you doing?" Maia asked when Taylor approached her with the cloth.

"I was going to wash you. You looked a little out of it. Don't ikthians ever do this for each other?"

Maia lowered her arms and allowed Taylor to run the cloth over her body in slow, careful movements. It felt surprisingly good, and some of the tightness in her chest eased under Taylor's soothing touch. "Only with partners, usually."

"You mean like a husband or wife?" Taylor asked, following the line of Maia's shoulders with the washcloth.

Taking a deep breath, Maia closed her eyes. "My translator seems to think we are speaking about the same thing. Partners are bound together, physically and emotionally, for however long they choose to be together, often until death parts one from the other."

"The translator's right. That's basically like a husband or wife," Taylor said. Her hands faltered. "Should I stop doing this if it's so personal?"

Somehow, the thought of Taylor's hands leaving her caused Maia to panic. "No!" She swallowed, a little embarrassed by her outburst as it echoed through the shower and lowered her voice. "I mean, no. Please, do not stop. It feels...nice."

Taylor smiled at her. "All right, but turn back around. I want to massage your back. It feels really tense."

"I...yes..." Maia whispered. She didn't know why she suddenly craved Taylor's touch, but the thought of being alone frightened her. Taylor reached out slowly, running her free hand across Maia's shoulders. Her touch was surprisingly gentle, but Maia could feel the strength behind it, and it made her shiver under the warm water. A soft whimper escaped her lips when Taylor's hand pulled away too soon, but it was quickly replaced by the rougher texture of the washcloth.

Taylor began moving it in circles, covering every inch of Maia's back in suds before the water from the showerhead washed them away. She even coaxed Maia into extending her hands, massaging the webbing of her fingers and stroking along each arm. After diligently cleaning Maia's back, Taylor crouched to begin washing her legs.

Maia let out a low sigh of appreciation as Taylor rubbed the stiff muscles of her calves, but as the cloth drew higher, sliding up along her thighs until it was nearly at the juncture between her legs, she held perfectly still, unsure what to do. Perhaps Taylor sensed her hesitation, because she left that area alone and ran the cloth over Maia's lower belly instead. Finally, she dropped it and stood back up, returning her hands to Maia's shoulders and massaging some of the tension from them.

She kept still, and her eyes remained closed as Taylor's hands wandered over her body. When Taylor reached around to cup her breasts, Maia shuddered, expecting the touch to turn heated and possessive. Instead, Taylor toyed with the hard tips, teasing them between her fingers. Warm lips brushed over Maia's shoulder, a sensation separate from the water. "I want to help you feel better," Taylor murmured against her neck. Maia remained silent, unsure what to say. Taylor drew closer, and Maia felt the hard muscles of the human's body pressed against her back. She pulsed involuntarily, her inner muscles clutching at nothing. "Will you let me?"

Maia didn't say yes right away. Her head spun. Water ran down her face along with confused tears, blurring her eyesight as Taylor turned her around, propping her tenderly against the shower wall. Instinctively, Maia parted her thighs and let out a quiet, breathless, "Yes," giving Taylor all the access she needed. She had no idea why she was crying, but she desperately wanted Taylor to touch her again for reasons she couldn't explain in words.

Taylor slid between her legs, parting her folds with two fingers. Their tips ran over the swollen ridge above Maia's entrance, although Taylor didn't apply nearly as much pressure as she had the previous times they'd done this. Maia rocked into the touch, deliberately seeking more. Taylor continued to rub her with slow, teasing strokes before withdrawing to caress Maia's inner thigh. "Just relax. Let me take care of you."

Maia melted, welcoming Taylor's touch completely. Their bodies met, wet limbs sliding past one another. Taylor lined her fingers up with Maia's entrance, but hesitated, obviously waiting for permission. Finally, Maia found her voice. She wanted Taylor to make her feel something good, to replace the constant fear and sadness with pleasure. "Please. Touch me."

Taylor caught Maia's lips in a tender kiss, stretching her with a slow, deep push. Maia gasped in response to the fullness within her. She could feel every small movement Taylor's fingers made. Her pelvis jerked forward, and she wedged one of her own legs in between Taylor's thighs. It was so difficult not to be involved with Taylor, even when she knew their end would only lead to more tears. Taylor drove her insane without even trying.

When they broke away from the kiss, Maia rocked into Taylor's hand, encouraging her to continue thrusting. Taylor filled her again, faster this time, fingertips dragging along her front wall. More tears streamed down Maia's face, mingling with the water droplets from the shower. Taylor kissed her cheeks, blotting them away with her lips before shifting to the column of Maia's throat. The hand on her hip tightened, and Taylor finally settled into a steady rhythm.

Maia turned her head, water cascading down one side of her face. Her lips parted, and she let out small, soft gasps every time she felt Taylor thrust back inside of her. It was difficult to take in air. Her chest felt heavy and light at the same time. She knew that they shouldn't be doing this, but she couldn't find it in herself to care. Right now, she needed the comfort Taylor was offering her.

"That's it," Taylor sighed next to Maia's fringe, kissing the line of her jaw and wandering down toward the dip of her throat. Maia instinctively tilted her chin back and offered Taylor her collarbone, not caring when the back of her head bumped the shower wall. "You feel so good, Maia."

Maia's face flushed, but not from the warmth of the shower. She was quickly discovering that she loved it when Taylor said her name. "Please..."

"Please?" Taylor repeated, holding Maia's hips steady.

"Please, say it again." When Taylor gave her a confused look, Maia swallowed down the knot of embarrassment in her throat. "My name."

"Maia," Taylor breathed, holding her gaze for a moment before lavishing kisses on her warm throat. "You're so ready for me," she murmured. Her fingers slid out again, and Maia released a sob of disappointment until she felt them settle on the hard ridge of her clit instead. The new touch was even more intense than before. She tried to press forward to relieve the pressure building inside her, but Taylor moved with her. "I love how responsive you are."

"I...cannot help it." Maia bit her lip as Taylor continued teasing her. Her inner muscles clutched down, clasping at nothing, but once again, Taylor knew exactly what she needed. She slid back inside, replacing her fingertips with the pad of her thumb. "You...your every touch..." Maia gave up on trying to explain and surrendered to Taylor instead.

Taylor leaned closer, and Maia shivered as blunt teeth grazed her neck. "You feel so good," she muttered between nips.

"Taylor, I..." Maia's words failed her, and for a moment, she was tempted by a thought that startled her with its intensity. She wished her collar was off. She wished she was free, and that Taylor wasn't her guard. Maia had never been with someone like this before, and she was ashamed that her first time was so far outside of normal circumstances. Most ikthians would never even consider touching a human, but Maia's research proved the differences between them irrelevant. All that remained now was the regret that she and Taylor would never have a chance at a normal relationship.

"Maia? Are you all right?"

Taylor's voice startled her, and Maia blinked. She had gotten lost in thought, something her colleagues used to tease her about relentlessly. "I...I am sorry," she said, her voice shaking a little. She looked down to see that Taylor's hand was still buried between her legs, and the pleasant stretch of the fingers inside of her suddenly stole her attention again. "Please, do not stop. I promise to explain later, but now..." She reached up to cup the side of Taylor's face, drawing it closer to hers. "Now, I just need you."

Taylor pressed her cheek into Maia's hand, turning to kiss the center of her palm. The simple gesture of affection made Maia's heart swell. For a moment, they simply stared at each other, and Maia could see her own need reflected in Taylor's brown eyes. Even though they could have no future together, at least she wasn't alone in this.

Taylor resumed the motion of her hand, and Maia felt the pounding ache center back between her legs, making her forget everything else. Every time Taylor's fingers entered her, she pushed her hips down, searching for something, anything to ease the tightness in her core. She knew what she sought, but couldn't find words. Instead, she clutched desperately at Taylor's back, hoping her lover would know what she needed.

"Oh, Taylor, I want..." Maia's voice was soft, tinged with embarrassment, but also alight with desire. "I want..."

"You want to come," Taylor finished the thought, cradling Maia's hip in her free hand and running her thumb just above Maia's hipbone.

The touch made Maia's clit pulse. "Please."

Taylor pumped into her one more time, harder than before, and Maia screamed. Her release tore through her, and she pulsed around Taylor's fingers, barely able to breathe. Each press, each curl inside of her was bliss. Tears leaked from her eyes as she spilled into Taylor's palm, finally releasing the pressure that had been building deep within her. She cried out again when she felt Taylor buck against her thigh, grinding down and covering it with warmth. Maia dug her fingernails into Taylor's back, trying to draw her closer even though no space remained between them.

Somehow, they untangled themselves, and their pleasure faded to a satisfied, exhausted feeling. Maia slumped against the shower wall, hot water rolling over her body. Taylor's weight pressed on top of her, but it was comforting instead of constricting. Slowly, Taylor's fingers eased out of her, but she kept an arm wrapped around Maia to hold her up. "God, I didn't think I could come that way," Taylor muttered thickly. She gave Maia's temple a kiss. "Are you all right?"

"Yes," Maia said after a long moment, "I am now." And to her surprise, it was the truth.

"Wow." Taylor placed a soft nip along the cord of muscle that ran between Maia's neck and shoulder. Maia tensed, but soon relaxed into the gentle bite. It didn't hurt. In fact, the sensation was soothing. Taylor let her go, nuzzling the sensitive crook of her throat just above her gills, but Maia could still feel her pulse pounding insistently beneath the place Taylor had bitten.

She drew in a shuddering breath and ran her hands down Taylor's arms. "It was incredible," she whispered back.

Taylor dipped her head and brushed her lips against Maia's one more time. "Let's do that more often," she said when they finally pulled apart.

Maia laughed a little. She didn't know how to sort through all the things Taylor had just given her, but she was grateful to have them anyway. She lowered her foot to the shower floor, trying to stand on her trembling legs. Taylor offered some extra support, then reached out to shut off the water.

When Taylor prepared to step out of the shower, however, Maia clung to her, unwilling to let her go. Taylor didn't object. She allowed Maia to huddle against her arm as she reached for a pair of towels that hung from a bar on the wall, wrapping the first one around Maia's shoulders before grabbing the other for herself.

Skin still dripping, they headed back into the bedroom. Maia remained pressed against Taylor's side, and when the human urged her to lie down on the bed, she pulled Taylor with her, determined to maintain skin contact.

"You're okay, Maia," Taylor said, stroking the top of her fringe. Maia crooned at the touch, nestling further into Taylor's embrace. She breathed deeply, inhaling Taylor's scent. It wasn't like an ikthian's, but it was warm and comforting, and its salt reminded her of the sea. "So, did it feel different that time?" Taylor asked, her voice sounding a little unnatural as she broke the silence between them.

"The...sex?" Maia propped herself up beside Taylor on one of the pillows.

"Yeah. I didn't mean to pressure you, but...you just looked like you needed that."

"I did," Maia said. "I know we should not pursue this any further, but I cannot seem to help myself around you, Taylor. Not when the rest of the galaxy is against me." Despite her clear explanation, Taylor still looked worried, and Maia was far too tired to offer a better one. "I did not want to connect with you before, because I hoped it would discourage us from trying this again."

Taylor's lips twitched into a frown. "Is that why you pulled away from me in the shower? Because being with me made you feel guilty?"

Maia shook her head. "Of course not," she protested. The hurt written on Taylor's face made her chest ache. "I was simply uncomfortable. My collar reminded me that we cannot have a normal relationship. I often find myself wondering how things would progress if I were not a prisoner."

Taylor seemed to relax. "It's okay. I wonder the same thing sometimes. Probably more than I should." She flopped back against a pillow, appearing pleasantly tired. "Hey, you're smiling again. What's on your mind? I didn't say anything stupid, did I?"

Maia shook her head. "Nothing. I was just drifting off."

Taylor patted the spot next to her. "The bed's all ready," she teased. "That is, if you want to share it with me tonight."

Even though she knew it was probably another mistake, Maia couldn't find it in herself to say no. She still felt vulnerable after her experience in the shower, and she wanted to stay close to Taylor. "I think would like that very much." Maia joined Taylor under the covers, snuggling against her side and pulling one of the human's arms around her waist. "Thank you," she said, though for what, she wasn't entirely sure.

Taylor placed one last kiss against the back of her neck, just above her collar. "Any time."

# Chapter Twenty

THE DETACHMENT OF REBEL soldiers from Nakonum touched down on Earth a few days after Taylor and Maia's moment in the shower. Although the naledai were unquestionably humanity's allies, Taylor had been looking forward to their arrival more than most of the other soldiers on base. Rachel and Andrew had looked at her like she was insane when she had tried talking about what she'd experienced with Maia, so she'd stopped trying. Who better to talk to about her strange obsession with an alien than another alien?

Akton was just that alien. The naledai was cocky, with an outward veneer of smart-assery that hid a warm heart as large as his big shaggy body. He was also one of the best hand to hand fighters Taylor had ever seen on the battlefield. Despite her pride in Earth's military, she would have bet all her wages the Coalition couldn't find a brawler among their ranks to match him. Action movies couldn't compare to watching Akton when he got within range of an enemy, and he was a crack shot, too—which he had proven the first time he and Taylor had met, when his squad had come to the rescue of a besieged transport ship she'd happened to be escorting.

Taylor found herself waiting slightly apart from a small crowd of other human soldiers as the naledai disembarked from their complement of ships. From the looks of it, they hadn't brought much else besides themselves and some basic weaponry. Taylor suspected their ships would be leaving with a lot more supplies than they'd arrived with.

Since Nakonum and almost all of their colonies were in the Dominion's hands, the naledai didn't have ready access to the resources required to sustain a war, even an underground rebellion that was *literally* underground. So far, not even the deadly and determined seekers had managed to dig all the naledai out of their burrows.

Taylor watched the action for a while, hanging back as the new arrivals spoke with the dockmaster. From a distance, she couldn't be sure which naledai was Akton at first, but she soon spotted him among the cluster of rebels. He was easily two heads taller than her five foot nine, and even among his own species, he was big enough to be noticed.

"Akton!" she called out, raising her arm and waving.

Akton turned. "Well, well, well, if it isn't Lieutenant Taylor Morgan," he growled, heading over to join her.

He had a loping gait that made him look more graceful in motion than his stocky body appeared to be while he was standing still, but it was underground that he truly thrived. His oversized arms were built for burrowing, as evidenced by the thick cluster of claws extending from his hands. Taylor remembered Roberts saying that the naledai looked like giant groundhogs crossed with pissed off werewolves, and he wasn't completely off base. Streaky silver scars crisscrossed every visible portion of Akton's furry pelt, and he hadn't even collected enough to be considered old yet.

"I see you've managed to keep all your limbs attached, puny as they are," Akton said. "Or do humans have three arms? I can never remember." His pointed snout trembled in a way that represented a smile, or at least, Taylor had learned to interpret it that way.

Taylor clapped him on the shoulder. "It's four. I've had some bad luck." They chuckled together, though Akton's came out as more of a deep rumble.

"So, the rumor is that you've got an important visitor on base," Akton said as they began walking, not heading for any particular destination. "My C.O. was pretty tight-lipped about it, but I know that's part of why we were sent here."

"Yeah. An ikthian prisoner of war. I'm in charge of looking after her." Taylor's smile widened as she thought about Maia, and this time, she didn't bother suppressing it.

"And I guess that's gone well," Akton drawled.

Taylor's smile faded. "I'm not sure that's how I'd describe the situation. I was hoping to talk to you about it, actually." She glanced around to make sure no one else was within earshot before continuing in a whisper. "I accidentally slept with her. A couple of times."

Akton interrupted her. "You're sleeping with the ikthian you're supposed to be guarding? There's no accounting for human taste, I suppose, but are you sure that's a good idea? My superiors would kill me for even thinking about it."

"Mine don't exactly know," Taylor confessed. "Neither of us meant for this to happen. And then we swore we wouldn't do it again, but...we can't stop. I don't want to stop." She paused, considering how best to explain what had happened. At last, she settled for, "I'm starting to care about her."

"You're in a heap of trouble, Taylor," Akton said, with worry rather than anger. "This is more than just burrow gossip. You could end up risking the entire exchange, and from what I've picked up with my nose to the ground, it's a big one."

"I know, I know," Taylor sighed. "I didn't want any of it to go like this. It just happened."

Akton shook his shaggy head in sympathy. "Be careful, Morgan. You're playing a dangerous game with this one. Even if this ikthian doesn't turn on you, they could send her back to the Dominion in an exchange, or decide to execute her. A broken heart on your part sounds like one of the least terrible outcomes."

The thought of the Coalition deciding to execute Maia made Taylor's stomach churn. "I try not to think about that."

"But you need to keep it in mind," Akton insisted. "She's a prisoner, not a fling you can forget about after shore leave is over. She could have a lot of lives resting on her valuable shoulders."

"You think I don't know that?" Taylor snapped.

Akton came to a stop by one of the squat cement buildings, shepherding Taylor around a private corner with one of his giant paws. "Look, I'm just worried about you," Akton said, leaning back against the wall. "I heard what happened to your squad on Amaren. Now this? It would be a lot for anyone."

She sighed. "Thanks. I'm managing, though. Maia has helped with that a lot, actually."

"Wait, did you say Maia?" Akton pushed away from the wall. "As in Kalanis?"

Taylor nodded, then grunted in surprise as Akton grasped both of her shoulders. "Hey!"

"*You're screwing Maia Kalanis?* Oh, Ancestors. You're dead. We're all dead. Do you have any idea who she is to the ikthians?"

Taylor shook off Akton's surprisingly strong grip. "I know her mother is one of their leaders..."

"Irana Kalanis and the rest of her family aren't just leaders," Akton said. "They control a good portion of the Dominion all by themselves. There's even an ocean on Korithia named after them. They're the closest thing the ikthians have to royalty."

Taylor's eyes widened. "So, you're saying that trading her for a couple of hostages is probably a bad deal?"

Akton snorted. "That's an understatement. Famous family aside, she's one of the Dominion's premier geneticists...or was, until she started refusing to let them use her research. They cite her older findings in propaganda all the time, and she *hates* it. She made tons of videos claiming all our species are distantly related or something, and there's no proof that ikthians are genetically superior and destined to rule the galaxy. The ECO office on Korithia scrubs them, of course..."

"ECO?"

"Executive Media Coordination Office. Ancestors, Earth really is a backwater planet, isn't it? Anyway, as long as you have Maia, you'll be able to convince the ikthians to leave Earth alone, at least until they figure out where she is. Then, they'll probably come looking for her, and I hope I'm not around when they do."

Taylor struggled to get a grip on her bewilderment. She hadn't actually believed the Dominion's offer of a solar system wide ceasefire was legitimate, which was one reason she'd advised General Hunt to turn it down. "Maia said it was a crazy deal. I just didn't realize how crazy."

Akton's furry brow lowered over his small eyes. "Trust me, Taylor, you don't want an invasion on your home planet. You don't want to become a protectorate nation. I've lived that life, and it amounts to galaxy-wide slavery...and the ikthians have *never* failed to conquer an alien home world once they find it. Never."

Taylor ran a nervous hand through her hair, exhaling loudly. Before she could dwell on the thought any further, however, her stomach grumbled. "This conversation is freaking me out. Want to take a break and hop into the mess? I could use some food."

"Sure," Akton said. "It's not like the ikthians are going to invade in the next twenty minutes."

Taylor rolled her eyes. "My luck isn't that bad, believe it or not."

Akton laughed, and they continued on to the mess hall. It was fairly crowded when they arrived. Fortunately for Akton, there was a small, separated section in the chow line with naledai options. Someone must have informed the cook in advance that their allies were paying a visit.

"Ancestors, this place reeks," Akton grumbled as he picked through the available food. "How do you deal with so many competing smells in one place?"

Taylor took a whiff. The mess did have a distinct smell, reminiscent of watery canned vegetables and industrial plastic, but it wasn't overpowering by any means. "Guess I don't really notice it."

Akton piled some stringy looking tubers onto his tray before moving onto some rather bloody looking meat. "You humans might have akilan eyes, but you couldn't smell your way out of a tunnel with only one exit."

Once they finished piling food onto their plates, they headed toward one of the smaller, more private tables available. "I guess I don't understand what's happening," Taylor said as she set her tray down. "The two of us didn't want this to happen. We just fell into it."

"Oh. Right. Sleeping with the prisoner. Kind of forgot about that, since you have *Maia fucking Kalanis* on your planet and the Dominion's temporarily agreed not to wipe Earth off the Milky Way map."

Taylor had the decency to feel embarrassed. Those were more important issues, and yet it was Maia's tender smile that kept resurfacing in her mind. "I feel drawn to her, Akton. Sometimes it feels like in another life, we could have pursued an actual relationship, as crazy as that sounds."

Akton chewed loudly while he considered what to say. "I'd tell you to avoid her except when you have to guard her, but it sounds like that plan isn't working out for you so far." He wolfed down another bite of food, a string of tuber hanging from the corner of his toothy mouth. "Plan B would be communing with your ancestors so *they* could smack some sense into you, but I know not all humans go in for that the way my people do. Do you?"

Taylor shook her head. "Dad was English. Mom was Japanese. There's a little background there, but neither of them were religious. Honestly, I don't know what higher powers I believe in."

"It's hard not to be skeptical in the middle of a war like this. But if you ever find yourself in a tight spot, Taylor..." Akton glanced around, and then lowered his voice. "You know how to contact me. I'm your man."

Taylor grinned. She had hoped Akton would come through and support her, and she was relieved she'd been right. "You're a good soldier, Akton, but I won't do anything to compromise you with your superiors. Or myself with mine, if I can help it."

Akton nodded. "I know, but things change. I'm willing to help if you need me. I have a feeling things are going to get very complicated for you very quickly."

Taylor noted the solemn tone in Akton's gravelly voice. Naledai culture valued personal bonds to family and friends almost as much as it valued ancestral wisdom. She accepted the gesture of friendship for what it was. "Thanks. I'd do the same for you."

"What're you planning to do, Morgan?" Andrew asked in a loud voice, plopping himself onto the bench opposite Taylor. She straightened up, taken completely by surprise. She'd been so focused on her conversation with Akton that she hadn't even noticed Andrew approaching their table.

"See? Humans can't smell anything," Akton told her with a wolfish smirk.

"Hey, fuzzy," Andrew said, nodding at Akton. "Good to see you in one piece. Heard your people took a few hits recently."

"More like twenty thousand casualties at our biggest base on Nakonum before we moved burrows," Akton sighed. "But let's not talk about that. Taylor and I were just discussing maintenance protocol differences between our ships."

"Sounds boring," Andrew said. "Here I was, hoping you were talking about something juicy. I thought naledai were all about gossip."

Akton smirked. "You'd fit right in on Nakonum."

Taylor wasn't so amused. "Andrew, I don't know what you're up to, but stop being vague," she grumbled. With displeasure and unease, she noticed that several other soldiers seated at nearby tables were listening in. Andrew's loud voice had gotten their attention, or maybe they had encouraged him to come over in the first place. Taylor thought she recognized a few of them as some of his lower-ranking buddies.

"We were just wondering how the *special* prisoner was doing," Andrew said, looking from his audience to Taylor. "There are all kinds of rumors, but I know you've got the inside scoop."

Taylor knew she had to say something, but didn't want to encourage the group. "The ikthians opened negotiations for the prisoner's return, if that's what you're wondering. I don't know much else."

"Everyone knows that, Lieutenant," said another soldier. His voice sounded familiar, but Taylor wasn't able to place it until she caught sight of Sergeant Bower standing nearby. Immediately, her shoulders tensed and her hands flexed at her sides, threatening to form fists under the table. Even though Bower had addressed her by her rank, his tone had been anything but respectful.

"I thought I told you to stay out of my fucking business, Bower," she said through clenched teeth, resisting the temptation to rise from the bench and stare him down.

"I think she's everybody's business at this point," Bower replied. "She seems willing enough to *play nice* with you."

His implications were obvious, and they made Taylor fume, but Akton placed his heavy paw on her head to keep her in her seat. "Well, soldier...Bower, right? That's because even the fish have some standards. If you're into aliens, you could always try a voldak. I hear they're pretty undiscerning...and they only go into blood rages and kill their mates about half the time."

Bower sneered, clearly insulted, as the other soldiers began hooting and hollering. Still angry, but also pleased with how Akton had handled the conflict (not to mention the disgusted expression on Bower's face), Taylor grabbed her tray and stood up, nodding to her friend in thanks. "You say the sweetest things, Akton. Now, if the rest of you idiots don't mind, I have guard duty."

She headed for the door with Akton walking beside her. They dropped off their trays at the front of the mess, not speaking until they were outside and well away from the group. "What's the story with you and that guy?" he asked once they were out of earshot.

Taylor scoffed. "Don't get me wrong, I love Andrew, but sometimes he hangs around some really shitty company. Bower got up in my face a few days after Maia was put in my charge. Can you believe the dumbass actually tried to touch her? I mean, she had a collar on, but still."

"Sounds like someone's got a death wish in addition to an attitude problem," Akton said. "Maybe he really *should* go fuck a voldak."

"You wouldn't hear me complaining," Taylor said.

Akton laughed at first, but then his expression grew worried. "It's easy to laugh at rock-heads like that, but if he gives you more trouble than you can handle, remember what I said before. You can always contact me. I have a secure channel we can use." He brought up his datapad and sent her the info.

"Thanks," Taylor said as her wrist buzzed, "but I'm hoping I won't need to beg you to save my ass again."

Rae D. Magdon & Michelle Magly

# Chapter Twenty-one

"THIS IS RIDICULOUS! I told you before, these ikthians are uncompromising. They will refuse our offer, and we will be back where we started!"

Taylor caught Roberts' eye as Bouchard continued ranting. Hunt and the other generals had finally sent their offer back to the ikthians, and they had aimed for the stars—allowing the humans to govern Earth's solar system themselves in exchange for granting the Dominion access to resource mines within the outer human colonies.

"Do you want Earth to end up like the naledai home world?" Roberts asked. "At least this way, we'll stay in control of our own planet."

"The offer is already sent, Chairman, Captain," General Hunt said, trying to act as mediator even though it was obvious that he was as frustrated with Bouchard's antics as Roberts and Taylor were. "Save the arguments until after the Dominion gives us their answer."

"And what about the naledai?" Bouchard countered. "They came here in a gesture of cooperation and goodwill, and we asked for nothing that would help them."

Taylor rolled her eyes. Bouchard wasn't military, and he wasn't technically her superior either, so she couldn't resist challenging him. "You didn't seem particularly interested in helping the naledai yesterday afternoon, Chairman. I thought your first allegiance was to humanity?"

"The naledai are our allies," Bouchard said stiffly. "Surely they deserve some consideration. Perhaps a few prisoners..."

"Prisoners?" Roberts barked in disbelief. "We can't just trade her for prisoners! She's a Kalanis, and her propaganda is essential to the Dominion's efforts at brainwashing ikthian citizens, if what the naledai say is true. I'd rather keep her here than accept such a terrible offer. At least then the ikthians would think twice before initiating more drone strikes on Earth."

"It's pointless to argue the issue anymore," General Hunt said. "Judging by their usual timelines, the ikthians won't contact us again for a few more days at least. When we get their response, I'll gladly let you both fight about it." He turned to Bouchard. "Can you at least wait until then?"

"It seems that the only thing we do in these meetings is agree to wait. I don't appreciate being shut out of decisions, General. This may be a time of war, but humanity has not ceded all its power to the military yet." He glanced at Taylor. "Additionally, I find it upsetting that you continue to attempt to outnumber me in these discussions."

"That's not what we mean by bringing Lieutenant Morgan into this," Roberts said before Taylor could react in defense of herself. "She's been watching over Kalanis almost constantly, and has valuable insight to share with us."

Bouchard clenched his fists, and Taylor suddenly felt uneasy. She took a step back, looking to General Hunt. "I think I'll return to my quarters, if that's acceptable to you, Sir. The Chairman would obviously feel more comfortable with fewer jarheads present."

"Dismissed, Lieutenant," General Hunt said. His sympathy for her was written on his face. "It probably isn't wise to leave the prisoner alone for long anyway."

"We'll be sure to let you know when we hear back from the Dominion," Roberts added. Although Taylor was flattered that the upper brass valued her opinions and wanted to include her in the negotiations, she was beginning to feel like the new responsibility was more trouble than it was worth. Since Maia's capture, the only thing she'd actually enjoyed about the job was spending time with her charge.

Roberts followed her out into the hall, telling the others he would only be a moment. "It'll be okay, Morgan, " he said, though the tightness in his shoulders indicated too much stress. "Bouchard and the generals are just scared, that's all."

Taylor ran a hand through her hair. "I understand. But it would be nice if they'd actually listen to me when I show up to these things.

"About that, Lieutenant." Roberts glanced over his shoulder to make sure the door was shut and no one lingered the hallway. "Have you discovered anything about Kalanis? Anything I should know?"

Taylor shook her head. "I didn't realize interrogating her was part of my job, Sir. We have people for that."

"The brass isn't interested in questioning her anymore, but I've got a feeling. We know now that her research is used in war propaganda on Korithia. That's huge. It makes you wonder what the ikthians plan to do with her when they get her back."

Roberts gave Taylor a knowing glance, and she swallowed. He wasn't alone in his fears.

"I'll see what I can find out, Sir."

"Good soldier. I'll make sure you get a bonus after this is all settled. Report back to me with anything you find."

Taylor gave Roberts a farewell salute, turning to exit the building. The ache in her chest settled somewhat as she crossed the base, returning to the officer's barracks. Her shoulders and neck were killing her, and a hot shower and some rest sounded like the perfect cure. The stress just kept piling up, and sooner or later, she was going to have to find some way of soothing it that didn't involve sex with Maia.

After riding the elevator to the top floor, Taylor stepped into the hallway. She frowned when she noticed that no one was standing outside the door. There were always at least two armed guards posted during the day, especially when she met with the brass. She was in charge of scheduling their rotations herself. At first, Taylor thought that perhaps there had been some confusion about the shift calendar, but she still felt uneasy.

*What if Maia escaped? What if…* Taylor reached down to her hip holster and drew her pistol. When she opened the door, her worst fears were confirmed. Maia was in the living room, but she wasn't alone. Three soldiers, all of them from the mess hall incident, had closed in around her. Sergeant Bower held her by the wrist while the other two hovered nearby. All of them sported bruises and scratch marks, clear evidence that Maia had put up a fight.

Maia's eyes widened when she noticed Taylor. "Help!"

Taylor switched off her pistol's safety, aiming it right at Bower. "Let her go before I blow a hole in your head."

All three men jumped, but Bower didn't let go of Maia. He looked at Taylor with his annoying, cocky grin, probably trying to figure out if she was bluffing. "She's not your property, if I recall."

Taylor's hand remained perfectly steady. "I'm her guard, and she's my charge to look after. Let go of her before I kill all of you. Don't think for a second the brass cares what I do to you." It would be all too easy to shoot them and be done with it. Captain Roberts wouldn't care. Neither would General Hunt. Bower and his friends had broken into a secure room and almost jeopardized the Coalition's most valuable prisoner of war. Taylor had every right to take action. It was her *job* to take action.

Instead of yielding, Bower yanked Maia closer, taking hold of her other arm. "She's an ikthian, Morgan. They live for fucking. Are you going to deny her something she's probably aching for right now?" He leaned over Maia's shoulder, inhaling beside her neck close to her toxin suppressor.

Maia flinched away, her expression an outright war of disgust and fear.

Taylor's grip on the gun wavered. Bower had her enraged. She didn't trust herself to make a clean shot, one that would leave Maia entirely unharmed. But before she could act, Bower went stiff. His grip on Maia loosened, and he fell to the floor, scrambling across the carpet. His eyes flew open, rolling wildly with fear, and his limbs began to jerk. He screamed and clawed at his skin, as if he was trying to tear it off and rip out whatever was underneath. The sound reminded Taylor of Jackson.

The other two soldiers backed as far away from Maia as possible, sprinting for the door. Taylor made no move to stop them. Instead, she looked at Maia, who took a staggering step backwards. The collar around her neck sparked, and she screamed, collapsing to the floor. Her muscles began twitching, and her eyes rolled back into her head.

Taylor hurried over, crouching down and watching helplessly as shockwaves coursed through Maia's body. She thought she caught the scent of searing flesh, and she was horrified when she realized that the skin around Maia's throat had been cooked down to a raw, ugly shade of purple.

When Maia stopped moving, Taylor reached to check her pulse, only stopping herself at the last moment. Touching Maia's skin so recently after she'd used her toxins could very well be deadly. Taylor looked at Maia's chest instead. There, she could see the ikthian's heart beating rapidly but steadily just above the dip of her collarbone.

Praying Maia would last a minute longer, Taylor sprinted through the living room, the bedroom, and into the bathroom, barely stopping long enough to open the door. She fumbled through the medicine cabinet, and her hands shook as she pulled out the completely inadequate-seeming first aid kit.

It would have to do. She rushed back out to the living room and knelt beside Maia, examining her again. She was relieved to see that the ikthian's spasms had stopped, and her breathing was steady and slow. Maia's brow was still knitted with pain, and she hadn't regained consciousness, but otherwise, she seemed all right.

Although her first instinct was to wash the toxins from Maia's skin and begin treating the burn around her neck, Taylor knew she had to take care of Bower first. She headed toward his limp form, but paused when her foot kicked a discarded hall pass. It was probably how Bower had broken in. She picked it up, frowning when she noticed the name 'Bouchard' written beneath an unpleasantly familiar photograph.

Taylor closed the distance between herself and Bower. He was still on the ground, but he was slowly regaining consciousness. Angry, weeping red blisters had been burned into his flesh, obviously from Maia's toxins. Taylor didn't know whether to be relieved or disappointed that Maia hadn't killed him.

"You know stealing is wrong, don't you?" she said to Bower, dangling the card in front of him.

Bower glared at her, but didn't try to retrieve it. He spat on the floor to clear his mouth, limbs still trembling. "So, what are you going to do about it? Report me?" His words were slurred, and his eyes were cloudy with pain.

Instead of leading him on, Taylor tossed the card to him. "I'll let you return this to him however you want. You get out of here, and never come near the prisoner again. Nobody needs to find out what happened, especially the part where you got your ass beaten by an ikthian in a fully functioning suppressant collar."

Bower didn't respond. Defeated, he staggered to his feet and dragged himself into the hallway, falling back to his knees more than once when his shaking legs gave out. Taylor waited for the door to shut and watched the lift descend all the way before returning to her quarters, and Maia.

# Chapter Twenty-two

TAYLOR RETURNED TO FIND Maia still passed out on the floor. Her silvery-white skin was bruised in several places, and jagged scratch marks slashed down her right cheek. Apparently, there had been quite a fight before Taylor's timely arrival. The worst injuries lay around Maia's neck, right underneath the collar. The top layer of skin had burned away, leaving welts and a ring of cauterized flesh where the collar had reacted.

Taylor deactivated the suppressor with her wrist unit and carefully pried it off Maia's throat, trying to do as little damage possible. She'd seen worse on her tours of duty, but this was a major wound for a civilian to experience. She dug out an application of antibacterial and injected the serum into Maia's shoulder. Aside from a few shuddering breaths, Maia didn't react.

Next, Taylor ripped open a packet of topical gel and rubbed it into the wound around Maia's neck, careful to avoid direct contact with the ikthian's skin. The slick, oily coating on Maia's flesh seemed to have evaporated, but Taylor wasn't going to chance it. Gingerly, she scooped Maia off the floor and deposited her on the couch.

In a few minutes, Taylor saw improvement. Maia's complexion looked better, and her breathing returned to normal. She slept peacefully rather than lying in an unconscious heap due to shock. The injection Taylor had given her was a rapid healing agent, primarily used to keep soldiers from blacking out from bullet wounds, but the damage done to Maia's neck had been worse than a clean, cauterized shot to the leg.

When Maia groaned and began to stir, Taylor sighed with relief. She had been worried about Maia, more than just for the sake of her job. Maia opened her eyes, staring up at the ceiling for several long seconds before looking at Taylor. She drew in a shuddering breath and tried to sit up, but quickly settled back down. With some effort, she reached up and touched her throat, whimpering when her fingers came into contact with the raw, open wound.

"Take it easy," Taylor said. "You're lucky you aren't dead."

Maia gave a weak nod. "It felt as though I might have been for a moment. Thank you for helping me. I assume I did not recover on my own."

Taylor smiled, pleased to hear that Maia could still speak without much difficulty. "Yes. I helped you after I took out the trash. Those men won't bother you again."

Maia didn't acknowledge the statement right away. First, she pulled herself up into a slouched position on the couch. "They were animals."

Taylor had no idea how to respond to the charged emotion in Maia's voice. There was something strangely familiar about it, but she couldn't quite place where she had heard that tone before. She shook herself, putting the question aside for later. "There were supposed to be more guards here, people I trust. I won't let this happen again."

"I know you won't," Maia murmured. "What happened while I was passed out?"

"I went to get a first aid kit. Once I checked to see that you weren't dead, I made sure Bower and his goons got out of here quick. You must have put the pain on him, because he was screaming like he was about to die."

"I am glad I did not kill him," Maia said. "I tried not to...I simply wanted him to let me go."

Taylor nodded, remembering the way Bower had twitched and writhed on the ground as the poison flooded his system. "I think he got the message. Anyway, we're in a stalemate now. They broke in here and threatened the safety of a valuable prisoner of war, but I'm worried they might guess that we've been..." Taylor's voice trailed off, but Maia seemed to realize what she meant.

"Are you afraid that they will tell your generals what we have been doing?"

Taylor sighed. "I'm worried that they'll strip me of my rank and assign someone else to guard you." She left the worry that her replacement might treat Maia poorly go unvoiced.

"I do not want another guard," Maia said, but the words came out scratchy, and she raised her hand to her throat. Apparently, some of the pain was inside as well as outside.

Taylor touched Maia's shoulder. "Here, I'll get you some water. You probably need it."

"Do we have any leftover food?" Maia asked.

Taylor stood and headed to the refrigerator. A few moments later, she returned with a full glass of water and a box filled with rations. Maia drank half of the glass before setting it aside and opening the box of food.

"Thank you," she breathed, picking up the first thing she could reach and biting into it. Taylor watched her devour the sandwich before moving onto another, and another. She would need to get more food before Maia finished.

"It's not a problem. If you have everything you need, I'm going to make a call."

Maia only made a vague gesture with her hand as she continued devouring the meal.

Taylor returned to the bedroom and activated her wrist comm. "Contact Andrew." The device blinked in acknowledgement and had the muscular soldier's face pulled up on the tiny holoscreen a moment later.

"Hey. What's up?"

Taylor glared at him. "I need to have a discussion with you."

Andrew must have picked up on the venom in her voice, because his brow furrowed. "Uh, sure. When do you wanna talk?"

"Now," Taylor said coldly.

"What's the problem?"

"Remember your 'friend', Sergeant Bower?"

Andrew's dislike for the Sergeant was obvious in his expression. "I wouldn't call him a friend."

"Whatever you call him, he just tried to assault my prisoner!" Taylor said, on the verge of shouting.

She was somewhat gratified to see Andrew's eyes widen, and then shift away guiltily. "And when you say assault, you mean…"

"The situation was taken care of before it escalated, but I'm pretty sure we both know where it was headed." Taylor deliberately left out the fact that Maia had stopped Bower herself. The last thing she wanted was for the generals to hear that Maia's collar wasn't calibrated high enough. "Now, I wonder who he could've gotten the idea from?"

"That's not fair," Andrew protested. "Yeah, I told a few people what you were doing. Maybe that put some ideas in Bower's head, but that's because he's a sick creep, not because I encouraged him. I didn't tell him to break in and hurt her."

Taylor wondered if she was being too harsh on Andrew. Her run-in with Bower at the mess hall had certainly been a contributing factor, but the irrational part of her wanted to pin the blame on someone. "You shouldn't have told Bower anything about the prisoner. Your big mouth almost cost us everything. If she had been killed, we wouldn't have anything left to bargain with. The Dominion could start bombing runs on Earth again!"

Andrew looked sufficiently chastised, and Taylor started to calm down. "I want you reporting for guard duty tonight. You're personally going to make sure that Bower and the rest of them don't come back for another try. There's no way in hell I'm going to lose this prisoner." Even as Taylor said the words, they sounded strange. She didn't view Maia as just a prisoner anymore, and referring to her that way felt wrong.

Andrew mumbled his reluctant agreement and ended the call, leaving Taylor to deactivate her comm and stare down at the floor. She'd expected to feel better after yelling at Andrew, but all she'd done was point out her own mistakes. Guilt crept up on her, guilt for allowing Maia to be hurt. The thought of what might have happened if Maia hadn't been able to override the collar made her sick.

Taylor pushed those thoughts down and went back into the living room. To her surprise, Maia was still awake and sitting up on the couch instead of sleeping. Taylor tried to offer her a smile, but was greeted with only a cold, distant expression in return. "Sorry if you overheard any shouting. You'll have another guard outside the door tonight, and I'll stay with you in the bedroom, just in case."

Maia offered a brief nod of thanks, although she didn't speak. Taylor could guess where the sudden hostility was coming from. The more she replayed the conversation with Andrew in her mind, the more horrible it sounded. She had referred to Maia as a prisoner and talked about her like a bargaining chip instead of expressing any sincere concern for her. It had been to make Andrew understand the serious consequences of his actions, but if Maia had overheard...

"Do you think you can stand up and get to the bed on your own, or do you need help?" Taylor asked, wanting to push past the awkward moment as quickly as possible and make sure Maia got a proper night's rest.

"I...I think I will need your assistance," Maia said, although her reluctance was clear. "Do not worry, you can touch me safely now."

Taylor bent down, sliding one arm beneath Maia's knees and folding the other under her shoulders. "Wrap your arms around my neck," she said, and Maia obeyed.

It only took a few moments to carry her into the bedroom and deposit her gently on the mattress. "Try and get some rest," Taylor whispered. She let her hand linger on Maia's shoulder, and then tugged the sheet up over it, making sure to leave the burn on Maia's neck exposed to the open air. Taylor moved to climb into bed on the other side, but when she wrapped an arm around Maia, she noticed the ikthian was already fast asleep.

Rae D. Magdon & Michelle Magly

# Chapter Twenty-three

THE NEXT MORNING, MAIA woke to find herself draped across Taylor. She sighed, breathing in the human's comforting sea-scent. It was familiar, even though they had only shared a bed for a short time. Maia's heart sank as she remembered what Taylor had said the night before. No matter how comfortable they were together, Taylor still only viewed her as a prisoner.

With a groan, Taylor shifted beneath her. Maia rolled off to the side and watched her wake up. Taylor's dark gaze roamed along her body, pausing at her throat. Maia touched the flesh there, now nearly healed. She sighed in relief. The pain was gone, and hopefully, there would be no major scarring.

"How's your neck?" Taylor asked. "It looks a lot better than yesterday." She reached out and touched the tender skin, resting her fingertips less than an inch away from Maia's. "It's probably healed enough to put the collar back on. I can't let my superiors find you without it."

Maia blinked and removed her hand. She had completely forgotten that the collar was missing. "I..." She swallowed back the protest forming in her throat.

*What did you expect, Maia?* she thought. *That Taylor would simply let you walk around without the collar? As far as humans are concerned, you are a living weapon, and Taylor still sees you that way, despite everything we have shared.*

Bitterness welled up inside her. Taylor had gone back and forth between disappointing her and giving her hope ever since she had been brought to Earth. She barely registered Taylor's regretful, "Here. I'll be right back," or her departure from the room. Instead, she waited in numb silence until Taylor returned with the collar, holding it out expectantly.

Maia felt as though an opportune moment hovered in front of her. She could escape right now. She had the capability. She could destroy Taylor like she had done to Bower. And then what? She would be hunted down by the other humans and slapped into another collar, removed from Taylor's care, and thrown into a cell where she would have no one. Hesitantly, she reached out and took the collar, snapping it into place around her own neck.

"There," she said, her voice hollow. She settled back on the bed and stared at nothing.

The mattress sagged as Taylor tried to resume holding her, but Maia deliberately moved a few inches out of reach. "What's wrong? Besides...well, pretty much everything."

Maia swallowed. She was torn between sobbing and crying out in anger. She was hopeless, completely hopeless, and probably sick for allowing her feelings for Taylor to grow for as long as they had. She should have fought more. She should have taken her freedom, no matter how remote the chances. Instead, she had shackled herself and sealed her fate, binding herself once again to a woman who struggled between seeing her as a person and as an asset of war. "I am just wondering..."

"Wondering what?"

Maia hesitated for a moment. The words waited like water behind a floodgate. She knew that they would only serve to drive Taylor away, but did it even matter? "I am wondering why I keep letting us do this. Why do I want to be close to you when it will only bring me pain? Sometimes, I think it is because of some strange bond we share, pursuing something we both know is unrealistic. But it does not matter. I will be dead in a few weeks anyway, and you will go on with your life."

Taylor gave her a blank stare. "You don't know that. There's nothing I can do to help you yet, but I..."

"No. That is not true. We trick ourselves into believing that our problems will magically solve themselves. We play at a relationship, but when the outside world intrudes, I am a prisoner, and you are my guard. That is what you said last night, is it not? If you wish to behave like we are lovers, I cannot allow us to do so while you are unwilling to consider me anything more than the Coalition's prisoner."

Taylor looked stunned. Maia half expected her to get up and walk away, but she only pushed herself into a sitting position. "I...I'm your guard..."

"What we have is no longer a normal relationship for a guard and prisoner, Taylor."

"So what, we should just stop?" Taylor asked, a hard edge creeping into her voice.

Maia sat up as well, shifting further away and pulling the sheets tight around her. "If you are incapable of engaging with me as a person, then yes. I have no idea why I allow you to do the things you do to me."

"That's not fair." Taylor stood up, tossing the covers aside. "You initiated things between us, too. I always asked you."

"I am imprisoned here, awaiting my death, and you and I have shared things that I have not shared with anyone else. Yet the second you are reminded of my place, you expect me to remain complacent and content as your prisoner." Taylor tried to speak, but Maia continued. "I am not expecting a happy ending. That could never happen between us. But if you cannot even see me as more than a prisoner, even after what we have done..."

"You never said anything," Taylor stammered at last. "You didn't tell me you'd never..." Her mouth opened, then closed again.

Maia looked away. "I do not regret sharing my body with you. I regret sharing my heart."

Those words were too much. Taylor crouched and began gathering up her clothes from the floor, hurrying to put them back on. Maia almost asked what she was doing, but Taylor said, "I'm leaving." She pulled her shirt over her head before struggling into her pants. "Andrew's on his way. If anyone comes in besides me, lock yourself in here."

"Taylor..." Maia reached out, hoping Taylor would stop and turn back, but the human hurried from the bedroom as if something were chasing her away. Maia heard the front door hiss open then shut again, leaving her completely alone. Taylor was gone.

After a few moments, it became clear that Taylor wasn't coming back. When Maia realized that the emptiness in the pit of her stomach was because she hadn't wanted Taylor to leave, she began to cry. Tears leaked from her stinging eyes, and she buried her face in her hands. Wetness ran over her fingers. It wasn't fair. She didn't know why she wanted Taylor's comfort now, when Taylor was the source of her pain, or why she felt so empty.

Although she desperately wanted to continue being furious, the last of her anger burned out quickly. Instead, Maia's thoughts returned to the many confusing occasions during which Taylor had treated her with kindness, and even tenderness. *She offered me clothes when I first arrived. She gave me the sandwich. She defended me against that awful man the first time and the second. She took care of my injuries. And there was that moment in the shower...*

Maia didn't understand. Taylor's eagerness to put her collar back on had stung precisely because Taylor usually did treat her like a person, like someone she valued above a simple prisoner. Like a friend, or even something more. Taking physical pleasure from Taylor was bad enough. Acknowledging an emotional connection was worse. She tried to push the thoughts from her mind, unwilling to consider them. But alone in the room, there was little else to think about other than the dull pain around her neck and in her heart.

# Chapter Twenty-four

TAYLOR HADN'T KNOWN WHERE she was going when she left the room, but she had a destination in mind as soon as she exited the elevator. She didn't want to be alone after leaving Maia. She needed to talk to someone, but she couldn't go to Andrew. Even though Rachel hated ikthians, she was the best friend Taylor had. Hopefully, that friendship would be strong enough to convince her to listen.

When the lift stopped on the first floor, she exited the building and headed for the barracks, where the rest of the soldiers and the junior officers had their quarters. She found Rachel in her bunk, going over some paperwork. "Hey," she said, looking up when Taylor came in. "How's your assignment going?"

"Bad, but since when is that new?" Taylor groaned, sitting down on Rachel's bed. Rachel's shared room was much smaller than hers, and it didn't have its own private shower. There wasn't any space for a couch or other large items of furniture. The only other place to sit was at Rachel's small desk, where she was currently settled, or the other bed belonging to her bunkmate.

Taylor sat patiently while Rachel studied her. "You look like you need a drink."

Despite her awful mood, Taylor tried to force an unconvincing smile. "Definitely need a drink." Taylor watched Rachel walk over to the small cabinet in the corner of the room and pull out a bottle.

"Is the brass riding you? I hear the negotiations are stalled." She sat on the bed beside Taylor and passed her the bottle. "Here, take it. You probably need it a hell of a lot more than I do."

"Thanks, and not exactly." Taylor hesitated, not sure how much she wanted to open up. Rachel wouldn't understand her feelings for Maia. "Some grunts tried to mess with Maia the other day. They swiped Bouchard's ID card."

"Really?" Rachel asked.

Taylor took a swig from the bottle without bothering to check the label. She coughed as the liquid burned her throat raw. "Maia didn't even need me. Somehow, she managed to poison Sergeant Bower when he tried to touch her. Bastard deserved it. The others just ran."

Rachel's eyes widened. "Shit. That isn't good, Taylor."

"She was only protecting herself," Taylor said. "Besides, she didn't kill him."

"I'm sure she was. But if she could poison him while her collar was on, imagine what she could do to you."

Taylor frowned. "She didn't do anything to me. The pain made her pass out. Overrode her nervous system with the shock. After I fixed the burns, I put it back on." An image of Maia's numb, hopeless expression as she had clicked her own collar back into place nearly had Taylor in tears, but she washed them back with another mouthful of fire.

Rachel didn't look convinced. "You need to go to the brass and tell them her collar isn't turned up high enough or something."

"I will," Taylor said, although she knew she wouldn't.

"So, what else happened? That can't be the only reason you're here downing my private stash of liquor?" Taylor took one last long gulp before Rachel took the bottle away from her. "This stuff is impossible to come by anymore, and I think you've had more than enough."

"You let me have it," Taylor said, her syllables running together.

"Because I thought you'd only take one shot!" Rachel pulled out a glass from her desk drawer and poured out a measured amount of the drink. "There." Taylor took the shot glass and downed it instantly. "That's all you're getting. Now, why are you really in here getting shit-faced off my good alcohol?"

Taylor shuddered as the drink settled in her stomach. "They just...they treated her like less than a person. And she's not...less than a person, I mean."

"Still not seeing where all the angst is coming from. You said she was fine." Rachel poured herself something to drink as well.

"I treated her that way, too," Taylor whispered. She was close to tears, and the burning in her throat from the alcohol only reminded her of Maia. "I slapped that collar back on her without a second thought, even after it hurt her. And I'm supposed to be better than them."

Rachel frowned. "She's just an ikthian," she began, but her voice trailed off when Taylor gave her a murderous glare.

"She's not just an ikthian. Thinking like that is what made them try to hurt her. It's a damn good thing she protected herself." For a moment, Taylor wanted to confess, to tell Rachel about her conflicted feelings, but she knew her friend wouldn't understand. "I've spent time with her, Rachel. She's just as...human...as we are." She buried her face in her hands, her back shuddering as she began to sob.

Rachel sat on the bed beside Taylor, placing a hand between her shoulders. "Hey...I know you're an asshole sometimes, but the ikthian can't hate you that much if she hasn't killed you yet." That only made Taylor cry harder, and Rachel pulled her hand away. "Listen, I don't know anything about aliens, but usually an apology is the place to start when you've hurt someone's feelings. You did say she has them, right?"

Taylor hung her head. She wanted to apologize for the way she had treated Maia, but she didn't know where to start. "You make it sound simple," she said in a hoarse voice. She was definitely starting to feel the effects of the alcohol. Her head was spinning, and Rachel's face was becoming blurrier by the second.

"It is simple. It's just not easy. If you think you've treated her badly, tell her you're sorry. If the prisoner...she... really is a *good* ikthian like you say she is, she could probably use at least one friend in this place."

Taylor almost laughed. "I'm the last person she needs as a friend. But she is a good ikthian. The truth is, she's harmless unless you attack her first, and I..." The words stuck in her throat. She cared for Maia. Deeply. Perhaps it was moving beyond just affection. The thought of falling for an alien terrified her. Falling for Maia, however, seemed perfectly natural...if only she wasn't the only thing standing between Maia and freedom.

"And you think she really cares about you?"

Taylor didn't hesitate. "I know she does."

Rachel took a deep breath. Even through the hazy effects of the alcohol, Taylor could tell that she was conflicted. Finally, she said, "It sounds like you should be talking to her about this instead of me, then. Tell her."

"I'm not sure I can. But I guess I have to." Gathering her resolve, Taylor stood up, swaying slightly on her feet. "I'll do it. I'll tell her I'm sorry. Tell her I..."

"Not now," Rachel said, pulling Taylor back down. "Sleep it off first. I'll let you have my bunk."

"Okay," Taylor muttered. It was probably a good thing to wait before talking to Maia. She was a mess in this state, crying one minute and forgetting all of her words the next.

"Lie down." Rachel stood up to give Taylor room. "And if you puke on my sheets, I'll kill you, superior officer or not."

As Taylor stretched out obediently on her side, Rachel went back to her desk, returning to the paperwork she had started. Taylor closed her eyes, sighing with relief as the room stopped tilting at strange angles. Tomorrow. Tomorrow, she would tell Maia she was sorry and confess her feelings. Hopefully, she would be able to come up with the right words. Unable to think of any now, Taylor gave up and pictured Maia's face, trying to remember what the ikthian's smile looked like.

Tomorrow, after she apologized, she was going to make Maia smile. Maia deserved that much from her, at least.

# Chapter Twenty-five

APOLOGIZING TO MAIA HAD seemed like an easy task while under the influence of alcohol, but once Taylor stood outside her door, the idea of going inside seemed impossible. The two guards that had been stationed in her absence looked at her with curiosity. One of them had already asked if Taylor had lost her pass or needed assistance, but she shook her head and kept staring at the door.

"Um, Lieutenant?" one of the guards said, "I don't know what the problem is, but you should probably just go inside." Taylor nodded and took a step forward. The door opened when she presented her wrist comm, but she didn't see Maia anywhere in the living room. She swallowed and went to check the bedroom.

She found Maia sitting on the bed, staring at the opposite wall. That seemed to be all the ikthian did with her free time, but it wasn't like she had many other options. Eventually, Maia looked up, giving Taylor a clear view of her face. There were dark purple circles beneath her blue eyes, and her body was limp with exhaustion. She looked as though she'd been crying for most of the night.

Taylor felt another stab of guilt. "Hey." She took a few steps forward, but stopped at the edge of the bed and made no motion to sit down.

"Taylor?" Maia frowned, shifting closer to her. "Is everything all right?"

Taylor closed her eyes and took a deep breath. If Maia's expression was anything to go by, she probably looked horrible, too. Still, Maia's persistent concern for her kindled a spark of hope in her chest. "I can't imagine it's all right for you. You've been through so much, Maia, and a lot of it is because of me."

Maia hesitated. "I...I am not sure what to say. You treat me kindly one moment, and then seem to remember that I am your captive the next. But I was too harsh on you yesterday. I enjoyed what we did. I just have no idea what to call...this...anymore. It defies everything I thought I knew."

Instead of comforting her, Maia's gentle tone made Taylor's chest tighten. She could barely look at the ikthian, and each soft word struck her like a blow. This was it. She had to apologize, and to tell Maia how she felt. "I'm sorry. So sorry for everything. The last thing I want to do is hurt you. I...I realize that I'm the one trapping you here, not just the Coalition, and it only makes things harder." She blinked to clear her eyes and forced herself to stare at Maia, who had gone strangely silent. "I can't just think of you as a prisoner anymore. Not after I've started to see you as a lover."

"A lover?" Maia whispered. Warmth surrounded Taylor's hands, and she realized that Maia had wrapped her fingers around them. "Is that how you have come think of me?"

Taylor ran her thumbs over the backs of Maia's knuckles. She knelt so that they were on the same level, bringing Maia's hands close to her chest. "Yes. That's how I think of you. How I feel for you."

Maia took a shaking breath, and Taylor saw a little of the pain leave her eyes. "So, what should we do now?"

"We take it one day at a time, and I'll see you as...you. Not just an ikthian or a prisoner of war. Just as Maia." Taylor brought Maia's hands to her lips, pressing a kiss against them. "I don't know when it happened. When I started seeing you differently. Somewhere along the way, I just forgot we were supposed to be enemies, and by then, it was too late to go back to being just your guard. I didn't mean to fall into bed with you so quickly, though. I'm sorry that happened."

Maia's face brightened. "I am not sorry," she said, drawing her hands back. She patted the edge of the bed beside her, and Taylor climbed off her knees, taking the offered space. "Taylor, you let me experience things I never would have otherwise, and I do not mean just physical pleasure. It has been an experience getting to know you, and one I am glad to have had."

A little of Taylor's guilt eased. Their desire had seemed mutual at the time, but she was terrified that she might have pressured Maia into being intimate with her. It was a relief to hear that Maia had wanted her. She lifted her arm, allowing Maia to settle under it and rest against her shoulder.

"Sometimes, I wonder what our first encounter would have been like without this war," Maia said, still comfortably tucked in her embrace.

Taylor looked down at her. "You mean, if the Dominion and Coalition weren't trying to kill each other?"

"Yes. If we all saw each other as equals. If we had met casually, just as two people..."

Taylor tucked her chin overtop of Maia's crest, pulling her closer. "I don't know. My pick-up lines are kind of terrible. I might have scared you off."

"But you are so kind," Maia said. "Perhaps that gentleness would have been enough."

"Or perhaps I would have gotten a slap across the face," Taylor teased. Her heart soared when she saw a smile tug at Maia's lips. *Mission accomplished.* She was grateful to have made Maia smile at least once. "So how would we have met? Maybe in a bar? Or would you stay away from those kinds of places?"

A light blush tinged Maia's cheeks as she considered the question. "I suppose I would have frequented a bar...eventually. Perhaps a colleague would force me to go after successfully compiling a report."

"I guess geneticists compile lots of those," Taylor said.

"Unfortunately, yes."

"So, you'd probably have a pick-up line about DNA sequencing or something, right?"

Maia's brow furrowed. "I do not understand what you are implying, Taylor. I was not under the impression that bars were an acceptable place to discuss genetic theory."

"That isn't quite what I meant," Taylor said. "I was just kidding. We really need someone to update these translator chips. You never get my humor."

"Perhaps it is because your delivery leaves something to be desired."

For a moment, Taylor was stunned. Then, she burst out laughing. She pulled her arm from around Maia's shoulders and braced her elbows on her knees instead, leaning forward until she could catch her breath.

"That was a joke," Maia said, sounding concerned. Her hand rubbed circles on Taylor's back.

"I know it was a joke." Taylor straightened up again, still a little winded from laughing. "I just didn't expect you to tell one."

"If it makes you feel better, it has always been difficult for me to detect humor or sarcasm, even in my native language. It is not just you." Maia's hand fell away, and Taylor saw a dark flush start to spread beneath her silver cheeks. "If we had met in a bar, I probably would not have realized that you were interested in me. Still, I suppose it would have been nice to have someone sympathetic to talk to. Since many ikthians disagreed with my discoveries, I had very few friends back home."

"What exactly were your discoveries, anyway?" Taylor asked. "All I know is that you think ikthian genetics aren't all they're cracked up to be."

Maia's face fell. "That is a fair summary, I suppose. I am ashamed to admit that the Dominion funded most of my research in the hopes that I would bring my species greater glory, and they often interpreted the results the way they wanted to instead of the way I presented them. Most recently, I have been studying the genetic codes of various sentient species across the Milky Way. Ikthians, naledai, humans...there are some surprising similarities that convergent evolution cannot fully account for."

"Wait, slow down." Taylor held up her hand. "What do you mean by convergent evolution?"

"In closely related environments, sometimes two species will evolve to function the same way. Their appearances become similar."

"Is that why you look so much like me?" Taylor asked, unable to resist studying Maia's body. She hoped Maia wouldn't notice, or mind the attention.

"Our similarities cannot all be attributed to evolving in equivalent environments," Maia said. She brought a hand up to Taylor's face, tracing her features lightly. "We have plenty of differences, but our basic structure is the same, all the way down to our DNA."

Taylor had considered how odd it was that so many of the spacefaring species looked vaguely 'human' before, but she had never given it much thought beyond that. "I guess it explains why we all look alike, but what does it mean?"

"The aliens I was studying did not just look like ikthians. They also shared several DNA sequences with us. It would be like a family trait showing up in several relatives."

Taylor frowned. "But how did we all get similar genetics? We're all from different planets. It doesn't make sense."

"We were even more similar to each other millions of years ago. We still do not know for certain what created life, but my research suggests that, at some point in the distant past, an ancient spacefaring species was genetically modifying all of our ancestors. They came to our home worlds and seeded life there, guiding our evolution. I believe each planet was home to a different experiment."

Taylor was stunned. Of all the explanations for why human life had evolved the way it did, this was the strangest she had ever heard. Humanity had been exploring space for the several decades, but they were certainly not the first to leave their home worlds. The ikthians had dominated the galaxy for over a century before their arrival. It wasn't inconceivable that another, much older race had laid claim to the galaxy even earlier. "I'm not gonna lie. That sounds...kind of crazy. Not in a bad way! Just...it's a lot to process. I can see why some people might not want to believe it. The thought that someone was manipulating your species isn't easy to swallow."

"Perhaps for your species. For the ikthians, it is not a strange concept. We already knew that some ancient force had been guiding our evolution. There is a great deal of evidence for this hypothesis in our own solar system. However, most of my people believe this force chose us specifically, and modified us to become the greatest beings in the galaxy: their successors."

"But why is the Dominion so afraid of your research?"

"Think about it, Taylor. Imagine the political implications. The Dominion justifies their rule by claiming that other species are inferior. Discovering that we are actually related, in a sense, to the people we are trying to subjugate would tear apart the very foundation of the ikthian belief system." Maia stopped, glancing away when Taylor tried to look at her. "But I am rambling. Forgive me. You must find all of this terribly boring."

Taylor shook her head. "No, you aren't boring...I mean, it isn't boring..." She gave Maia an awkward look, rubbing the back of her neck. "Sorry. Sometimes I'm not really good at figuring out what to say."

"That makes two of us," Maia admitted. "I fear that somewhere along the way, my research prevented me from socializing with other ikthians...or any other species. Not that my mother would have allowed it. But something about you makes me want to spend time with you, Taylor." She paused, lifting her hand to cover her mouth as she let out a yawn. "I apologize. I did not sleep last night."

"I guess that was my fault." Taylor wanted to ask Maia more questions about her research, but they could wait until later. The ikthian was clearly exhausted. "I'll let you get some sleep. You can tell me more tomorrow."

Taylor put her hand on Maia's shoulder, giving it a brief squeeze before standing up. "Are you going to bed as well?" Maia asked with a hopeful look.

"Probably," Taylor said. "I could use a good night's sleep. I'll take the couch for now while we...start over. You've given me a lot to think about, and I'm not sure I even understand half of it."

Maia's eyes fixed on Taylor's. "Are you talking about my genetic research, or...whatever is between us?"

"Both. Just give me a little time. Then, maybe we can..." Taylor let her voice trail off, too unsure of herself to suggest what she was thinking.

"Yes," Maia said, but her voice sounded reluctant. "Perhaps some space would be helpful to both of us." Taylor knew that if she asked, Maia would allow her to share the bed, but she didn't want to tempt herself. Before she was intimate with Maia again, she wanted to get to know her better. She still felt some lingering guilt for rushing into sex with Maia so quickly.

There was a pause between them, and Taylor took a pace back toward the door. "Sleep well." She turned away, forcing herself not to look back. She knew if she did, her resolve would shatter.

# Chapter Twenty-six

FOR THE NEXT WEEK, Taylor worked hard to discover new ways of making Maia happy. During the days, she usually found some excuse to go out for a little while and pick up gifts. Sometimes she brought back food, and she provided Maia with meals more often than was strictly necessary. When she noticed that Maia had a sweet tooth, Taylor bribed the line cook into giving her extra rations of fresh fruit, which the ikthian took a liking to immediately. She'd given Rachel a piece of the haul, too, as repayment for the alcohol and friendly ear that she had provided.

Taylor also started looking for books to bring to Maia, since she had caught her glancing over the limited selection in her quarters more than once. She handed over the first one she found quietly, hoping for a positive reaction. Maia studied the book she had chosen with hesitant surprise. "I thought you might like this," Taylor explained, wincing a little at how awkward her own voice sounded.

The sad smile she got in return was almost enough to dishearten her. Maia took the book and looked it over. "I appreciate the thought, and I probably would enjoy this book, but I cannot read any human languages."

"I know, but…I thought I might be able to read it to you," Taylor said, unable to conceal her hopefulness. She didn't consider her own reading voice to be any good, but she and Maia had nothing else to do while they waited for the generals and the ikthians to come to an agreement.

"Yes," Maia said, smiling broadly. "I would like that very much. "

The book, *Pride and Prejudice*, delighted Maia. They never got very far in it, considering she constantly interrupted Taylor's attempts at reading aloud. "This is quite archaic," she said more than once. That was her favorite note. "Imagine, assuming the females of a species needed to be enslaved, or traded around like property...although I suppose we did not treat our males very well in the past, either."

"It's an old book," Taylor said, feeling the need to defend the work.

"And if you'd let me get farther, you'd realize Elizabeth is undermining that stereotype."

"I like that character. The one who ruined her clothes in the mud?" For some reason, Taylor had suspected that Maia would latch onto the defiant main character. "I dislike her mother, though."

Taylor smirked. "Does she remind you of anyone?"

"If you are trying to infer that my mother is like the controlling human in that story, then...you would have a point. The male character, though. Darcy. That is what he is called, yes? He seems rude."

Taylor shrugged. "He just doesn't know how to talk to women, especially one as lovely as Elizabeth."

"Does he remind you of anyone?" Maia asked, a playful edge to her voice.

Taylor laughed and shut the book. "I refuse to acknowledge what you're implying. I'm hardly a wealthy Englishman."

"A what?" Maia asked.

"Englishman. It just means someone who is from England."

"Is that a neighboring planet?" Maia asked. Her eyes were wide again with scientific curiosity. Taylor liked seeing it in her gaze.

"No. It's an island here on Earth. We like to divide up where people are from that way."

Maia furrowed her brow as she processed the information. "So where would you be from?"

Taylor sighed and placed the book on top of the nightstand. She ran a hand through her hair and thought of the simplest way to explain it to Maia. "Well, most humans would consider me to come from two places. I grew up about seven hundred miles north of San Diego, where we are right now, but my mom is actually from Japan. It's a set of islands west of this continent."

"But if you always lived on this continent, why would other humans assume you belong to both?"

Taylor shrugged. "It's a heritage thing. What about you? You don't have just your mother, right? What does your father do, or where is he from?"

"My father is on Korithia. He has always been there." Maia glanced out the window, looking wistful. "We rarely speak, though. He mostly focuses on keeping up with my mother and her career. It was always...exhausting for him to live such a public life, but he is expected to remain with my mother, and so he does." Taylor nodded and waited for the inevitable question. She knew Maia would ask it, even though she was an alien. She would ask just like any other woman Taylor had dated. "And what about your mother and father?"

She took a deep breath. "They died when I was young." Maia's face fell, but Taylor gave her a small smile anyways. "Don't feel too bad for me. It was a long time ago, and I've had time to come to terms with it." She reached for the book and opened it again. "I can read more for you, if you want." It seemed like a suitable time to change the subject.

Unfortunately, reality interrupted before Maia could agree. Taylor's wrist comm buzzed with a message from Roberts, requesting her presence at another meeting. Normally, Taylor hated meeting with the brass, especially when Bouchard was involved, but this time, she was grateful for the excuse to leave for a little while. Bringing up her parents always made whatever woman she was seeing feel pity for her, and while Maia hadn't rushed to soothe her, she could tell the ikthian needed a moment to process the information.

It only took her a few minutes to say goodbye to Maia, put the book away, and hurry over to the meeting. Taylor reported to Roberts' office early. She could hear muffled voices shouting at one another through the door, and for once, things were almost normal. She nodded at the guard, and he activated his communicator. "Sir?" he said. The voices in the next room grew quiet. "Lieutenant Morgan is here."

There was the silent crackle of static, and then, "Send her in." The guard nodded and opened the door.

Inside, Generals Hunt, Lee, and Moore were waiting for her, along with Captain Roberts. Bouchard had made an appearance again as well. Taylor held her salute until General Hunt nodded. "At ease, Lieutenant Morgan. We wanted to check up on your progress with Kalanis. Anything to report?"

Taylor thought for a moment. What had she learned about Maia that would prove useful to a war effort? She had learned she was a person, and that she had a new appetite for human literature, but the generals probably weren't interested in hearing any of that. "Maia told me some more about her genetic research," she said instead.

"We knew that already," Bouchard said. "She confessed that during the initial interrogation."

"But you don't know what she was researching." General Hunt and the others seemed intrigued, but Bouchard looked like he wanted to slap her for contradicting him. "Her latest study suggests that the ikthians and most species in the Milky Way are more closely related than the ikthians like to think. We share some DNA sequences with them, and the way Maia put it, we're almost like distant relatives. That's why the Dominion wants her back so badly. Her discoveries would undermine their deepest-held convictions. One of the naledai on base, Akton, even told me that the ECO offices on Korithia scrubbed every attempt she made to talk about her findings or issue corrections when they were misused."

General Lee stroked his dark beard, studying Taylor intently. "She told you this, Lieutenant Morgan?"

"Yes. That's why the seekers were chasing her, and why we captured her so easily."

"I can see why," Bouchard said sourly. "Perhaps we should modify our negotiation tactics. Surely the Dominion has little use for someone who challenges their doctrine..."

Even though she didn't like the idea of returning Maia to the Dominion, Taylor was alarmed by Bouchard's dismissal. If he didn't perceive Maia as valuable anymore, it could put her in serious danger sooner rather than later. The Coalition had no reason to house a prisoner they couldn't use, and as much as Taylor still wavered on the issue, she knew she needed to find a reason for the generals to keep Maia around.

General Moore spoke before she could. "The ikthians have been open to negotiating with us so far. Things are moving slowly, but they seem invested in getting her back. She's obviously still valuable to them."

Taylor breathed a sigh of relief.

"We cannot just ignore this information," Bouchard insisted. "Making deals to trade an unfavored prisoner of war could be extremely detrimental to us. If the Dominion views Kalanis as a traitor..."

"It doesn't matter what they value her for as long as they value her," General Hunt said. "If her people consider her research so subversive, it might even drive up her price."

Taylor's stomach churned. Although she admired him, hearing General Hunt discuss Maia like a piece of property was difficult, almost painful. It reminded her too much of her own actions. *No wonder Maia's feelings were hurt.*

"What if her research is valuable to us, Sir?" Taylor asked. If she wanted to help Maia, now was the time to act. "What if it could help end the war?"

Bouchard rolled his eyes. "Do you honestly think some bleeding-edge theory about genetics will stop the Dominion from conquering any planet it wants? Kalanis is obviously playing you, Lieutenant. Don't let a pretty face distract you from your true loyalties."

Taylor froze. In that moment, she realized that Bouchard knew. She wasn't sure whether Bower had told him, whether he had heard it from some other source, or whether he had simply guessed, but he knew. Taylor was certain that if he got the chance, he would use the information against her.

"You're being harsh, Bouchard," Roberts said, breaking the tension. "The lieutenant may have a point. This research might not do much for the leaders, but what if it incites a riot among the masses? Large regimes aren't kept together without layers and layers of lies."

"The ikthians won't care," Bouchard said dismissively.

"Not all of them, but some," Roberts continued. "Besides, the Dominion has a lot of other planets under their control. If we could get our hands on Kalanis's research and make the Dominion look weak, it might encourage some of them other species fight back. Most naledai worlds are already on the brink of revolution."

General Hunt frowned, and Taylor's stomach sank. "That might take too long, Captain. And it's a huge risk. Human lives could be saved if we stick to negotiations. If we could guarantee safety for Earth..."

"There is no guarantee that the ikthians won't turn around and go back on their word once Kalanis is secured," Bouchard said. "We should bargain for something of substance, not an empty promise."

"What do you suggest, Chairman?" General Hunt asked.

"Other prisoners, resources, anything we can use to try and boost our war efforts. I guarantee that this conflict will not end until the Dominion is destroyed, or they are convinced that we are capable of defending ourselves."

Taylor grew more upset as she watched the three men fight. General Hunt was too optimistic, and Bouchard was far too cynical, as well as completely inconsistent in his opinions. She was suspicious, but she kept her mouth shut.

Noticing Taylor's distress, General Moore was kind enough to offer her an escape route. "We can't do anything until we receive our next message from the ikthians," she pointed out, glancing between Hunt, Bouchard, and Roberts. Her words seemed to soothe them. "We can decide what to do after we hear their offer. And Lieutenant Morgan, good work on the intel. I'm sure it will guide our decision."

"Thank you, General." Taylor couldn't help admiring Moore's calm, rational tone. If she had been a general instead of a lieutenant, she might not have been so patient with Bouchard.

"See if you can find out any more from Kalanis," General Lee added. "We need to know more about her research." Taylor saluted to show that she understood. "The rest of us will call you for another status report in the next two days. You're dismissed."

For what felt like the hundredth time, Taylor hurried out the door, eager to be anywhere but Roberts' office. She took the stairs two at a time down to the first floor, bypassing the elevator, and she wondered what she should do. Bouchard was obviously working some kind of angle, but until she figured out what it was, she couldn't be sure of the best way to respond. Until then, she'd have to live with the sick feeling of fear in the pit of her stomach.

# Chapter Twenty-seven

MAIA LOOKED DOWN AT the book that lay open in front of her. The words slipped past her eyes, none of them making sense. She wished she had the time and the necessary tools to learn the language. The story was charming, even if it had been written hundreds of years ago by this Austen human. Maia had grown up with stories to read and watch, but there was something fascinating about discovering another species' art. If she had been allowed, she might have taken to studying the major texts from other cultures as a child, though that would have ostracized her even further from her people, in addition to disappointing her mother. The ikthians never considered anything that came from other cultures to be useful.

With a sigh, Maia allowed her thoughts to float elsewhere. Where they wandered surprised her. She pictured Taylor, naked and well-muscled, pinning her down to the bed, and her body pulsed in response to the vivid mental image. She was somewhat ashamed by the swiftness and strength of her physical reaction. Taylor hadn't tried to initiate anything more between them since the incident with Bower and the other humans. Instead, she had made an effort to be kind while maintaining distance.

Unfortunately, Maia's need had only grown worse since then. Though Bower's attack had made her even more fearful than before, Taylor always made her feel safe. She blushed, shaking her head to dispel a particularly intense memory of Taylor's lips meeting hers in a searing kiss beneath the spray of the shower. She missed the taste of Taylor's mouth.

"Stop it," she murmured. Perhaps it was time for another shower, alone. It would offer her some privacy if she became desperate.

The sound of the door opening gave Maia an excuse to abandon her book. Taylor was back. Her heart rate spiked with anticipation. Taylor had asked for time after confessing her feelings, but Maia had been fighting off her pent-up need for nearly a week. She could do it no longer.

She met Taylor out in the living room. The human had slumped onto the couch, hunched over with her head in her hands. Maia resisted the urge to initiate physical contact. Obviously, something was wrong, and she had to be considerate of Taylor's feelings. Not knowing where to begin, Maia sat down in the empty space next to her. "Hello."

Slowly, Taylor glanced up. "Hey."

They both stared awkwardly. Taylor was clearly waiting for her to say more, but Maia didn't know how to continue. "Are you all right? You seem upset. Tense." She was worried first and foremost, but the greedy, amorous part of her couldn't help hoping Taylor would allow her to help relieve some of that tension.

"Just a meeting with some people I really didn't want to talk to."

"Is there anything I can do?" Maia leaned forward slightly, shifting closer. She desperately hoped that Taylor would pick up on the hint, or at least react to their close proximity.

Unfortunately, Taylor was either oblivious, or not in the mood. "No, but thanks for asking. It was just hard to hear the generals talk about you like a bargaining chip. Guess it reminded me too much of my own behavior." She straightened, giving Maia a weak smile. "I asked them if we could use your research to undermine the Dominion. All of them except Roberts thought that was a terrible idea. I tried my best, but they don't understand."

It was a surprising confession. Maia hadn't expected Taylor to suggest her research as a potential tool for the Coalition, but it was somewhat flattering. "You honestly think my research would make a difference in this war?"

Taylor looked at her in disbelief. "Are you kidding? You're brilliant. You know everything about the ikthians and their propaganda machine, and your research threatens to subvert their entire belief system. If you were human or even naledai, they wouldn't hesitate to ask you for help."

Maia blushed. "You really believe that?"

"I do. And I haven't given up hope of convincing them yet. It seems impossible right now, but I want to find a way. I think you should stay here and help us, as an ally instead of a prisoner."

*She wishes for me to stay. Taylor wishes for me to stay, and not as a prisoner.* Maia knew it was a pipe dream at best, something she shouldn't dare to hope for, but simply hearing that Taylor wanted it filled her heart with joy.

Before she could stop herself, she leaned forward. When Taylor didn't pull away, Maia kissed her. After a few seconds, Taylor began to kiss her back. Maia moaned at the warmth and softness of Taylor's lips. Tasting them was like sinking into a warm, comforting pool of water, and it relaxed every inch of her body even as a more urgent heat churned low in her belly. She placed her hands on Taylor's shoulders, whimpering when they broke contact.

"Hold on," Taylor muttered. Her breathing had grown heavy, and she stared at Maia with wide, dark eyes. Maia could read arousal there, but there was also hesitance, and hope. "I didn't say any of this to just get you to sleep with me again."

"I know. I am doing this because I want to." Maia tipped Taylor backwards onto the couch, hovering over her to join their lips again.

Taylor cupped the side of Maia's face, easing them out of the kiss and pushing her a few inches away. Maia withdrew, a small pout settling on her lips. She was about to protest, to counter any arguments Taylor made, but the human only smiled at her. "We should move to the bedroom," she whispered, and Maia felt the nervousness in her chest unravel. Taylor wasn't rejecting her after all.

"I suppose this couch is not very comfortable," Maia agreed. Reluctantly, she climbed off of Taylor and stood on unsteady legs. Her hands trembled too, but with desire rather than nervousness. She wasn't afraid of the way her body reacted to Taylor anymore, although the intensity was still overwhelming.

"Actually, I had other reasons for wanting to go back there."

Before Maia could ask Taylor to explain the cryptic comment, she found herself being scooped up in a pair of powerful arms and lifted off the floor. She let out a squeak of surprise, but Taylor only grinned. "Is this too Darcy for you?"

Maia laughed and placed a hand on Taylor's chest, enjoying the rise and fall beneath her palm. She could feel Taylor's heartbeat, and for some reason, the fast and steady thump aroused her even more. She hoped that it was beating quickly for her. "*Pride & Prejudice* would be another type of story entirely if Darcy carried Elizabeth away for activities like these."

Taylor shrugged Maia up higher into her arms as she carried her down the hall and across the threshold to the bedroom. Maia looped her arms around Taylor's neck, settling against the solid warmth of her chest. "I'm sure there's a book like that somewhere in the library if you're interested," Taylor whispered, pressing their foreheads together and stealing another kiss.

A groan broke in Maia's throat as they finally pulled apart. It took her a moment to find her words. "I think we can find better ways to occupy ourselves."

Taylor lowered Maia onto the mattress, but didn't join her right away. Maia frowned and reached out, running her fingertips down Taylor's arm. Even through the fabric of Taylor's shirt, she could feel the strength there, the muscles that had so easily lifted her up. "Where are you going?" she asked, wanting to touch Taylor's bare skin more than anything.

Taylor blushed, although she didn't try and shrug off Maia's touch. "I...uh...wanted to try something, actually? Something a little different. If you don't mind, that is."

"Try something?" Maia had often heard jokes between her colleagues about sexual partners revealing their odd requests, but since she rarely joined in such conversations, she had no idea what her reaction was supposed to be. She wondered what Taylor could possibly ask of her, but hoped that it was a desire she could fulfill. Thinking back, she realized Taylor had always taken the initiative before, and she hadn't made the same effort to reciprocate. It was a habit she wanted to change.

Taylor sighed. "Maybe it will be easier if I just show you." She turned away from the bed, hauling out the duffel bag tucked away next to the nightstand. Even though she'd been living in this suite with Maia for several weeks, she still hadn't bothered to unpack everything.

Maia fidgeted, torn between impatience and curiosity as she watched Taylor rummage through the pack. After a few moments, she seemed to find what she was looking for. She stood back up and turned, holding something in her hands.

A soft gasp escaped from Maia before she could stifle it. The shape of the object was instantly familiar to her. *Yet more proof of the genetic similarities between our species*, her scientific mind couldn't help adding as she tried to gather her thoughts. It had a thick, veined shaft and a flared head with a small dip at the very top. Although the color wasn't silver like ikthian flesh, the shade was a perfect match for Taylor's skin. Taylor cleared her throat, and Maia blinked, suddenly realizing that she was staring. "I...was not expecting this," she stammered.

Taylor's face fell, and she moved to turn back around, the shaft of the toy still clutched in her hand. "It's all right, we don't have to—"

"No!" Maia interrupted. This was definitely a surprise, and a pleasant one. The more she thought about it, the more curious she became, and she felt the insistent pressure between her legs begin to rise again. "I mean, no...you do not have to put it away." She swallowed, her tongue thick in her mouth. "I...I think I would like to try."

Taylor broke into a smile. "Good," she said, radiating excitement. "This is something I love doing, but..."

"But?" Maia prompted as Taylor climbed onto the edge of the mattress, kneeling beside her.

"I guess it's something I'm a little insecure about. Past girlfriends didn't always react positively to my 'gender stuff'."

Maia's brow furrowed. "Why not? I admit that I am not, um, very experienced with such things, but would this toy not feel pleasurable to them?"

"Not just for them," Taylor said, turning it around in her hand.

Maia leaned in, curious to get a closer look. She noticed the shaft didn't end the way typical ikthian anatomy did. Instead, it curved back up on itself, flaring into a short, round bulb. Positioned on the seat between the bulb and shaft were a few carefully-placed circles, and Maia's eyes widened in understanding. "Does this transmit sensation?"

Taylor nodded. "Among other things."

"That would make it ideal to use. I do not understand why your previous partners objected."

"I guess it was too realistic for them. I don't know what your culture thinks about gender, but...mine's kind of complicated."

Maia sensed this was a very serious topic of discussion, but there would be time to ask questions later. She placed a reassuring hand on Taylor's arm. "Well, I have no objections. I have been drawn to you from the beginning, and I feel no differently now. Will you show me how it works?"

Taylor bit her lip, but nodded, scooting back on the mattress and shucking her pants and underwear. "Just, uh, give me a second to put it in."

Maia's eyes zeroed in between Taylor's spread legs. The odd tuft of black hair there made her smile, but seeing the sheen of wetness that clung to Taylor's lips excited her the most. She knew she was the cause of that wetness, and her fingers twitched with longing. She wanted to gather it up and spread it around the red bundle of Taylor's clit, which was already prominent.

"Uh, Maia?"

Maia realized Taylor was looking at her worriedly. "Oh, I am sorry. Was I staring?"

"A little, yeah," Taylor said, and Maia couldn't tell whether she was feeling sheepish or smug about it.

"You are very striking, Taylor. Please, keep going?"

Taylor exhaled and brought the toy between her legs, positioning the shorter end at her entrance. For a brief moment, Maia was jealous, remembering how good Taylor had felt around her fingers. But then, she forgot everything else as she watched Taylor press the toy into place, wincing a little as it slid inside of her. When she pulled her hands away, it remained where it was, jutting outward from between her thighs. Taylor seemed to radiate with newfound confidence.

"So…how do we begin?" Maia shifted even closer to Taylor on the mattress, stroking the top of her thigh

Taylor smiled, and though she was still blushing, Maia could tell she was swiftly regaining her courage. "We could always just start out slow." She tucked her fingers beneath Maia's chin, tilting her face up to kiss her. Maia couldn't resist sliding her tongue forward, flicking it into Taylor's mouth briefly before retreating. First, she wanted to become more familiar with Taylor's new, temporary anatomy. She had restrained herself from touching Taylor for long enough.

Maia reached down and wrapped a hand around the shaft, giving it a slow, gentle stroke. Taylor gasped, bucking up into her hand. "Oh God," she blurted out. "This…this isn't slow…and it's so much better…"

"Better than what?" Maia asked, giving the warm length another curious pump of her hand. She couldn't help admiring how perfectly it matched Taylor's skin. She could still see the outline of Taylor's lips flared open around the base of the toy, but otherwise, it looked surprisingly realistic.

"Better than…" Taylor hesitated, as if she wasn't sure whether to continue. Maia halted the motion of her hand so that Taylor could find her words. "Better than when I touch myself," she finished, torn between looking into Maia's eyes and watching Maia's hand as it began to move again.

"You mean, you use it when you are alone?" Emboldened by the confession, Maia tightened her grip around the shaft. Even though she had never done this before, Taylor's reactions seemed more than promising. Her panting breaths came quicker with each passing second, and the blackness of her pupils blended with the dark, glossy brown of her eyes.

"I…uh…sometimes. It makes me feel…good?"

"Oh, does it?" Maia pumped her hand one more time before

leaning in to give Taylor's lower lip a teasing nip. She enjoyed having this kind of power, at least for the moment. Perhaps later, she would allow Taylor to pin her down and have her turn, but she had waited what felt like ages to be the one in charge.

"Yes," Taylor gasped. "Not just physically...like, emotionally. *Fuck,* I can't do words right now."

The toy twitched in Maia's hand as her fingers brushed the swollen head, and a glistening bead of wetness spilled from the tip, sliding against the pad of her thumb. "Taylor?" she asked, her voice rising with excitement. "Is this wetness from you?" She repeated the motion, and a low groan broke in Taylor's throat. Maia instantly decided that she loved the sound, and wanted to hear it again.

Taylor could barely stammer out an answer. "Y...yes..."

Maia licked her lips. Taylor had tasted her during their second time together, but she'd never had an opportunity to return the favor. Even though this wasn't the way she had planned on doing it, Maia's heart pounded heavily in her chest at the thought. As Taylor had done earlier, she summoned her bravery and asked, "Would you like my mouth on it?" Judging from the whimper Taylor made, she would like it very much. "Lie back," she said with a gentle nudge.

Rae D. Magdon & Michelle Magly

# Chapter Twenty-eight

AS TAYLOR SETTLED AGAINST the pillows, Maia leaned over her, placing kisses along her neck and stopping to suck at her pulse point. Taylor's skin tasted of warmth and salt, and Maia found she didn't have the patience to linger in one place for long. She found the hem of Taylor's shirt and gave it a questioning tug. Taylor curled up, lifting her arms, and Maia took that as permission to pull it over her head.

Once it was gone, Maia forced herself to stop and appreciate the visual. The word she had used to describe Taylor before, 'striking', suddenly seemed inadequate. She wasn't sure there were any words in any language that could properly convey how she felt as she gazed upon Taylor's bare body. What words could capture the fascinating mixture of hard muscle and vulnerable softness, of alien-ness and familiarity?

Hers. She wanted all these things to be hers. Maia returned to where she had left off, at Taylor's neck, and began kissing lower. She paused at Taylor's breasts, letting her breath wash over one of the stiff brown nipples, but one of Taylor's hands touched the top of her fringe, not pushing, but politely guiding her down. "Not that. Lower? Please?"

Maia was more than happy to fulfill that request, but as she approached the juncture between Taylor's legs, she slowed down. She passed her tongue over one of Taylor's hip bones, swirling there until she felt Taylor's legs clench on either side of her shoulders. Only then did she turn her attention to the tan colored shaft in front of her.

"You know," Taylor said, causing Maia to glance up. "You don't have to do this if you don't want to."

Maia gave Taylor a reassuring smile. "Of course I want to."

Taylor let out another needy groan, and Maia's gaze shifted back down between her legs. At first, she simply stared at the shaft resting inches away from her mouth. She had little experience with situations like this, and she wasn't sure where to begin. Eventually she chose to focus on the flared head first. It tapered to a blunt point, and a narrow slit ran through the tip. Wetness glinted there. *Another of the toy's features,* Maia guessed.

Finally, her curiosity got the better of her, and she placed a soft kiss directly on the tip. It didn't taste like much of anything yet, but it was very warm, and similar to Taylor's skin.

Taylor's abdominal muscles tensed, and the small, strangled noise she made encouraged Maia to slide her lips further down. She took the rest of the head into her mouth and waited, expecting Taylor to guide her. But Taylor simply stared down at her, caressing the back of her neck as she drew in a shuddering breath. "God, yes. Please...please, don't stop..."

Thrilled with the power Taylor had handed to her, Maia circled her tongue over the slit again. This time, she tasted something there, salt more concentrated than that of Taylor's skin, and also a hint of sweetness. In her eagerness, Maia accidentally pushed too far, and she coughed as the head bumped the back of her throat. She wrapped a hand around the base, hoping to prevent herself from making the same mistake twice.

Fortunately, Taylor didn't seem to notice the error. She was lost to the moment, hair a tousled mess, face flushed with pleasure. Her expression pleaded for more, so Maia tightened the seal of her lips, maintaining eye contact all the while. A few more drops of warmth spilled from the pulsing head, and Maia lapped them up, sighing as the taste spread across her tongue.

"Oh God," Taylor grunted, stroking the back of Maia's neck. "Your mouth...you feel incredible." Her hips twitched, as if she were fighting the instinct to thrust.

Maia found it more and more difficult to concentrate. Taylor's words of encouragement kept running through her head, fueling her own need. She tried squeezing her thighs together, but it did nothing to ease her discomfort. There was a cramping hollowness deep within her belly, and every time she moved, she felt her own wetness drip further down her thighs. She needed to be touched. To be filled.

Instinctively, Maia reached down to cup herself. She explored with her fingers, desperate to ease some of the ache. Taylor's eyes widened, and Maia could tell she was watching. "You like doing this enough to touch yourself, huh?" she teased, stroking Maia's cheek. Maia froze, embarrassed, but Taylor gave her shoulder an encouraging squeeze. "Don't stop. Keep touching yourself. I want to watch."

Maia needed no further encouragement. She ran her fingers on either side of her clit, then did her best to re-focus on her task: pleasing Taylor as much as she possibly could. She tried everything she could think of: light, dusting kisses, broad, flat licks, and of course, a sucking motion that drew deep, rattling groans from within Taylor's chest, as well as more wetness into Maia's mouth. She shivered as she realized that she wanted more of the heavy taste.

Taylor's body went rigid. "Maia," she said, her voice a little frantic, "I...I need to..."

Maia suddenly realized what was about to happen. She knew Taylor was trying to warn her, but instead of pulling back, she ran her tongue over the sensitive tip one more time before sliding her lips as far along the pulsing shaft as she could. Taylor jerked and clutched the back of her head, shouting something that resembled her name.

Even though she was expecting it, the flood of warmth that filled Maia's mouth startled her a little. Some of it escaped from the corner of her lips, but she corrected herself, holding her breath and swallowing instead. She had been the one to make Taylor come, and she didn't want to waste her reward. The taste of Taylor's release was strong, but pleasant once she became accustomed to it, and Maia sucked harder in the hopes of earning more.

A heartbeat later, her own orgasm came crashing down over her, a mighty wave overtaking the shore. Her inner walls quivered, squeezing around nothing, but she compensated for the emptiness by focusing on her clit, rubbing in quick circles and whimpering around the shaft filling her mouth.

Their shared high lasted for some time. Taylor relaxed first, melting into the bed, but Maia took a few moments longer, keeping her hand pressed tight over herself. Slowly, she let the toy fall out of her mouth and scooted up along the bed, sprawling onto the mattress beside Taylor. Taylor draped an arm around her waist, pulling her close.

"You are wet all over," Maia murmured in astonishment when she came into contact with Taylor's sticky, cooling skin.

"What, my sweat?" Taylor chuckled breathlessly. "Don't ikthians sweat?"

"My translator is using a word in your language," Maia said. "I do not understand."

"Sweat," Taylor said. "Uh, there are these tiny holes in our skin called pores. You can see them if you look close. They pump out water and salt to keep us cool."

"So, that is why your skin tastes so good! The salt explains it."

Taylor smirked. "So I'm basically a giant salt lick to you?"

"I suppose you are." Maia squinted at Taylor's face. She could indeed see tiny holes there, as well as flakes of skin far smaller than ikthian scales, and hairs so sparse and fine that she had scarcely noticed them before. "You are fascinating," Maia said. "And not just because you are human."

Taylor gave a satisfied grin. "You too, and not just because you're an ikthian." She propped herself up on her side. "How are you? Is everything okay after, uh, all that?"

Maia blushed and let her hand wander to Taylor's hip. "I...enjoyed myself very much, actually."

"How much?"

The teasing tone in Taylor's voice made Maia smile. "Enough that I am very interested in experimenting with this new toy some more."

Taylor took the hint and eased herself over Maia. "I think I can arrange that...but you'll have to take off your clothes first. I can't believe I let you get away with that."

Maia wove her fingers through Taylor's hair, pulling their mouths together in a deep kiss. "Then why don't you help me out of them?"

Taylor did, although with some difficulty, because Maia was reluctant to release Taylor's mouth for more than a moment at a time. Once Maia was finally naked, Taylor broke away, panting slightly. "How long can you hold your breath, anyway? Kissing you is great, but I need air sometimes."

Maia might have been embarrassed, but the look of happiness on Taylor's face made her see the humor in the situation. Besides, need was building within her again, and she was incredibly aware of Taylor's warm shaft as it brushed against her thigh. Her desire for Taylor reminded her very much of the floating sensation that came with shortness of breath, even when her lungs were full.

"A very long time, by your standards. But Taylor, please..." Maia's lips grazed Taylor's chin as she nuzzled just beneath her jaw. "I want you inside of me. I want to know how it feels."

Taylor's stomach muscles tensed above her, and Maia knew she was about to get what she was begging for. "Go ahead," Taylor said in a strained voice. "Take it at your own pace."

Maia's hand left the tangle of Taylor's hair, stroking down her back and around her side to reach between their bodies. She gripped shaft of the toy, guiding it carefully between her legs. She stopped breathing for a few seconds, and her heart skipped a beat. As she rubbed against the head, little sparks of heat rolled over her skin. She tilted her pelvis down, feeling the tip slide through her folds until it rested against her entrance.

Taylor trembled above her, bracing herself on tense, powerful arms, looking down into Maia's eyes. Their lips met in another kiss, and Taylor's hips pushed forward to meet hers. Maia whimpered at the stretch, but it was a pleasant sensation, not completely unlike her own fingers or Taylor's. Soon, she found herself rocking to try and take more.

Taylor moved slowly, carefully, taking her time to ease the first inch of the shaft inside. Maia cried out, raking her nails lightly between Taylor's shoulder blades. It was almost too much all at once, but thankfully, Taylor gave her a few seconds to adjust. As she grew accustomed to the stretch, Taylor leaned down and kissed her again. Maia let out a soft whimper, losing herself in Taylor's lips.

It didn't all go smoothly. Sometimes the angle of their bodies wasn't quite right, and once, Taylor slipped out of her on accident. "Sorry," she mumbled sheepishly, but Maia didn't mind at all. Discovering this together made it special, and real, and she didn't want or expect perfection. Eventually, though, the two of them picked up a slow, steady rhythm, moving against each other with more ease and fluidity.

Maia relaxed into a warm, melting sort of heat, and Taylor was finally able to slide all the way into her. She heard Taylor's breath hiss as their bodies joined, and she ran her hands up and down the human's back, feeling her shoulders rise and fall with each breath. For a moment, words hovered on Maia's lips, words she desperately wanted to say. But she knew she wasn't ready, and Taylor probably wasn't either. *Perhaps someday, if by some miracle I do not end up dead, and Taylor is still around to hear them...*

Maia forgot everything else as Taylor began to move, thrusting inside of her, pulling out again, catching against sensitive places deep inside of her that she hadn't even been aware of before. She couldn't focus on anything except the pressure between her legs, and the ache that was steadily growing with each pump of Taylor's hips.

Taylor paused, stroking the side of Maia's face. Then, the tender moment broke, replaced by a deep current of need that dragged both of them back into motion again. Maia shivered as Taylor's hand left her face, sliding down her throat and over her breast before making its way down her stomach. She brought it between their bodies, skimming over the ridge of Maia's clit.

Maia gasped as Taylor pushed back the hood, pressing down firmly with the pads of her fingers. Taylor's hips resumed their rhythm, driving deep, and Maia realized she was already hovering on the edge of release. It would only take a few more thrusts for Taylor to send her over the brink.

"Maia, please..."

Maia suddenly realized that Taylor was almost as close as she was. She squeezed down, deliberately tightening her inner muscles around Taylor's length. She pulsed, wondering what it would feel like when Taylor finally released inside of her. Taylor lowered her lips to Maia's throat, kissing her pulse point. "I want to feel you come around me...I need to..."

The words and circling fingers were enough. Maia went rigid, digging her nails into Taylor's broad shoulders and throwing her head back. Her inner walls clenched, then loosened in a series of harsh flutters. A few tears leaked from her eyes and rolled down her cheeks as she dove over the edge, plunging into bliss.

Taylor came after Maia did, exhaling sharply and bucking forward one final time. A burst of warmth flooded Maia's core, and her own pulses came faster. The rhythmic slips of heat were a powerful reminder that Taylor was within her. No, that Taylor was *with* her. She was no longer alone in this galaxy. She was in someone's arms, someone who cared for her, and they were joined in one of the most intimate ways possible.

Once the two of them stopped quaking with the aftershocks of their release, Taylor shifted her hips back and pulled out. She took a deep breath, smoothing a hand through her tousled black hair. "How are you?"

Maia looked up at her with wide eyes, amazed that Taylor even needed to ask. She sat up, kissing Taylor's lips one more time. "I am wonderful. You were wonderful."

Taylor reached down and eased the shorter end of the toy out of herself, placing it on top of the dresser before collapsing on the bed. "Good," she muttered, her eyelids drooping with exhaustion.

"May I hold you?"

Taylor nodded, suppressing a yawn. "Yes, please," she murmured against Maia's shoulder. "I'll just...shut my eyes for a bit. Is that okay?"

Maia could hear the sleepiness in Taylor's voice, and reached down to pull a cover over them. "Stay in bed with me as long as you like. I do not mind your company." She heard Taylor's deep, even breaths and knew she was asleep. *In fact,* she thought, *I am starting to wonder what I will do without you.*

# Chapter Twenty-nine

THE NEXT DAY, TAYLOR found herself wandering the base, unsure where her feet were taking her. She'd left the apartments and Maia with a gentle, mostly-wordless goodbye, hoping the crisp morning air would banish some of her restlessness. The fog outside turned out to be as bad as the fog in her head. It blurred the world around her in smoky grey colors, and breathing it in didn't do any favors for the tight knot of stress in her chest.

After what she had shared with Maia the night before, she wanted to talk through her feelings, but she wasn't sure where to go. She thought about visiting Rachel, but decided that she didn't want to impose on her friend twice in such a short period of time. She didn't trust Andrew to keep her secrets anymore, although they had come to a sort of truce over the past week when he'd shown up for guard duty even during hours he wasn't scheduled.

As she passed the mess and spotted a group of naledai strolling down the steps, she thought of Akton. He had told her to find him if she ever found herself in a tight spot, although he probably wasn't expecting her to pop by and ask for relationship advice. Deciding he was still the best of her three options, she followed the group past several buildings and over to the docking bay. A large naledai frigate was at rest there, and Taylor walked toward its looming, shadowy shape in the fog until it became clearer.

The naledai standing guard outside the ship was surly at first, but once she mentioned her name and told him that she was looking for Akton, he seemed more at ease. "You said your name was Taylor?" he asked, studying her for a moment. "Akton's mentioned you. Says he met you running supplies in our solar system. Not many humans are brave enough to go in the middle of an alien warzone."

Taylor could tell he was grateful. The Coalition vastly preferred to send resources rather than troops to the naledai, a decision she didn't agree with—but she'd had the opportunity to fight ikthians on someone else's doorstep instead of just Earth's, and she'd taken it gladly. "I killed a few ikthians there," Taylor admitted. The resistance on the naledai home world was bloody, and she had seen both humans and naledai die defending it.

"Well, go on in." He stepped aside, opening the door to the decontamination chamber for her. "He's probably down in the engine bay."

Taylor nodded. "I'll keep it in mind." She stepped onto the ship. The naledai crewmembers inside seemed slightly surprised to see a human, but none of them objected to her presence. She walked by them without comment, heading for the elevator. She had been on enough naledai ships to understand their basic layout.

As the guard had predicted, Akton was in the engine bay. He had taken a panel off one of the processors and currently had it in pieces. He stared at the pile of wires and parts as if calculating his next move, but looked up when Taylor entered. "Taylor." Akton straightened up and turned around to greet her, tangled cords dangling from his giant claws. "What brings you onboard?"

Taylor crossed the width of the small room and stopped beside him. "I was wondering if we could talk."

"Sure. I don't need to have this put back together for a few more days." Akton gestured at the pile of parts. "What's on your mind? This is about Kalanis, isn't it?"

Taylor nodded. "I need some advice."

Akton leaned against a wall, dropping the cords on the floor with the rest of the mess. "Well, start at the beginning. I have a feeling this is going to take some time. You have that look on your face like...something bad happened. If you were naledai, I'd say you looked as if a greskar had ripped your mother's right arm off." Taylor raised an eyebrow, and Akton shook his head. "Well, it sounds better in the native tongue."

Taylor laughed, feeling some of her tension ease. She tried to think about how to best word what she wanted to talk about. "Well, I've been spending a lot of time with Maia." She waited for Akton to say something, but he only nodded for her to continue. "And...I think I'm in too deep to go back."

She told him everything. About Bower and the other guards, about her fight with Maia, about how they had made up and tried to get to know each other better. The whole time, Akton listened patiently. After she finished, he paused for a moment, staring thoughtfully at nothing. Finally, he said, "You really care about her, don't you?"

Taylor was taken aback by the question. "Of course."

"And you think she cares about you?"

Taylor hesitated. "I don't know. I think so. That's how she seems to feel when I'm around, but...how can she? I'm standing between her and freedom." She leaned against an engine box and her fingers flexed over the edge of the casing, drumming anxiously on the metal. "The worst part is, I know what will happen to her if the Coalition sends her back to Korithia."

Akton released a low growl from within his chest. "You're not the only thing keeping her here, Taylor. Remember the armed guards and the mounted turrets on top of all the buildings? Even if you left the door unlocked, it's not like she would just be able to walk out of here."

"No. But...I am...I was...her guard." Taylor sighed. She didn't feel like Maia's guard anymore. That part of their relationship had disappeared long ago.

"You're also the only human on base that views her as a person now, even if it took you a while. I know what the Coalition tells humans about ikthians. It's somewhat disturbing. But you know that they're not all evil, no matter what the Dominion does."

Taylor groaned, massaging her temples. "I know. You should see the way people act around Maia whenever she leaves her chambers. They think she can kill them with just a look."

"But you don't." Akton gave her a long stare, as if he were considering something. "If you met other ikthians...ones like Maia, who weren't a threat to the Coalition...would you consider them your enemies?"

Taylor was surprised by how easily the answer came to her. "No, I wouldn't. Not anymore."

Akton looked around the room before stepping close to Taylor and lowering his voice. "Not all ikthians are members of the Dominion."

Taylor studied Akton intently. Obviously, he knew more than he was telling. "I didn't think naledai soldiers associated with ikthians, unless you count shooting them."

"The situation is desperate on my home world," he said, sounding almost too casual. "My superiors will work with anyone that wants to help set the naledai free. If they happen to be ikthian rebels who want to bring down the Dominion, why should we reject their help?"

Taylor was floored. She'd had no idea that there were ikthians actively working to fight against the Dominion and help the naledai. "Does the Coalition know about this?"

"For the most part, no. A few of the generals might, although I doubt they would admit it in public. It looks bad for them. I've seen this sort of psychological play before. They tell you the enemy is without exception. That way, soldiers never hesitate when it's time to kill."

Taylor pushed off the engine, folding her hands behind her back. She looked at Akton, a plan forming in her mind. Perhaps she could do one small thing to make up for her mistakes.

"How much do you know about Maia's genetic research?"

"Just what I told you. She had the scars to come out and say the theory of ikthian genetic superiority was full of bunk, and we were all too similar to be enslaving each other."

"It's more than that. Our DNA—naledai, human, ikthian—is more similar than the Dominion is comfortable with. She's betting some ancient species helped with our genetic development. You know, introduced a common ancestor we all share on different planets and let evolution do its thing."

Akton's shaggy brow lowered. "That's...a big claim, Taylor. My people won't like that. The thought that our ancestors also gave rise to the ikthians... It'll be hard for them to swallow, but I bet it would be even worse for the Dominion. Their whole doctrine, their rationalization for taking over the rest of the galaxy, is based on the theory that they're a superior species. Something like this?" His voice trailed off as he seemed to imagine the possibilities.

"If some of Maia's research magically appeared in your hands, would you know how to get it to someone who could use it?"

"Definitely. The Dominion's argument falls apart if we're all genetically similar to each other. And while some ikthians will overlook it, this might lend us the support we need to turn the tide of this war." Akton considered the possibilities further. "It will still be difficult to completely undermine the Dominion's authority, but things will go faster when reason is allowed to speak.

Taylor began pacing again. "Maia didn't have anything on her when I brought her here. She would probably need access to an interstellar network in order to get a copy...and my superiors would never sign off on that."

"You remember what I said the last time we talked, Taylor? If you're going to break the rules, you might as well break them all the way."

"The politicians aren't interested." Her fingers clenched into fists as she remembered Bouchard's face. "I tried to explain about Maia's research, but they didn't understand. I'll need to sneak it to you somehow. Hopefully you can get it to go public, and then the brass will have to revise their strategy for dealing with the ikthians."

"And what about Maia? What happens to her?"

Taylor felt like she was being torn in two. She didn't know what to do. She wanted a magical solution that would allow Maia to go free without betraying the orders of her superiors.

"Taylor." Akton took a step closer. "I can get her to safety. Just...consider that if you do decide to hand over the research."

Taylor ran a hand through her hair and sighed. "I won't let her get hurt, Akton. Not anymore." That was one promise she felt comfortable making.

Rae D. Magdon & Michelle Magly

# Chapter Thirty

FOR THE NEXT TWO days, Taylor managed to avoid Maia and her superiors almost entirely. She spent a lot of time lurking around the mess hall, sitting mostly by herself and ducking out of conversations. Her talk with Akton had been both enlightening and conflicting, but she was still having difficulty sorting through all of her options

Although she hadn't discussed it with Maia yet, Taylor knew that getting her research to the rebellion might turn the tide of the war. At the very least, it would be a blow to the Dominion. Perhaps it would convince the brass to cooperate more effectively with the other species, including the ikthians who were part of the rebellion.

Then there was Bouchard. He obviously didn't trust the ikthians and wanted to end negotiations as quickly as possible, even if it meant settling for something less. If the Chairman got his way and Maia was returned to the Dominion, Taylor was sure that she would die. Her stomach twisted into unpleasant, slippery knots at the thought.

But all those problems didn't even begin to sort through the mess of emotions Taylor felt for Maia. She wanted the ikthian to be safe, but she also craved her company and her touch. However, she knew her feelings would lead to nothing. Things between them were already complicated enough, and she didn't want to make them worse.

By the third day, Taylor realized that stewing over her problems would lead nowhere. The Coalition and the Dominion would reach some kind of agreement soon, and no matter what they decided, Maia would end up suffering. She entered the suite hesitantly after dinner, passing the guards without a word. Aside from sleeping on the couch every night for a few hours, she had been spending her time anywhere but here in an effort to avoid this decision.

Maia was in the bedroom, and when Taylor entered, she glanced up from the book she had been examining. They stared at one another for a few moments, both uncertain. Finally, Taylor took another hesitant step closer. "Maia, can you tell me more about your research?"

Maia's brow furrowed at the question, but she didn't appear upset.

"What about my research do you wish to know, Taylor?"

Taylor leaned against the wall. She scuffed the carpeted floor with one of her boots, and she couldn't decide what to do with her hands. Eventually, she shoved them in her pockets. "How has the Dominion reacted to it so far? Aside from sending seekers to kill you, I mean."

"The public has not seen it yet. My initial findings were presented to a committee, and they chose to think my research suggested that ikthians were genetically engineered for superiority. They granted me the funds to continue my research, but what I managed to uncover only seemed to contradict what the Dominion hoped to find. I sent them regular updates, but did not even have time to put together a formal presentation before they sent the seekers after me."

Maia sighed. "I attempted to release portions of my research by myself, but the Executive Communications Office—ECO—maintains strict control over broadcasts in Dominion space. Aside from one or two small video messages, I was unable to discuss any of my findings in depth with the scientific community at large, or with the public. Most ikthians on Korithia believe I am simply a rebel, although they know only a few factual details about me or my situation. They need only hear that I reject ikthian superiority, and that is enough to offend their biases. "

Taylor took a deep breath. She had been waiting around and feeling sorry for herself for far too long. If she really wanted to help Maia, the naledai, and her own people, this seemed like the best way. "What do you think would happen if I got your research out there? Showed it to the people on Korithia and all the interior ikthian planets? There are rebels on Nakonum who might be able to use it."

"I am not sure." A small worry line creased the middle of Maia's forehead, and Taylor had the sudden, irrational impulse to smooth it away. Instead, she removed her hands from her pockets and folded them behind her back, curling her fingers into her palms. "Many will close their ears and their minds, but making my research public to the citizens of the Dominion might cause a few of them to change their attitudes. It will certainly embolden the dissenters who already claim that we are not predestined to rule the entire galaxy, and there are more of them than you may think."

"Is the Dominion's control over their own people really that shaky?" Taylor asked. She hadn't even known that there were ikthian dissenters before Akton had informed her. From the outside, the ikthian empire looked firm and unshakable.

"It is weaker than they would like to believe. Not all of us are monsters, Taylor. I admit I was rather neutral on the subject before I began my research, but the more information I uncovered, the less reasons I could find to support subjugating other intelligent life." Maia paused and looked up at Taylor from her seated position. "If I could change my mind, perhaps others can too. Besides, not all of the aliens I have encountered have treated me badly."

Guilt lanced through Taylor's stomach. The weight that never seemed to leave her shoulders was suddenly crushing. "Maia," she said, struggling for words. "The way I used to treat you...the things I did..."

"The things we did cannot be undone." Maia stood up from the bed, closing the distance between them. "And I would not want to undo them, even if I could. Those moments are very precious to me, Taylor."

Taylor could still see the wet shimmer of tears in Maia's eyes. "I didn't mean to hurt you," she said, desperately wanting Maia to believe her.

Maia took both of Taylor's hands in hers. "You are the only human to show me kindness here." She ran her thumb over the back of Taylor's knuckles. "That means so much to me."

"I should have shown more. I shouldn't have initiated anything sexual with you while you were my prisoner. I should have treated you better from the beginning instead of seeing you as a bargaining chip. And I don't expect repayment for what I'm doing right now. I just want it to be the right thing."

"This is not about repayment. Nothing in the world could force these actions from me...these feelings." Maia's thumb continued tracing over the back of Taylor's hand, lingering over each callous and scar, and she felt her heart thump faster.

"Maia..." Taylor looked up, and her breath caught in her throat. She'd always thought Maia was beautiful, but it had never struck her this way before. Simply looking at her face threatened to stop her heart. "I don't want to hurt you. And it seems like no matter what happens, both of us are going to end up grieving."

They drifted closer, until their faces were only inches apart. "No, we won't," Maia murmured softly into Taylor's lips. "Not for this."

Taylor took her mouth in a soft kiss, asking for permission without words. Maia granted it, parting her lips and sliding her hand up along Taylor's arm. Taylor trembled at the gentle gesture. Although she knew she had missed Maia's touch over the past few days, she hadn't realized how much she had missed her taste. Her scent. The sounds she made. Everything about Maia overwhelmed her. It seeped into her pores and made her crave more.

In a matter of moments, Maia had pushed her down onto the bed and crawled on top of her. Maia's hand cupped the side of her face, and Taylor's chest constricted. She wanted this, wanted it badly, but at the same time, she knew it was a horrible idea. She opened her mouth to protest, but before she realized what was happening, their lips were pressed together. This time, she didn't have the strength to resist.

Maia's kiss was inexperienced, tentative one moment and overly eager the next, but Taylor didn't care. She simply wanted more. She parted her lips, allowing Maia's tongue to dart out and taste her, and then repeated the motion herself. She pulled Maia closer, wrapping her arms around her neck and tracing the folds of her crest. She felt a surge of pride when Maia shivered and whimpered softly into her mouth.

They finally pulled apart, allowing Taylor to pant for breath. "Maia...I'm sorry about being so indecisive. I just...I haven't wanted to make another mistake and I..."

Maia looked almost hurt at that comment. She slid her hands over Taylor's stomach, feeling the muscles there beneath her shirt. Gently, she traced the hem, pulling it up to reveal the first strip of tan skin. "This is not a mistake. It never was."

"But..." Taylor's protests were lost as Maia's warm hands slid beneath her shirt, lifting it further. Instinctively, Taylor raised her arms over her head. Soon, the shirt was tossed aside, and Maia began exploring, running her hands over Taylor's torso. Being touched so near to her breasts wasn't always Taylor's favorite activity, depending on her mood, but Maia's hands melted her fears. She relaxed, letting go of all her worries, simply enjoying the feel of Maia's skin against hers.

"Please..." The pain and need in Maia's eyes made Taylor's heart ache. "Let me have this. Do not tell me to stop because you are worried you have harmed me in the past."

Maia's warm hands cupped her breasts, and Taylor's eyes fluttered shut as she swallowed down a moan. "Maia," she whispered instead, arching into the touch. Teasing fingers captured the hardened peaks of her nipples, twisting gently. "I..." She managed to open her eyes again. Meeting Maia's gaze convinced her, just for a moment, that everything would be all right. "Yes."

Maia smiled and kissed her again, pushing her down onto the bed. Her lips lingered over Taylor's collarbone before trailing steadily downward. "I do not know why I feel this way for you," she muttered, and Taylor groaned as Maia's tongue swiped at the tip of her breast, not sucking, simply teasing. She released it a moment later and Taylor whimpered in disappointment. "But I cannot help it. I need you."

Taylor tried to reply, but all she could manage were breathy moans and whimpers. It had been so long since she had trusted another person enough to have sex this way. Her previous lovers had always been timid, or judgmental, or they had stared at her expectantly, as if she always knew exactly what to do. Although she usually loved taking charge, allowing someone else to lead for once was a relief. It was freeing to be with someone like Maia, someone she could open up to without fear of judgement.

Taylor's hands wandered to Maia's shoulders, and she gripped them like a lifeline. Maia began kissing along her stomach, and Taylor's body pulsed in anticipation. Slowly, Maia's hands drifted down to Taylor's hips. Her fingers dipped beneath the hem of Taylor's pants, and Taylor felt herself pulse against the seam. When Maia withdrew, Taylor pushed forward ever so slightly, encouraging her touch.

Maia took the wordless offer and cupped a hand between Taylor's legs. "By the Ancients, you are so warm, so ready for me. I can even feel it through your clothes..." She lowered her head, placing a kiss on the button of Taylor's pants before undoing them.

Taylor wanted to speak, to tell Maia how much this meant to her, but no words came. She could only look down at Maia and hope the ikthian read some of her feelings in her face. She raised her pelvis when Maia began tugging at her pants, eager to be out of them. They were tossed aside, and her underwear quickly followed.

As soon as she was naked, Taylor spread her legs, leaving herself completely open to Maia's gaze. It seemed to burn into her, and Taylor felt a heated flush crawl up along her chest. Maia was studying her, examining her, blue eyes darker than the deepest ocean. Taylor had never been more happy to drown.

# Chapter Thirty-one

FOR A MOMENT, MAIA froze, taking in the sight. Although she had touched Taylor here before, she realized that she had never taken the time to look closely, to memorize the details. Taylor's anatomy was similar to hers, but the color was deliciously alien. Her inner folds were a reddish-brown color, different than the rest of her skin, and they glistened with wetness. Slowly, Maia trailed her fingers through them, entranced by the silky feeling. She smiled when her fingers hit the hard point of Taylor's clit, causing the human to gasp. Maia ran her finger over the tip, and her heart jumped in her chest when Taylor's thighs twitched.

Taylor moaned softly, inclining her hips toward Maia's retreating touch. "Don't stop," she murmured. Maia began rubbing in slow circles, noticing the way Taylor's breath became uneven. She kissed along Taylor's exposed thigh, sucking the skin in between her teeth momentarily and swiping her tongue across it. She continued up along Taylor's muscular leg that way, alternating between light kisses and small bites. Taylor began to tremble, and while she was distracted, Maia removed her hand.

Before Taylor could whimper at the loss, Maia closed her mouth over the point of Taylor's clit, sucking inward and lashing her tongue across the tip.

"Maia!"

At the sound of her name, Maia moaned against the swollen bud trapped between her lips. She could catch a few traces of Taylor's flavor this way, but after a moment, she couldn't resist moving down. The taste became heavier when she slid her tongue past the tight ring of muscle at Taylor's entrance, curling it forward to coax out as much delicious salt as she could.

Taylor groaned, and Maia felt the grip on the back of her head tighten. Every time her tongue swirled or pushed forward, Taylor's hips rose off the bed. Sensing that she was close, Maia moved back up to her clit, sliding a hand between Taylor's legs and pressing two fingers forward to take the place of her mouth.

"Is this all right?" Taylor answered by groaning and rocking against her fingers, so Maia slid them inside, curling forward. She was absolutely fascinated with Taylor's responses. Wetness spilled around her fingers, coating her hand along with Taylor's inner thighs. It was lovely to have such physical proof of Taylor's arousal.

She released Taylor's clit for just a moment, grinning when she heard Taylor huff at the loss. "I have wondered what this would be like for a while," she murmured, continuing to push her fingertips against the spot inside of Taylor that made her stiffen and clench down. "To see all of you, to know all of you...to explore you at my own pace."

"Explore to your heart's content," Taylor breathed, continuing to run her fingertips over the dips in Maia's fringe. Maia smiled. This might be the last chance they had, and she was determined to enjoy it. Her touches were exploratory as she coaxed Taylor into rocking against her mouth, but there was urgency behind them as well, a desperation for closeness, for lost time that had slipped by them.

Maia could see and feel the tension coiling in Taylor's abdomen, and she knew it wouldn't be long before she brought about her lover's release. Taylor arched further with each swipe of Maia's tongue, every push of her fingers. "Maia...oh God, Maia." Taylor's grip on the back of her head faltered. " I'm..."

Taylor pulsed between Maia's lips, and Maia rejoiced as the warm silk of her inner muscles tightened and fluttered. Maia kept up her slow thrusts, drawing forth as much pleasure from her lover as possible. Taylor moaned above her, and her hands clutched desperately at any part of Maia she could reach. Maia hummed with pleasure as more wetness coated her tongue.

As Taylor's contractions subsided, Maia withdrew her mouth and slowly pulled her fingers back. Taylor reached down, beckoning for Maia to join her. She crawled up and settled against Taylor's side, resting her head on the human's sweat-slicked chest. Taylor's heart was still racing, although her breathing had begun to slow down again

"Maia..." Taylor whispered, cupping her cheek and lifting her chin. She looked up with soft, trusting eyes, and Maia felt her heart break and begin to mend itself at the same time. She let her thumb brush over Taylor's cheekbone, then her lips, shivering slightly when she realized that her fingers were still covered with Taylor's wetness. On impulse, she urged Taylor's face closer, bringing their mouths together in another kiss. They melted into each other, sharing the taste.

When the kiss broke, Maia whimpered in protest, but Taylor surprised her by rolling her over, easing her onto her back. Taylor's lips trailed down her throat, covering it in a line of light kisses. She was a mess of emotions—confusion, desire, fear, and affection—but she smiled through all of them. She wouldn't give up this moment for anything. "Taylor," she breathed, running her hands up and down along the human's lean back. She could feel Taylor's muscles moving beneath her palms. "You make me feel so much that I..."

"I want to make you feel," Taylor pleaded as one of her hands slid between their bodies. She started with Maia's stomach, tracing patterns around her navel, gradually dipping lower. All the while, she kept her eyes focused on Maia's face, as if to make sure there were no signs of doubt or reluctance. And then her gaze flicked down to the collar cutting into Maia's throat, and Maia felt her pulse flutter above the tight band. She knew what Taylor was thinking, but she didn't dare to hope.

"Hold still," Taylor whispered, lifting her wrist. She was still wearing her comm unit, and in total silence, she entered the code that would unlock the front of the suppressor. It opened with a hiss, and Maia felt the sides of the collar pull apart. There was still a soft indent in her skin where the collar had been, outlined by a faint purple ring. Taylor glared at the collar with a look of hatred before tossing it aside, not caring where it landed.

Maia couldn't breathe. She stared into Taylor's eyes, feeling tears well up in her own. She was free. That in itself should have been exhilarating enough, but somehow, Maia was even more touched by the fact that Taylor trusted her. She knew that Taylor was going against everything she had been taught, and the orders she had been given. All for her.

"I...I cannot believe..." Taylor silenced her with a kiss. Their mouths opened to each other, giving and taking, and for a moment, everything else in the world faded away. Finally, they pulled apart, breathless but happy.

"I should have done that a long time ago," Taylor said, skimming her fingers down along Maia's abdomen. Maia whined when they paused just above the juncture between her thighs. She parted her legs, praying that Taylor wouldn't make her wait any longer. Taylor took her unspoken invitation, sliding her fingers forward and grazing the tight ridge of Maia's clit. She traced it with the pad of her thumb, still gazing into Maia's eyes.

Maia bit her lip, pushing up into Taylor's hand. Taylor's fingers slid over her with every subtle movement she made. They brushed past her entrance every time, but didn't push inside. "Taylor..." Maia tightened her grip on Taylor's back. "Please, take me."

Her plea was enough. Taylor's fingers slid inside of her, filling her at last. She pulsed, squeezing down around them as Taylor took her mouth in another kiss. It was a perfect rhythm. Feeling their bodies press together only made her ache more. Her mouth broke away from Taylor's, and her lips sought skin, sucking and nipping at the sensitive flesh along her lover's neck. The soft moans she drew from Taylor made her heart swell.

"I want you to come," Taylor whispered, her hot breath washing over Maia's cheek. "Please. For me."

The words sent a spike of arousal through Maia's core. She was ready to surrender herself completely She brought a hand to Taylor's face and drew her gaze up. Their eyes met, and she smiled. She wanted to say something, to tell Taylor how much this trust meant, but no words would ever suffice. The ache inside of her was growing unbearable, and she desperately wanted to come so that Taylor could share her pleasure.

Taylor pushed deeper, trying to find the best angle, and Maia could hold back no longer. She closed her eyes, allowing herself to swim in every sensation. The waves of her release were powerful, but steady and sure, just as Taylor's thrusts were. Maia sought Taylor's neck, kissing and biting every available inch she could reach. Tears crawled down her cheeks, and her inner walls rippled desperately around Taylor's fingers. She needed Taylor to fill her, to be with her.

Finally, the storm began to break. She and Taylor melted into one another as they settled into the mattress, a mess of limbs and slick skin. Both of their heartbeats hammered together, and Maia suddenly realized her predicament. The burn of lust had eased, and she knew that desire hadn't been her sole reason for making love with Taylor. She had wanted something else, and the thought of what that might be was terrifying.

Her heart sank as she realized that no matter what she was feeling, or what she might want, the known universe was against them being together. More tears welled in her eyes. This time, they were full of loss and regret instead of pleasure and belonging. She buried her face in Taylor's chest, crying against her shoulder.

Taylor stiffened above her, but instinctively tried to soothe her, pressing their foreheads together and stroking the side of Maia's face with her free hand. "Sweetheart, please don't cry," she murmured.

Maia shuddered beneath her, fighting back sobs. "Taylor, I...I cannot...We cannot..."

Taylor removed her fingers as gently as possible, pulling away from Maia so that their bodies wouldn't have to touch. "Oh God, Maia...I'm so sorry, I..."

Maia propped herself up on her elbows and reached out to prevent Taylor from leaving the bed. "No. Stop. Please do not diminish what we just did. It was...everything I wanted."

"It was? Then what's wrong?"

Maia drew in a shuddering breath. "I cannot lose you after this. I..."

"I'm right here," Taylor said. She eased her weight onto her elbows and nuzzled her face into Maia's neck, placing light kisses against her gills. "You won't lose me."

That only made Maia cry harder. Her leg wrapped around Taylor's waist, and her hands clung desperately to her back. "They are going to send me away," she said through half-sobs. "I will be taken back to the Dominion, and they will kill me."

Taylor lifted her head away from Maia's warm skin. "I'll explain your research better to the generals. They won't get rid of you if you're an asset..."

Maia sniffed, and though she didn't sob anymore, a few tears streamed down her cheeks. "Taylor, these humans see me as currency. They are not like you. They will send me back to Korithia." She left the rest unspoken.

Taylor was silent for a long moment. Finally, she rolled onto her back and pulled Maia close, kissing her forehead. "I don't know what's going to happen, but I won't let anyone hurt you. Not the generals, the Dominion, or anyone else. I promise."

Maia relaxed, easing into Taylor's embrace. They rested against the pillows, breathing evenly although neither of them could fall asleep. Tomorrow, they would have to face reality, but lying in Taylor's arms allowed Maia a brief window of fantasy. She wanted just a few more hours of pretending that they could find happiness together.

Rae D. Magdon & Michelle Magly

# Chapter Thirty-two

THE NEXT MORNING, TAYLOR'S spirits sank even lower as she stood outside Roberts' office, listening to the raised voices within. General Hunt, Chairman Bouchard, and Roberts were clearly in the middle of a big argument, and she was reluctant to interrupt, even though they had summoned her. The last thing she wanted to do right now was insert herself into a disagreement. Instead, Taylor thought about Maia. After a few long, quiet hours spent holding each other, the ikthian had fallen asleep on her chest, most of her tears dried.

The muffled voices behind the door grew louder. "Earth must accept this offer!" Taylor recognized Bouchard's voice. "The most powerful empire in the galaxy has agreed to spare us. This may be our only chance to preserve a future for our people."

"What about the colonists? If we take this deal, millions of them could be overwhelmed by the Dominion's forces." Taylor recognized that voice as Roberts, and it prompted her to scan herself through the door. She found all three men staring at each other in front of Roberts' desk. The lines of their shoulders were tense and their faces were somber. All of them turned to look at her.

"Lieutenant Morgan," Roberts said to Taylor as she gave a crisp salute. "Right on time. There's something you need to see."

"The Dominion has made an offer, Sir?"

"An unbelievable offer," General Hunt said. He circled the desk to face Roberts' terminal. Roberts and Bouchard followed him, and Taylor approached reluctantly, standing a foot apart from the others. A holographic image of the same three ikthians from before hovered over the display.

Roberts activated the recording, and the three ikthians began moving. This time, the ikthian on the right spoke, the one with the elaborate pink markings. The expression on her lovely face was surprisingly placid. "The Dominion has agreed to stop all aggression towards the planet Earth in exchange for Maia Kalanis's safe return."

The other ikthian spoke next, the one with blue on her crest. "We cannot extend such promises for the rest of your system, but we consider our offer more than favorable. Respond within the next sixty standard hours, or this gesture of goodwill shall be rescinded."

Taylor looked at the ikthian in the middle. Now, she knew for certain that it was Maia's mother, Irana. She looked older than the others, stern with age and experience. The resemblance to Maia was uncanny, and even the exhaustion and obvious pain in her eyes was familiar. Taylor wondered if that pain for her daughter had been there before, and she had just been too blinded by prejudice to notice.

The transmission ended, freezing Irana's face, and Taylor forced herself to look away. Fortunately, or perhaps unfortunately, Bouchard distracted her by beginning another rant. "We must act quickly, before they change their minds. Agreeing to leave an entire planet to its own devices? According to our naledai allies, it is completely unheard of..."

"We won't be able to call them our allies anymore if we pull all our troops and surrender just to save Earth," Roberts snapped.

"Enough," General Hunt said. "Your arguments aren't helping. And I fear Bouchard is right. The Dominion is too powerful for us to fight off forever, even with our naledai allies and the help of our colonists. It might be time to start thinking about preserving Earth's future."

"The Dominion isn't as powerful as you think," Taylor blurted out, remembering what Akton had told her. She could see her chance slipping away, and her heart raced after it. "There are already a few dissenters among their own people—good ikthians who don't believe in the Dominion's doctrine."

Bouchard gave her a condescending glare. "What dissenters? Why have we not heard about them? How have *you* heard of them?"

"A naledai soldier currently on-base told me."

"Oh, really?" Bouchard drawled. "Where are these ikthian rebels, then? Where is their help when we need it most? Where are their troops on our front lines?"

"There's no need for your sarcasm, Chairman" Roberts interrupted. "You make a good point, General Hunt, but I'm still worried about the colonies. We can't just leave them to fend for themselves. We have responsibilities to them, too."

"I agree with you, Sir," Taylor said, squaring her shoulders. "We shouldn't be so quick to give up. Let's send more troops to protect the colonists and the naledai. We'll make contact with the ikthian dissenters and use Kalanis's research to destabilize things on Korithia. Hearing the truth will inspire more people than you think to rise up—I know it will."

"Make contact with the enemy?" Bouchard said with blustering disbelief. "You would have the ikthians obliterate us all!"

"I understand your concerns," General Hunt said, glancing from Taylor and Roberts to Bouchard. The somber look on his face and grave tone of his voice made it clear that he was deeply torn by his options. "Lieutenant Morgan, your spirit is admirable. I will make sure we investigate these claims of ikthian dissenters. If they exist, we will find some way to use them to our advantage, whether they become our allies or not. In the meantime, we must protect Earth at all costs. Even a temporary ceasefire will give us time to evacuate as many colonists as possible from the outer worlds and rebuild our defenses here. This buys us time to decide on our next move—time we desperately need."

"Time isn't enough, Sir," Roberts said. "Now more than ever, we need to come together and act decisively."

General Hunt gave him a look of obvious regret. "I'll meet with the other generals tomorrow. I expect a vote on the matter immediately before we make our recommendation to the Coalition."

Taylor's heart clenched. That was as good as a guarantee. Despite General Hunt's lip service about the colonies, she knew Earth was the Coalition's first priority. The chance to protect their home world, even if only to buy some time until the Dominion inevitably went back on its word, would be too much for them to resist. Most, if not all of them, would probably vote the way General Hunt expected. The Coalition would likely go along with it, especially thanks to Bouchard's fearmongering. In all likelihood, Maia was going back to her people.

The thought sent an ache through Taylor's chest, and she suddenly found it difficult to breathe. "Sir, you can't do this. Letting the ikthians push forward and hunkering down on Earth for the backlash isn't a plan. It's just delaying the end. But we have other options. Maia's research—"

"I know that during your time watching over her, you have been able to develop a relationship with Kalanis," General Hunt said. "It's not unusual for a guard to become sympathetic after spending time with a prisoner. Perhaps, like Maia Kalanis, not all ikthians believe in the Dominion's doctrine. I had the opportunity to view some of her videos recently." General Hunt stared at Irana's frozen holographic image, and in that moment, Taylor knew he realized the full ramifications of his decision. He knew Maia wasn't evil, and he knew abandoning the colonies and the naledai resistance would result in more death for everyone except the people living on Earth. "But this is war, and difficult decisions must be made. Our own interests must come before the unlikely chance of toppling an Empire, and the survival of the Coalition depends on protecting Earth first."

Taylor stepped forward, a protest already rising in her throat, but Roberts grabbed her shoulder before she could directly challenge the general. "I suppose there isn't anything more to be done until the generals and the Coalition vote on the matter. I understand the difficult position you're in, General."

"I know you do," General Hunt said sadly.

A victorious smirk spread across Bouchard's face. "Well, if we have nothing further to discuss, I have other meetings to attend. I must discuss our options with some of my colleagues in order to prepare for the vote. This is a time-sensitive issue, after all." He strutted away from General Hunt, brushing dismissively past Taylor and Roberts. "As for you, Lieutenant Morgan, I suggest you try and remember why we are fighting this war in the first place: to *save* human lives, not sacrifice them for nothing." He left the room, allowing the door to hiss shut behind him.

General Hunt sighed. "We'll let you know the results of the vote tomorrow afternoon, Captain. Then, I'm fairly certain Kalanis will need to be processed. Get her ready, Lieutenant."

Reluctantly, Taylor saluted, her arm unnaturally heavy. Never before had she been given orders that she so vehemently opposed. "Yes, Sir."

"Good, Lieutenant. Goodbye, Captain." General Hunt departed the room as Bouchard had, and once he was gone, Taylor finally allowed herself to break down. She buried her face in her hands, wanting to scream in frustration.

"Taylor?" Roberts' firm grip on her shoulder became a fatherly squeeze instead, and Taylor glanced over at him, blinking away tears. Her mentor looked worn down, and she couldn't remember seeing some of the wrinkles around his eyes before.

"They'll kill her if she goes back, Captain. And she could help us take down the Dominion if they would just *listen*..."

"I believe that too," Roberts said, "but it's too much of a risk for the brass to take. They won't budge."

Taylor sniffed, struggling to regain control of herself. This wasn't the time to break down. "How many of the higher-ups know that not all ikthians are against us? That some of them have broken off and joined the naledai rebellion?"

"Too many to justify keeping it secret." Roberts let go of Taylor's shoulder, walking over to his chair and sinking into it. "It started out as need to know information, but some of our older troops have had the opportunity to be more involved with the naledai rebels as the war has gone on. The rebellion isn't picky about its allies. If an ikthian wants to blow up other ikthians, the naledai aren't going to stop them."

"So why are we the ones holding out? Why not unite under the same force rather than attempt to hold our own against impossible odds?"

Roberts shook his head. "Part of it is the war propaganda. Soldiers don't want to have to cope with the idea that humans and aliens aren't all that different underneath their physical appearances. It's harder to kill ikthians every day when you know some of them are on our side. But if you ask me, it's the people in charge."

"You mean Bouchard?"

"He and other old war hawks are all stuck in the past. General Hunt is liberal in terms of what the others think of this new galactic community, and even he can't see a better way forward." Roberts' eyes narrowed thoughtfully. "Now that I think about it, I'm going to monitor Bouchard a little more closely. I don't trust him."

Taylor snorted. "Can't imagine why not."

The joke was bitter and forced, but the corners of Roberts' mouth twitched up in a smile anyway. "You might as well return to your quarters, Taylor. I know things seem grim right now, but it's not too late. The vote hasn't happened yet. Maybe we can find another solution."

Something about the tone of Roberts' voice caught Taylor's attention. His words sounded determined rather than resigned, and she turned them over in her head again: *It's not too late...is he telling me to do what I think he's telling me to do?*

He was, Taylor was sure of it, but either way, her decision was made—and not just for Maia, either. She nodded once. "Understood, Captain.

Rae D. Magdon & Michelle Magly

# Chapter Thirty-three

AFTER HAVING DISMISSED THE regular guards at the door, Taylor hesitated outside the quarters that she and Maia had shared for the last several weeks. It was difficult to believe so little time had passed. It felt like she had known Maia for years. The promise she had made last night still echoed in her head. She had sworn to keep Maia alive, and that left her only one option. She sighed and opened the door.

Maia was sitting in the front room instead of the bedroom, resting uneasily on the couch as if she had been waiting for Taylor's return. When their eyes met, she smiled. "Taylor, you're back."

"Not with good news. I just got back from a meeting with the brass." Taylor folded her hands behind her back, staring down at her boots for several long moments before she gathered the will to look up. "The Dominion wants you back. They've made the generals a tempting offer."

Maia's skin blanched to a sickly, pale grey hue. The hope in her sparkling eyes died out, replaced with dull resignation. "When will I be leaving?"

"That's the thing..." Taylor swallowed, certain of her choice, but even more tortured than when she'd walked in. Before meeting Maia, everything had been so simple—follow orders, kill ikthians, serve humanity. Now, for the first time, she doubted her superiors and the very institution that she had sworn loyalty to. "I promised to keep you alive."

Maia's eyes widened. "What are you going to do?"

Taylor sat on the couch, resting a hand on Maia's thigh. "I'm still working on that, but I think I have one of my commanding officers convinced we need to get you out of here. I think your research is important to this war effort, and that we should make sure others see it."

There was a long, heavy pause. Finally, Maia spoke. Her words were a little unsteady, as if she were choking back tears, but a smile lit up her face. "If you are serious about this, I will need access to a terminal in order to download my findings."

Taylor nodded. "I know. I've known for a while. I just need to figure out the best way to do it...Wait, can you even download your research with our servers? The Dominion has their own network."

"Not through the Coalition's servers, no," Maia said. "But if you could get me to a naledai server, I would have everything I need. I uploaded my original research on Nakonum's network. It is ikthian-controlled, but not as heavily monitored."

"That's smart thinking. I need to take you to Akton."

"Akton?" Maia asked.

"A friend of mine," Taylor explained. "He's a rebel naledai visiting from Nakonum. There should be a terminal on his ship with access to the naledai servers."

"And he can help us?"

"Definitely. The generals aren't voting on the Dominion's offer to spare Earth until tomorrow morning, so we'll have time to sneak onto the ship."

Maia mouth fell open. "Are you saying the Dominion has offered to spare Earth?" Taylor nodded. "I...I cannot believe it. They have never offered to leave a planet alone before."

"Yeah, well, I'm not sure I believe them," Taylor muttered. "Either they really want to get their hands on you, or they're lying. Both of those outcomes are unacceptable."

Warmth folded around Taylor's hand, and she glanced down into her lap. Maia's fingers had curled around hers. She looked up again, staring into Maia's worried blue eyes. "Taylor, I know my research is important, but this will be dangerous. There are so many things that could go wrong..."

"It's not just about your research," Taylor said in a low voice. "I care about you, Maia. I want to keep you safe."

"I care about you as well, Taylor. Perhaps more than I should."

Taylor stood up from the couch and offered Maia her hand. "Come on. Let's put together a bag, just in case we need to get out of here in a hurry." The two of them retreated to the bedroom, fingers still laced together. They packed mostly without speaking, lost in their own thoughts, but they were never far from each other's touch. Taylor filled one of her smallest bags with clothes for both of them, water, rations, and extra ammunition for her pistol. "Anything else you can think of?" she asked, noticing that there was still a considerable amount of room in the pack.

Maia blushed, dipping her head in a nod. Without speaking, she walked over to the nightstand beside the bed and opened the top drawer, the same one where Taylor had left her strap-on. When she turned around with the toy in her hands, Taylor's eyes widened. "You never know," Maia said, smiling shyly. "We might need it."

A grin spread across Taylor's face, and she brushed Maia's fingers as she put the toy in the bag. If last night had demonstrated that there was something growing between them, this gesture cemented it. With her heart a little bit lighter, Taylor sealed up the pack and set it at the foot of the bed, where it would be within easy reach. She made sure her pistol was loaded before setting it on top of the nightstand next to her communicator. She hoped she wouldn't have cause to use it.

"All right, let's get some sleep," Taylor said. "We'll find Akton later, when the base isn't so busy and we're rested." Her voice suddenly became softer. "Maia...would you share the bed with me?"

Maia smiled as she took Taylor's hand. "I suppose there is no harm."

Taylor allowed Maia to get settled in the bed first before lying down beside her and wrapping a protective arm around her midsection. Before they fell asleep, she felt a sense of peace settle over her. Her decision was made, and she knew it was the right one. No matter what happened to her, she would make sure that Maia stayed safe.

# Chapter Thirty-four

"WAKE UP!" A ROUGH hand gripped Taylor's shoulder, and she blinked, trying to make out the large shape looming over her in the dark. It was obviously a person, but she was too bleary and confused from sleep to process what was happening. "We need to get you and Kalanis out of here!"

As her eyes adjusted to the dim light, Taylor sat up, recognizing the voice and shape of the person above her. "Roberts?" She reached for her pistol even though it wasn't at her hip. Fortunately, she and Maia had fallen asleep in their clothes.

"I was right to monitor Bouchard's communications. It isn't safe here anymore," Roberts told Taylor as she disentangled herself from Maia's arms. She hurried to grab her weapon from the nightstand, too startled to be embarrassed that her superior had caught her without it while Maia was nearby. "Bouchard is going to have you court-martialed. He's sending a squad to pick you up."

Taylor's eyes widened. "On what grounds?"

Roberts cleared his throat and looked from her to Maia. "Fraternizing with the enemy."

Taylor's face burned. She turned to Maia, who had just started to wake up and was staring at her with squinting, confused eyes. "Taylor," she gasped, clinging to Taylor's arm when she noticed Roberts' dark bulk standing over them. "What is happening?"

"Don't worry, he's a friend, but we have to leave right now." Taylor climbed out of bed, making sure that her ammo clip was fresh. She had so many questions she wanted to ask, but Roberts' urgency left no room for them. Instead, there was only time for one. "What's the plan?"

"You both need to get out of here as quickly and quietly as possible."

Relieved that she had known this was coming, Taylor reached to the foot of the bed and grabbed the small bag that she and Maia had prepared the night before. She swung the straps over both shoulders, retrieved her pistol, and followed Roberts towards the door. Maia continued clinging to her arm, but was quickly starting to understand the gravity of their situation.

"We might have to fight our way out," Roberts said as they hurried through the living room and left the captain's quarters. "They're coming to arrest you right now."

"Where the hell did he get the proof to court-martial me?" Taylor asked.

Roberts gave her a sad look. His brow furrowed with concern. "It seems another soldier approached him with the information."

Taylor's stomach sank. "How much does he know?"

"Everything." For a moment, Roberts couldn't meet her eyes. "I'm afraid your friend Rachel Harris is responsible. She told Bouchard you were getting too attached to the prisoner, and that you were probably being mind-controlled. Bouchard decided he needed to act now, before you tried to take Kalanis and run."

Taylor was stunned. She nearly came to a halt, searching for words, but none came. *Rachel betrayed me?* She didn't want to believe it, but at the same time, everything that Roberts had said felt true. Even though Rachel had probably convinced herself that she was doing the right thing, Taylor felt a tight knot of anger form in her chest.

But she could not focus on that right now. Maia was her priority—not Rachel. Taylor started walking again, faster than before. Maia and Roberts nearly had to sprint in order to catch up. Taylor bypassed the elevator, heading directly for the stairs. "I guess you know I have a friend on the naledai ship docked here. It might be our only chance now."

Roberts nodded. "Whatever you need to do."

Taylor activated her wrist comm, sending a call along the secure channel Akton had given to her. After several seconds, he picked up. "Taylor, do you realize how late it is?" His voice was rough with sleep.

"Akton, I need a lift off base."

Taylor heard a sudden crash over the speakers and winced. She wondered if Akton had fallen out of bed. "What did you do this time?" he asked, sounding a little more alert.

"I'm bringing Maia. Her research can help the rebellion, but she'll be dead if we don't get her out of here, now."

A few more seconds of silence followed. Taylor glanced at Maia. She didn't like the way her brow furrowed with worry.

"All right," Akton said at last. "Meet me in the docking bay as soon as possible. I'll alert my superiors. "

"Got it." Taylor closed the channel and reached for the stairwell door. "Let's go."

The doors burst open before she touched them, and a soldier barreled through, an assault rifle pressed into his chest. He seemed surprised to see them, but he shifted his weapon to one hand and reached for Maia's arm.

That was his mistake. A moment later, he jerked his arm back as though he'd been burned. The muscles in his face contorted, and he howled with agony, his entire body twitching. As he doubled over, Taylor raised her arm and struck the back of his skull with her pistol. He crashed onto the floor, still writhing at their feet, and Taylor hurried into the stairwell. She had no idea how much damage Maia's toxins had done to the soldier, but she wasn't going to stick around long enough of find out. "Come on!"

Roberts followed, pulling the door open and rushing down the stairs with them. When they reached the bottom of the stairs, he went to the door, but Taylor stopped and looked at Maia. She was shaking, obviously horrified by what she had just done. Suddenly, Taylor realized how vulnerable the ikthian was without a weapon. Her toxins wouldn't be much use against a gun at long range.

"Do you have an extra gun, Roberts?" she asked, although she wasn't even sure if Maia knew how to use one.

Roberts nodded. "I have a spare pistol."

"Maia needs one."

"I can protect myself," Maia said. She touched the spot where her collar had been. "My combat training is much more useful without worrying that I will be shocked."

If Roberts noticed the absence of the collar, he chose not to say anything. After what felt like an eternity, he gave her a slow nod. "I trust your judgment, Taylor. You know her better than anyone." He removed a second pistol from his hip and passed it to Maia. Her hands shook as she accepted it, but she held the weapon correctly.

Satisfied that Maia would be able to defend herself, Taylor glanced between Roberts and Maia to make sure they were ready. When both of them nodded at her, she hauled the door open. The three of them dashed for the nearest cover, the corner of a pathway flooded with shadow in the moonless night. Taylor only had a second to take in their surroundings before she saw figures moving into formation. Bullets flew by, and she heard an officer yell for them to stop.

Taylor stepped in front of Maia, all too aware of the fact that the clothes they were wearing wouldn't shield them. Even a single hit could end up being fatal. But Maia didn't need her protection. She raised the gun and placed a clean shot in the nearest soldier's calf, causing him to retreat.

The shot gave the other soldiers pause—not much, but enough to give Taylor, Maia, and Roberts a chance to duck around the building and follow the adjoining wall. The harsh drum of boots on cement followed, and Taylor looked around, trying to find a place to hunker down. Nothing. The other buildings were too far away.

Roberts unhooked a flash grenade from his belt. "Away!" He lobbed it behind him just as the squad of soldiers rounded the corner. As soon as it went off, Taylor sprinted for the next building without looking back, ignoring the shouts of surprise and pain that echoed behind her.

They ducked into the shadows behind another building, heading for the docking bay by the route that offered the most protection. Warning sirens began to blare from the tops of the base's towers, and Taylor cursed between her teeth. "Shit. I was hoping we'd get a few more minutes before they woke up the entire base..."

"Come on," Roberts said. "Keep moving." He waved her and Maia forward, and the three of them passed behind the rear of the mess hall building in a dead sprint. They didn't stop until they arrived at the docking bay, which was suspiciously free of guards. Taylor wanted to be relieved, but it didn't feel right. She could hear commotion in the distance, more soldiers rousing themselves at the sound of the sirens.

"Try the door," Roberts said.

Taylor scanned her wrist comm. The door remained closed. She flipped open the panel of the manual terminal beside the door instead and entered her passcode, but the screen flickered red. "Not working."

Roberts holstered his pistol and stepped up to the console. He didn't even bother with his comm, and the first passcode he tried didn't work. He swore and shook his head. "Should have known the bastard would do something like this." He tried another code, and then another. Finally, the doors opened, and Taylor heard Maia sigh with relief.

"Looks like he didn't get all of them," Roberts said. "Let's move."

Taylor hurried into the docking bay, glancing around at the dark, empty space. The massive ships were mostly shadow in the faint glow of the night-time floor lights, and she kept expecting soldiers to leap out and attack her, or to catch a glimpse of the red dot of a sniper's gun. When she heard footsteps finally echo in the darkness, she whirled around with her pistol drawn, but she almost lowered her arm when she realized who was standing there, with an assault rifle pointed straight at her.

Rae D. Magdon & Michelle Magly

# Chapter Thirty-five

"RACHEL?" TAYLOR BLURTED OUT.

"She's removed the collar!" another voice shouted off to her left. Taylor glanced toward the sound. Bouchard stood in the docking bay as well, sneering at them. He also carried a pistol, and was flanked by two more soldiers, both with rifles. "You were right to come to me, Harris. The ikthian clearly has her."

Rachel made a short gesture with the body of her own rifle. "Sir, let me handle this." Bouchard nodded, though he looked displeased. Rachel turned back to Taylor. "Put the gun down. I don't want to hurt you."

Taylor lowered her pistol. "I'm taking Maia to the rebels, Rachel. You don't have to get involved."

For a moment, Rachel faltered, but she didn't lower her rifle. She stared at Taylor with pain-filled eyes, obviously torn. "How could you do this, Taylor?"

Taylor stepped protectively in front of Maia, but that only seemed to make Rachel's frown deepen. "You don't understand what's going on," she said, keeping her own gun lowered. "I'm trying to help. If you'd just give me a chance to explain..."

"The ikthian has twisted her mind, turned her against her own kind," Bouchard interrupted. "She is no longer your friend. Lieutenant Morgan is gone."

"I didn't want to believe it..." Rachel's hand remained steady, but Taylor thought she could see tears of anger in her eyes. "This is my fault. I knew she was changing you, but I didn't want to see. I should have done something sooner."

From behind her, Taylor heard Roberts speak up in a calm voice. "Lieutenant Morgan is right, Harris. Dr. Kalanis has information that could help the rebels bring down the Dominion. Taylor is trying to keep us safe."

"Don't listen to him. Obviously, the ikthian has him under her control as well." Bouchard walked up beside Rachel, speaking directly into her ear. "Why else wouldn't they want to trade her for Earth's safety? Taylor is willing to let this ikthian go, even if it means leaving us to rot."

Rachel narrowed her eyes at Taylor. "Is that true?" she asked, tightening her finger on the trigger.

"We can save more lives this way. We can end the war." For a moment, Taylor saw Rachel hesitate, and continued on, hoping she could get through to her friend. "What about your family? They're in the colonies right now, aren't they? If we pull our troops back to Earth and abandon the colonies to the Dominion, they'll be the ones to suffer. You know I wouldn't do this unless I knew it was the right thing."

Rachel inhaled shakily, but there was still fire in her eyes. "I want to believe you, Taylor. But you're making it almost impossible." She glared at Maia, who was barely breathing at all, and hadn't made a single movement since Rachel's appearance. Her blue eyes were wide with terror.

"The generals haven't told us everything," Taylor insisted. "There are ikthians working with the naledai to bring down the Dominion. We can win this!"

"She's been brainwashed," said Bouchard. "The ikthian is using her."

"Bouchard's the one brainwashing you, Rachel."

"That's enough out of you!" Bouchard raised his gun and pointed it directly at her. Its nose wavered, but Taylor could see his finger hovering over the trigger, preparing to fire.

Suddenly, Taylor felt herself being shoved roughly to the side, trapped behind a muscular arm. Roberts pushed past her, standing between her and the gun. "Bouchard, don't..."

A shot rang out. Roberts lurched. He clutched his hand to his chest as Bouchard stared, wide-eyed, the gun still in his grip. Roberts stumbled forward, nearly collapsing against Maia's shoulder. When he looked at Taylor, she saw red dripping over his fingers. "Go," he whispered, his balance wavering. He let go of Maia, collapsing to the floor.

Taylor wasn't the first one to act. She stood there, staring at Roberts in disbelief for a second too long, until the other two soldiers raised their weapons. Something brushed her arm, and she saw Maia staring at her with watery blue eyes. They flicked down toward her webbed hand, and Taylor saw that she was concealing a stun grenade, the same kind Roberts had used. *He passed it to her. That stubborn bastard.*

Taylor blinked once to tell Maia she was ready, then closed her eyes and covered her ears.

The grenade went off with an ear splitting bang. It felt like knives were ricocheting around inside of Taylor's skull, but she had been forewarned. When she opened her eyes, she saw the guards and Bouchard reeling. Rachel was hunched over, obviously stunned, but she still managed to stare at Taylor, teeth bared in anger and tears streaming down her cheeks.

Turning away, Taylor knelt beside Roberts, trying to haul his arm around her shoulders. "Maia, help me," she pleaded, not caring when his blood spilled onto her shirt. He was still alive, but only just, and his eyes were unseeing as blood trickled from the corner of his mouth. Bouchard's shots had been in his chest.

"Taylor," Maia said, pulling at her sleeve, "it is not safe here. We have to run."

"I...I can't leave him," Taylor said, even though she could already feel the life seeping from Roberts' body. "He saved me. He was..." Her throat burned with tears as she realized that she had used the word 'was'. She had no way to save her mentor and friend. All she could do was take the chance he had given her. "I'm so sorry, Michael," she whispered, using his first name as a goodbye as Maia helped her up.

They sprinted to the rear of the docking bay, not daring to look back over their shoulders. Taylor's breath burned in her chest as she realized she was leaving Rachel behind as well. Blinking back tears, she took Maia's hand, hauling her past several human ships before stopping short. The naledai ship was gone, and in its place was a shuttle.

A swell of light flooded the docking bay as it opened, and Taylor saw Akton's silhouette emerge. He bounded down to meet them, hackles raised and assault rifle at the ready. "Ship's already in orbit. Came to pick you up, but I heard an explosion and—is that blood?" he asked, staring Taylor's fatigues. "Ancestors, what happened?"

"Not mine," Taylor said grimly. "We gotta move." She could already hear the clamor of footsteps approaching. Bouchard's soldiers were coming after them, or reinforcements had arrived.

"When I told you to contact me if anything changed, I thought you'd at least give me twenty-four hours' notice before making an escape." He looked between Maia and Taylor. "I'm going to lose a rank for this."

"Not if we get out of here alive. We're leaving—now!" Taylor pushed past him to board the shuttle, but Akton raised his rifle.

"Incoming!" She heard him fire at the approaching soldiers, and Maia shot another round from her pistol as well.

"Morgan!" Taylor turned and saw Bouchard approaching. "If you take the prisoner aboard that shuttle, you will officially be a traitor to the Coalition."

Taylor raised her pistol to fire, but then she saw Rachel run up behind Bouchard, weapon drawn. She realized that she could do it. She could pull the trigger and watch blood spout from Bouchard's head. But then she felt Maia's hand on her arm, silently asking her to lower her weapon. "Taylor, no."

"He murdered Roberts." Her arm shook slightly. "He should be dead."

"If you kill him, your friend will attack you," Maia reminded her in an urgent whisper. "You will never forgive yourself if you are forced to shoot her."

Taylor lowered her arm. Maia was right. She couldn't do this, not in front of Rachel. Her job was to protect Maia, not exact revenge for Roberts' death. He had given her a mission to complete. Still, her rage at the cold-blooded murder that Bouchard had committed made her chest burn. "You killed Roberts," she shouted. "You're the traitor."

Akton hopped into the shuttle, sitting in the driver's seat. Taylor kept her gun at the ready as Maia climbed in behind him.

Bouchard began barking commands at his terrified looking soldiers. "What are you waiting for? Don't let them escape!" The remaining soldiers charged, with Rachel at the front of the pack, but it was too late. Taylor clambered into the shuttle, closing the door behind her just in time to hear shots collide with the metal.

"Get us out of here, Akton," she said, taking her seat as she heard the hum of the plasma engines. The shuttle lurched and lifted into the air, powered from below as Akton drove them up and away.

"What are we going to do now?" Maia asked, reaching out to hold Taylor's hand. "Your people will kill us if we try to return."

"We're not going back," Akton said, flying the shuttle out through the open roof of the hangar. The boosters switched on, and the shuttle began to rattle slightly as it picked up speed. "There's a naledai cruiser in orbit. We should be safe there. They can take us to the rebels." He turned to glance over his shoulder at Taylor. "That is where you want to go, right?"

"Definitely." Taylor took a deep, unsteady breath, focusing on all of the things she needed to do. That would help take her mind off of Roberts, Bouchard, and Rachel. "We need to download Maia's research and give it to the rebels as quickly as possible. I'm sure someone there can spread it to the ikthian home world."

Akton nodded. "We can take care of the download while en route."

Taylor's stomach dropped as they cleared Earth's atmosphere. She wondered for a moment if she would ever return. No doubt Bouchard would spin some story about her. Even though she hated the thought of being labeled a traitor by the Coalition after years of faithful service, she knew she had made the right choice. She pulled Maia into her arms, ignoring their unfastened safety harnesses, and rested her forehead against the ikthian's shoulder. Their fingers remained laced together.

"I'm not going to let them hurt you," she whispered beside the folds of Maia's fringe. "I'm never going to let anyone else hurt you ever again."

Rae D. Magdon & Michelle Magly

# Epilogue

AS MAIA WATCHED TAYLOR emerge from the shower in a cloud of steam, she couldn't help noting the irony. They were in completely opposite positions from her first night in captivity. This time, Maia was the one waiting in the room that the naledai had provided for them, observing the water droplets that ran down Taylor's body. Taylor glanced at her, seeming slightly uncomfortable with her own nakedness.

"You know, I have grown to find your form rather pleasing to look at," Maia said. She winced at the awful phrasing of her words as they hit her ears. She had wanted to bolster Taylor's spirits, but apparently, she still hadn't overcome her social awkwardness. The translator didn't help matters. She would need to construct a more organic program to help their communication.

Taylor gave her a strange look, then forced a weak chuckle, running a hand through the dripping spikes of her black hair. "Thanks, I think."

Maia blushed. "You make it difficult for me to speak, Taylor."

"I do, huh?" Taylor inhaled, as if trying to summon strength, and made her smile bigger, approaching the bed. "You know, I wasn't exactly suave the first time I saw you step out of the shower naked either. You make it difficult for me to speak sometimes, too."

"Why is that?" Maia asked, scooting closer.

"You're..." Taylor paused, searching for the correct word. "Amazing."

Maia's flush crept further down along her throat. "Did you always think that way, even from the beginning?"

"It took me a while to come to terms with it. Falling for an ikthian was a bit of a head-trip. By the time I got used to the idea, we were fighting for our lives..." The joy drained abruptly from Taylor's expression, and she looked around their new room, away from Maia. "It's hard to believe we made it off Earth at all. And Roberts didn't."

Taylor's voice was thick with guilt, and Maia's first instinct was to soothe it. "His death was not your fault, Taylor. There was nothing you could have done to save him. Now, it is up to you to carry on for him. I know you will do everything in your power to stop this war. My data has already been downloaded. We will present it to the rebels as soon as we meet them."

"Thanks." Taylor blinked rapidly, but managed to suppress the tears Maia could see gleaming in her eyes. "You know, I think Roberts would've liked you if he'd gotten to know you. Maybe he even would have approved of us."

*Us.* The word hung between them, but this time, it made Maia feel exhilarated. Now that they had made it out alive, she and Taylor could finally begin to explore what they were to each other. "I hope he would have. I also know that he would have been proud of you."

"I'm not sure why," Taylor said bitterly. "I couldn't save him or stop Bouchard."

"Your Captain's death is a tragic loss, but it does not mean you failed," Maia protested. "You made all of this possible, Taylor. You chose to save me even though it meant going against your own people." She hesitated. "I do not know how to repay you for what you have done for me."

Some of the sadness left Taylor's face, and Maia saw something warm and bright fill her eyes instead. *Hope. Thinking about me makes her feel hopeful.*

"I don't need thanks or anything else," Taylor said. "I don't even expect you to stay with me long term...although I hope you want to stick around. I, uh, don't really have anyone else now."

Before Taylor's sadness could return, Maia leaned in to kiss her. She kept the meeting of their lips soft and light, although it took some effort. Taylor smelled wonderful, and her freshly scrubbed skin was incredibly soft. Maia pulled back before she could get carried away. Taylor might not be interested in anything too physically intimate, considering she had just lost her Captain.

"I have no plans to go anywhere."

"Thank God," Taylor said, with a low, relieved laugh. "I didn't want to assume—"

"I understand." Maia ruffled Taylor's dripping hair, pleased to note that texture was even more fascinating while it was wet. "I have lost all of my loved ones as well, for obvious reasons. I am grateful to have your company."

Taylor dipped her head, presenting more of her scalp for Maia's fingers to rub. "You really like the hair, don't you?"

"Yes," Maia said, a little embarrassed.

"You should ask to pet Akton's sometime. I'm sure he'll love that."

Maia giggled, more from relief than from the joke itself. If Taylor was feeling well enough to try her hand at humor, that was a good sign. "I think I prefer yours...although I am very appreciative to your friend for saving our lives."

"He's a good one," Taylor said. Her eyes went distant again, and Maia suspected she was remembering Roberts.

"Well then, I hope I have the chance to get better acquainted with him."

Taylor lifted her chin and heaved a sigh, taking up her favorite position on the bed: flat on her back with her hands behind her head. "Happy endings are never easy, are they?"

"What?" Maia asked. She rolled onto her side, stretching out beside Taylor and gazing down at her with concern.

"You know? Happy endings. Elizabeth and Darcy. Everything tied up in a neat little bow." She closed her eyes. "Maybe it's stupid, but I was hoping this would be a happier ending. Don't get me wrong. I'm so, so happy you're alive and safe..."

Maia shushed her. "You do not have to explain, Taylor. You lost your Captain. You were forced to flee your home. Your best friend betrayed you, and there is still a war all around us. Anyone would find it difficult to feel happy in those circumstances."

Taylor opened her eyes. "Difficult, maybe, but not impossible. It's not too late."

"No, it is not." Maia reached out to take Taylor's hand in her own, running a thumb over Taylor's knuckles and offering what she hoped was a comforting smile. "Something has changed between us. I did not allow myself to think about it before, because I was sure I was going to die. But now, I believe a relationship with you might be possible."

"A relationship?" Taylor repeated in a throaty voice, her eyes swimming with emotion.

Maia nodded, still holding Taylor's hand. "Yes. I wish to explore my feelings for you. It will need patience, but perhaps after spending some time as equals, as lovers, we might find our happy ending after all. That is, if you want to try..."

"I definitely want to." Taylor opened her arms, and Maia slid into them with a low sigh. "We'll take it slow, okay? One day at a time." She paused, then broke into a grin. "I just realized something."

Maia tilted her head. "Oh?"

"I haven't even taken you out on a proper date yet. What kind of lover am I?"

"The kind who has saved me so many times that I am beginning to lose count," Maia said, running her hands over Taylor's back.

"That's true." Taylor nuzzled into her neck, then said, "There's still a lot of work to do. We're part of the naledai rebellion now. I'm sure we'll have more than enough to deal with, but it'll be worth it, as long as I'm with you."

Maia's lips spread in a smile. "You say such lovely things. I hope what we are doing makes a difference."

"It will," Taylor said, not even pausing to consider any other possibility. She blinked slowly, and Maia noticed that exhaustion had crept into her face.

"You should rest," she ordered.

Taylor stuck out her lower lip. "Don't want to."

"Then *I* will rest, and you will lie here with me and close your eyes. Is that an acceptable compromise?"

Although she heaved a grumpy sigh, Taylor nodded her agreement. "Okay. Can't really say no to being close to you." She shifted into a more comfortable position, and Maia cuddled next to her, pulling Taylor's arm into its usual position around her waist.

Soon, Taylor was fast asleep, snoring away just as Maia had predicted. She took a moment simply to enjoy the puffs of Taylor's hot breath on the back of her neck, and the weight of the elbow draped over her side. She had gotten her happy ending, and she would do everything she could to make sure Taylor felt the same, someday.

Maia had no idea what the future would bring, but she was certain it would be the first step in dealing a significant blow to the Dominion. Perhaps after the fighting was done, if it was ever done, she would find some way to bring Taylor back to Earth. She liked the idea of allowing Taylor to show her the beautiful parts of the planet they had left behind, so her memories of Taylor's home world wouldn't be limited to a single room.

It was something to work toward. Something to hope for.

# The story continues in Starless Nights

In this sequel to Dark Horizons Taylor and Maia did not know where they would go when they fled Earth. They trusted Akton to take them somewhere safe. Leaving behind a wake of chaos and disorder,

Coalition soldier Rachel is left to deal with the backlash of Taylor's actions, and soon finds herself chasing after the runaways. Rachel quickly learns the final frontier is not a forgiving place for humans, but her chances for survival are better out there than back on Earth. Meanwhile, Taylor and Maia find themselves living off the generosity of rebel leader Sorra, an ikthian living a double life for the sake of the rebellion. With Maia's research in hand, Sorra believes they can deliver a fatal blow against the Dominion.

# Chapter One

LIGHT STUNG RACHEL HARRIS' eyes as soon as she stepped through the door. She winced and raised a hand to her forehead, shielding her eyes to get a better view of the room. She couldn't see much with the floodlights aimed at her face, but if she squinted, she could just make out a long row of shadowed figures seated in high-backed chairs. Her stomach dropped. Every person of rank near San Diego Base had to be here, though she could not see who they were. They would hide from her even at her own trial. The door shut behind her with a loud clang, and her shoulders suddenly felt heavier. It took effort to keep them straight.

"Rachel Harris," a deep voice said, coming from the middle of the group. She recognized it immediately. General Hunt was usually fair, but as the commanding officer of the base, he was ultimately responsible for the recent events that had brought her here. "You are charged with treason against the Coalition. According to reports, you aided Lieutenant Taylor Morgan's escape from Earth with a valuable prisoner of war. How do you plead?"

Rachel locked her hands behind her back and chose a spot on the wall to stare at. She was the scapegoat. That had been clear since they first accused her. They needed someone to pin their mistakes on, and she was the lowest-ranking soldier involved. Of course she had to take the fall. "Not guilty, Sir."

"So you've stated before." Hunt glanced down at the datasheet in his hand, scrolling down the glowing screen. "Your statement says that you followed Chairman Bouchard's orders in an attempt to capture the fugitives when they tried to escape."

*Fugitives.* The word made her stomach clench. Even though it was technically true, it felt like a mask. Taylor was a traitor, an outlaw. Yet only a few weeks ago, they had been close friends. Before that damn ikthian's arrival, this situation would have been unthinkable for both of them. She pushed the thought aside and nodded. "That's correct, Sir."

Hunt set the sheet back on the table and stared directly at her. Rachel kept her shoulders squared, refusing to cower under his gaze. Even though she was already guilty in his eyes, she didn't want to look it. "Chairman Bouchard is neither a military official nor your commanding officer. He is only a liaison between the Coalition and the military. Why did you defer to his orders instead of approaching your commanding officer with your concerns?"

Rachel had heard it all before. This might be her official sentencing, but she had already been found guilty a month ago, the night Taylor had escaped with Maia Kalanis. "Sir, I approached Chairman Bouchard because I also suspected Commander Michael Roberts of treason. He was close with Lieutenant Morgan, and—"

"You failed to follow the appropriate chain of command," someone else interrupted, although she couldn't tell who was speaking. "Your disregard for protocol came with too high a price."

"I know I failed. I'm not denying it." She had done worse than fail. She had kept quiet when Taylor had been assigned to guard the ikthian prisoner. She had done nothing when her friend started to show signs of being bewitched by the alien's powers. She had waited too long, and during her last chance to make things right, she let Taylor get away. She'd had a gun pointed at Taylor, but she hadn't been able to use it.

"We've also taken a statement from Chairman Bouchard," the voice continued. This time, she recognized General Lee's face through the glare. He was another of the Coalition's five generals, and if the number of seats in front of her was any indication, the rest of them were in attendance as well. She swallowed back a rising lump in her throat. "He claims the traitor, Lieutenant Morgan, was responsible for the death of Commander Roberts. Your statement claims otherwise. Would you care to elaborate?"

Rachel flinched. She had hoped it wouldn't come up. She was just a grunt with a couple of bars on her chest. Even though he had shot Roberts, Bouchard was untouchable. He was an elected representative, outside the military, and he didn't have to follow the chain of command. They would take his word over hers no matter what she told them.

"No, Sir," she said, struggling to keep her voice steady. "Everything I need to say is in my statement." Roberts was a traitor like Taylor, but watching him die had been ugly, in some ways uglier than watching ikthians slaughter their troops. With most of the galaxy against them, humans couldn't afford to start murdering each other, too.

The dark figures in front of her moved. A few turned to whisper at each other. Rachel's heart sank. They would never clear her of these charges. She would be stripped of her rank and sent away in shame. If she was lucky, they'd ship her off to an asteroid mine where she could work herself to death for the war effort. She would never see her family again.

At last, General Hunt spoke up. "We have one last question. Do you know anything about Lieutenant Morgan's whereabouts?"

Rachel tried to conceal her surprise. She knew the brass hadn't caught up with Taylor yet, or they wouldn't have called her here to take the blame. But if they were desperate enough to ask her, they had to be completely out of leads. "Taylor...Lieutenant Morgan is probably headed for Nakonum or maybe one of the other planets in that system. She escaped on a naledai ship with Akton. She's got this delusion about helping the rebels on their homeworld."

"A delusion indeed." Hunt peered down at the report again and furrowed his brow. "If we're to believe your assessment of the situation, you would have us accept the possibility that the ikthians are rebelling against their own kind and are in league with the naledai, our allies."

Rachel blinked against the bright lights. She had to choose her next words carefully. "I didn't want to rule out any possibilities in my report, Sir, but it's what Taylor told me. Whether it's true or not, she believes it."

"It's what Taylor told you while under the influence of a dangerous war criminal."

"Where else would you prefer to look, Sir?" Rachel asked.

None of the generals responded at first. Hunt stood and walked around the table, approaching her slowly. She stood at sharp attention, waiting without hope. "We are done looking," he said, staring at her with a stern expression. "Rachel Harris, as punishment for your act of treason, this tribunal court sentences you to exile from the planet Earth."

Rachel knew there was more. There had to be more.

"You are to seek out the fugitives Taylor Morgan and Maia Kalanis and bring them back to Earth if possible. This assignment is strictly off the records, and as such, you will receive minimal aid from military personnel. You will reveal to no one the nature of your assignment, and you will not enlist the help of the Coalition of Humanity. Should you fail to apprehend Morgan, you will execute her. Until you succeed in your task, you are not to return to Earth."

Rachel could see the pity in Hunt's face. This was not a special assignment. It was a death sentence. Hunt could no longer meet her gaze, but Rachel stared at him. She wanted to remember the guilt in his eyes so she would remember to kill Bouchard the next time she saw him. She had messed up, yes, but the slimy politician had left her to the wolves. Despite his rank, Hunt had no power in this matter.

Finally, Rachel took a step back. Her path was clear. There really was only one choice from this point. "I'll leave immediately."

"I suggest you do. You're dismissed, soldier." Hunt nodded, and Rachel threw one last salute before turning and exiting through the door. More whispers came from behind her, but whatever the generals thought of her fate didn't matter. On paper, their decision would look generous. They were offering her a chance to fix her mistakes and redeem herself. But in reality, they had sent her on a suicide mission. Even though Taylor had been bewitched by the ikthian, she was still a very dangerous fighter, and she would not be alone. Rachel would be outnumbered and outgunned, assuming she even managed to track her quarry down.

Once she stepped into the hallway, Rachel headed for the nearest wall and leaned against it. The two guards posted by the door stared, but she ignored them. She needed a moment to ground herself. She closed her eyes and sighed, trying to decide what to do. Despite everything, Taylor was still her friend. It wasn't her fault the ikthian prisoner had warped her mind. She didn't deserve to die, but she couldn't stay with the ikthians either. Not if she was going to help them.

Rachel opened her eyes again and pushed off the wall, striding down the hallway with new purpose. She would follow the brass's orders. She would find and stop Taylor, kill her if she needed to. She would make sure Kalanis never turned another human again. Then, if she survived, she would come back to Earth and take care of Bouchard. He was to blame for all of this. Now that she was exiled, there was nothing stopping her from taking justice into her own hands. The military couldn't touch him, but she wasn't part of the military anymore. If Taylor was going to die and Roberts was already dead, Bouchard deserved the same.

She stopped in front of the elevator and hit the pressure pad, waiting for it to carry her to the lower levels of the building. She needed to go to her room, grab her kit, and take one of the shuttles. If the brass really did want to keep this quiet, they wouldn't get in her way. If the look on Hunt's face meant anything, maybe he would feel guilty enough to give her a little money for food and ammo.

Once the elevator reached the bottom floor, she headed outside. The sky was clear, and she stopped to look up as a soft wind blew past her face. A brilliant blue flooded her vision. This would be the last time she ever got to see Earth's sky, the sun, or anything else familiar. She hadn't been born here, but Earth was her home and had been ever since she enlisted. She didn't want to leave.

"I'm not going to let them take Earth from me," she whispered. The ikthians, the brass, Bouchard. They had ruined her life, forcing her to abandon her home in the middle of a war. And they were all going to regret it.

# *Available now*

# About the Authors

## Michelle Magly

Michelle Magly is a queer writer and academic scholar. She lives for writing about far-off lands in the distant future and fantasy landscapes.

Michelle co-authored her first novel with Rae D. Magdon, All the Pretty Things, in 2013. Their second novel, Dark Horizons, was released February 2014. The sequel to Dark Horizons, Starless Nights, won a 2016 Rainbow Award for Best Lesbian Science Fiction. Look for the conclusion to the trilogy, Eclipsing the Sun, coming soon.

Michelle released her first solo work, Chronicles of Osota - Warrior, in July 2014. She is now working on the second book of the series, Thief. Warrior and Dark Horizons were both finalists in the 2014 Rainbow Award SciFi/Fantasy category.

When not writing, Michelle hikes, goes rock climbing, skis, and plays a lot of video games.

Connect with Michelle online

Facebook  Michelle Magly
Twitter  https://twitter.com/MichelleMagly
Email  michellemagly@gmail.com

## Rae D. Magdon

Rae D. Magdon is a writer of queer and lesbian fiction. She believes everyone deserves to see themselves fall in love and become a hero: especially lesbians, bisexual women, trans women, and women of color. She has published over ten novels through Desert Palm Press, spanning a wide variety of genres, from Fantasy/Sci-Fi to Mysteries and Thrillers.

Rae is the recipient of a 2016 Rainbow Award (Fantasy/Sci-Fi) and a twice-nominated GCLA finalist (Fantasy/Sci-Fi). In addition to her novels and short stories, she writes for queer video games and a queer webseries. When she isn't working on original projects, she spends her time writing fanfiction for Mass Effect, Legend of Korra, The 100, Wynonna Earp, and Overwatch.

Connect with Rae online
Website  http://www.raedmagdon.com/
Facebook  Rae D. Magdon
Tumblr  http://raedmagdon.tumblr.com/
Email  raedmagdon@gmail.com

Cover Design By : Rachel George
www.rachelgeorgeillustration.com

## Note to Readers:

Thank you for reading a book from Desert Palm Press. We have made every effort to edit this book. However, typos do slip in. If you find an error in the text, please email lee@desertpalmpress.com so the issue can be corrected.

We appreciate you as a reader and want to ensure you enjoy the reading process. We would like you to consider posting a review on your preferred media sites and/or your blog or website.

For more information on upcoming releases, author interviews, contest, giveaways and more, please sign up for our newsletter and visit us as at Desert Palm Press: www.desertpalmpress.com and "Like" us on Facebook: Desert Palm Press.

Bright Blessings

Manufactured by Amazon.ca
Acheson, AB